CLIFFORD THURLOW is a re
He has a diverse portfolio
travelogues and film script
Kent, he later became the
Greece, covering pivotal events.

Thurlow's passion for writing flourished during his time in India, where he studied Buddhism and authored *Stories From Beyond the Clouds*.

His career includes collaborations with notable figures and best-selling works such as *Today I'm Alice, Runaway, Typhoon* and *Sex, Surrealism, Dalí and Me*.

From the library of
The Book Fairies
... to read and pass on...

PLACE FOUND	READER	DATE	THOUGHTS ON THE BOOK

#ibelieveinbookfairies www.ibelieveinbookfairies.com

Luath Press Limited

EDINBURGH

www.luath.co.uk

First published 2025

ISBN: 978-1-80425-175-1

Printed and bound by
Clays Ltd., Bungay

Typeset in 11 point Sabon by
Main Point Books, Edinburgh

For Iris Gioia

To the world I leave my heart, to the Republic my gun, to men's slow eyes my unvanishing footsteps.
James Neugass
with the Lincolns at Villanueva da la Cañada

If you had asked me why I had joined the militia I should have answered: To fight against Fascism, and if you had asked me what I was fighting for, I should have answered: Common decency.
George Orwell
Homage to Catalonia

...tell your children how, coming over seas and mountains, crossing frontiers bristling with bayonets, and watched for by ravening dogs thirsty to tear at their flesh, these men reached our country as crusaders for freedom. Today they are going away. Many of them, thousands of them, are staying here with the Spanish earth for their shroud. You can go proudly. You are history. You are legend.
Dolores Ibarruri, La Pasionaria,
at the last march of the International Brigade

Prologue

SHERIDAN REMAINED ON the top step and watched as a black Daimler turned into Carlyle Square and stopped outside his house. His wife stood in the open doorway. He could not recall another time when she had waited with him for the car to arrive.

The driver trotted up the steps and collected the valise at Sheridan's feet. He placed it on the front passenger seat and opened the rear door.

'I should be back tomorrow,' Sheridan said.

Her lips tightened. 'We don't want to lose her.'

'She's suffering from depression. We won't lose her.'

'We've lost our son.'

'We don't know that, Charlotte. There's a great deal of confusion. There always is.'

He wondered whether to kiss her cheek but didn't.

'I have to go.'

He ran down the steps into the back of the car. The driver closed the door and returned to his seat. The vehicle circled the square and pushed out in front of a postal van on Old Church Street. Sheridan – General Sir Richard Sheridan – reached for his sunglasses. He was dressed casually in a fawn linen suit, brogues and a dark blue tie.

'No great hurry, Douglas. They'll wait,' he said.

They crossed Battersea Bridge. The river was dotted with small boats and barges carrying coal. Women in summer dresses and men with jackets hooked over one shoulder hurried back from lunch to offices and shops. It was Friday, 27 August 1937. The first foul whiffs of war were in the air and it seemed to have put a spring in everyone's step.

They picked up speed on Clapham Common and followed the A23 to RAF Biggin Hill on the outskirts of Bromley. They arrived in 40 minutes. A lanky NCO in shorts manned the entry gate. He bent to peer inside Sheridan's open window and stood back with a sharp salute.

The driver followed the road between a cluster of brick buildings. As he turned on to the runway, the engine on a Bristol 138 roared to life. The craft was an ungainly beast with wide wings on a narrow fuselage. It was still in the development stage and had set a number of high-altitude records. Every flight could be justified as research, Sheridan's justification to himself.

His driver handed him the valise. He climbed the boarding ramp and the door was bolted in place behind him. He was the only passenger. The Bristol shook as it accelerated along the runway and lurched into the sky. He stared down over the fields and orchards, everything green, stable, the Garden of England stretching reassuringly across Kent to the coast.

He closed his eyes. Soldiers learn to grab sleep when they can, not that sleep was possible with the noise and turbulence. In his long career from the Western Front to Whitehall, Sheridan had never used government facilities for private purposes. It was anathema to him. This overnight journey was the exception to his own rule, something he was not proud of.

The flight to Flughafen Salzburg was a little over four hours. A driver in livery waited for him at the wheel of a Maybach Zeppelin, the largest private motor car ever built. Sheridan stepped into the plush interior and was driven through dense forests to Schloss Fuschl, the 15th century castle where senior Nazis had met in secret in January 1933 to appoint Hitler as Chancellor.

The schloss, newly restored, the walls turning pink in the afternoon sun, was the summer residence of Count Joachim von Ribbentrop. He opened the door for Sheridan the moment the car stopped and shook his hand warmly.

'Pleasant journey?' he asked.

'Pleasant enough,' Sheridan replied.

A valet took Sheridan's valise and the two men passed through the wide corridors of the house into a park edged with mature trees. Tables with white cloths had been set up beside a marquee on lawns patterned in stripes by a mowing machine. Men in overalls carried cases of wine, boxes of glasses and blue-rimmed white plates decorated with a swastika.

Ribbentrop led him down to the lake where a table had been prepared with sandwiches under a bell jar and a bottle of schnapps with two glasses. Sheridan glanced back at the marquee.

'Joachim, I didn't know you were entertaining.'

'My dear fellow, I thought you were being terribly... British. It is the end of summer party. The Führer will be here. I thought you must know that?'

Sheridan sighed and took a deep breath. He should have known that. It was his job to know. You must forgive me, Joachim. I have made a stupid mistake.'

'Sir Richard, there is nothing to forgive. You must stay.'

'But I do not have the appropriate clothes...'

Ribbentrop stood back to study his guest. 'We are the same size, my friend. I have a closet full of evening suits. I insist.' His eyes grew brighter. 'This is a rare opportunity.'

They sat. Sheridan felt as if he had been outmanoeuvred in some way. But Ribbentrop was right. It was a chance to see Hitler up close, take the measure of the man who had risen from nowhere and appeared to have his entire nation in thrall. It was Sheridan's second visit to Schloss Fuschl since Ribbentrop's posting to London as the German Ambassador. The two men had what diplomats call a rapport, as well as an understanding shared by those who had survived the Great War trenches. Ribbentrop was a handsome, controversial figure, immaculate in a Savile Row blazer with shiny buttons and a blue and gold cravat. His English was clipped, to the point, fluent.

'You have intrigued me, Richard,' he began. 'I imagine it is too much to hope that you have come to discuss joining the Anti-Comintern Pact?'

'That discussion will take place, I assure you. But not now. I am here to ask you a personal favour. I thought it correct to do so face to face.'

The valet served coffee. Sheridan watched two swans glide by leaving chevrons on the surface of the water.

'It's about my son.'

'He is in Spain?'

Sheridan paused before he replied. Of course Ribbentrop knew. It was his business to know.

'I believe so,' he said.

'It always surprised me that he joined the International Brigade.'

'And me.'

Ribbentrop poured two glasses of schnapps.

'*Prost*,' they said, and drank them down.

'Whatever needs to be done, Richard, if it is within my power, I will do it.'

'Simon went missing after the Brunete campaign. And there is another man. A friend of my daughter...'

'The beautiful Alice. How is she?'

'Not at her best. She suffers a sort of melancholia. It's difficult to say. She won't speak. She barely eats.' He brushed back his hair. 'I would like to establish if my son and the other man are alive. If that is the case, I would like to bring them back to England.'

Sheridan removed from his jacket two sheets of paper which he unfolded and slid across the table. Each contained the personal details of the two men with a photograph held in place by a paperclip.

'They are young,' Ribbentrop said. 'Young and foolish.'

'Let me repeat. This is personal. Nothing to do with my government.'

Ribbentrop leaned forward and Sheridan felt the full force of his pale grey eyes. 'If there is another war, Richard,' he said, 'it would be a pity not to be on the same side.'

ROBBIE GILLAN WASHED his socks in the fountain and cast his eyes over the great gathering of men in Trafalgar Square. He was proud to be there and recognised in those men a certain dignity borne from triumph over hunger and hardship, something nowhere more apparent than in the pale, drawn features of Jimmy McGee.

It had taken 33 days to march 400 miles from Glasgow to London. Many had dropped out along the way. Not Jimmy. By an act of sheer will over physical strength, he had kept up as they foot-slogged south through a wasteland of silent factories, empty warehouses, dole queues and depression. In grimy cities across the North of England and wretched villages all along the way, the poor had come out with water and crusts of bread. People cheered. Small boys with swinging arms followed the procession. In the exhilaration of the moment, more unemployed men gave wives a peck on the cheek and joined the march.

They read the newspapers passed along the line, but reporters had little interest in men marching for jobs when there were dignitaries travelling to the capital to witness the coronation of Edward VII at Westminster Abbey. After the one-sided conflict in North Africa, the tanks had rolled into Addis Ababa and the Italians had seized Abyssinia. Hitler's Berlin Olympics would begin in August.

The marchers had reached London three days after the outbreak of civil war in Spain on 17 July, and the street battles in Madrid and Seville had replaced all talk of sportsmen and kings. Spain's Republican government with promises of land reform, a minimum wage and equal rights for women was under siege from its own generals.

*

The sun warmed the steps where Robbie sat wringing out his wet socks before putting them back on. He stood and gazed around at the circle of fine buildings, the statues of lions and monarchs, Lord Nelson high above it all on his column of shiny stone. A colliery band with blaring brass arrived from the direction of Admiralty Arch, the musicians followed by a choir of Welsh miners in mufflers and caps. The sky was patterned with banners from the Labour Party, the Unemployed Workers' Movement and the trade unions.

There was a marked lifting of spirits when word passed through the crowd that their presence in Trafalgar Square had been reported by the BBC in its nine o'clock broadcast. The next message to reach them was that the final march on Downing Street would commence at ten.

Jimmy McGee was lying flat out on the paving stones. Robbie pulled him up.

'Come on, Jimmy, we've got an hour to kill,' he said. 'There's something I want to show you.'

'Och, mon, leave me be. I'm fagged out.'

'Come on. This is going to change your life.'

'I want to stay here. I don't want to go and miss it...'

'We're not going to miss nothing. Hamish won't let them go without us.'

Hamish McDonald, whose authority was the result of occasional success in the boxing ring, acknowledged Robbie's conspiratorial look without understanding its purpose.

'Aye, we'll wait,' he said. 'If we haven't gone, we'll still be here.'

'Mary Mother of Jesus, now where the hell are you going?' It was Jamie Douglas, grim and wiry below his halo of orange hair. He was a Catholic from Ireland with a tongue coated in the bile of its colourful blasphemy.

'We're going for a promenade,' Robbie replied.

'We've promenaded all the bliddy way from Glasgow. You don't know no place in London.'

'You mind your business what I know.'

Jamie would have followed but Hamish grabbed his arm to stop him.

Robbie led Jimmy across the road in the direction of the National Gallery. The sound had been muted from the centre of the square but, by some sonic effect, from where they now stood the crowd roared like an express train hurtling into a tunnel. The Welsh band played 'Men of Harlech', the boom of the trombones and tubas filling the air as if it were trapped in the dome of a cathedral.

They turned into the backstreets that wind their way to Leicester Square. Robbie stopped outside a café with a handwritten sign tacked on the door: Fresh bacon and eggs daily.

'What are you doing, mon. We've got no money.'

Robbie placed his hands on Jimmy's shoulders. 'Do you trust me?' he asked and Jimmy shook his head.

'I trust you to get us into trouble.'

'That's what I like to hear, something positive.'

Robbie opened the door and led the way into a narrow space lit by the gas jets below a copper boiler. A chubby woman in an apron was rubbing a cloth over the machine.

'Good day, missus. I want two plates of breakfast and two cups of tea,' Robbie said. He dug into his pocket and held his palm outstretched. 'I've got a shilling.'

The woman's mouth dropped open. 'A shilling,' she repeated. 'This is London, not one of those places where you come from.'

'We walked all the way from Scotland and me mate could do with some decent grub,' Robbie told her. 'I'm sure a shilling will pay for one. As for me, I'm not even that hungry.'

The woman leaned over and took the coin. 'Go and sit yourselves down. Let's see what we can do.'

She dropped the coin into the drawer below a marble counter and they sat at a table with a salt cellar on the scarred wooden surface. Jimmy stared at Robbie as if he were a magician.

'Where'd you get the bob from?'

'From me mam. It's been burning a hole in my pocket for weeks.'

'You're really something, you are,' Jimmy said. 'You're the best friend I've got...'

'We're all friends. We need each other.'

'Aye, we do. But there's not many willing to share what they've got.'

'You are,' Robbie reminded him. 'You were the one who said if there were 20 of us with a bob each, we'd be able to pay my fine.'

'It's easy to be generous when you don't have nothing.'

'That's the best time.'

'I said it 'cos of what happened at the yard. We were all rattling the gates, but you were the one who got arrested.'

'Aye, I was born under an unlucky star.'

Jimmy shook his head. 'No,' he said. 'I don't think so.'

Robbie sat back and took off one of his boots. 'This is how lucky I am.' He poked his finger through a hole in the leather. 'I don't have a hole in one of me boots, I've got bliddy great holes in both of them...' Robbie loosened the red neckerchief at his throat and sniffed the air. 'Can you smell that? Smells like bacon.'

'Aye, and whatever it is, we'll share, half-n-half.'

In the dim light, the café interior had the appearance of a waiting room at a railway station with green tiles and pages from illustrated magazines on the plaster walls. Next to their table was a photograph from *National Geographic* showing a Canadian Mountie in hues of scarlet and gold, everything crisp and clean. Robbie read the caption.

'Canada. Land of the free.'

Jimmy nodded. 'That's where we ought to go.'

'Not me, I don't think I could walk another inch.'

Just then, the woman approached with two plates, each containing an egg, a rasher of bacon and two slices of toast. She placed them on the table and collected two mugs of tea from behind the counter.

'Here, that's all you're getting.'

As Robbie sprinkled salt on his egg, he watched Jimmy gobble down his food like a man possessed. Jimmy was 23 with small features, pale blue eyes and a finely tuned mechanism that only functioned when it was properly serviced. He finished the food before the plate had time to cool and blew steam from his tea.

'You saved my life,' he said.

Robbie wiped up the egg yolk with a piece of toast. 'Och, mon, it's only a dish of grub. It's not like it's a fag, is it?'

Jimmy glanced up at the woman. 'Thanks, missus.'

She waddled back to the copper boiler, then returned with an enamel teapot to refill the cups.

'That all right for you, was it?'

Robbie grinned. 'Best thing I've ever eaten. You're the embodiment of human kindness,' he said.

She rummaged through the pocket at the front of her apron and produced a red tin. She removed two cigarettes, placed them on the table and snapped the lid shut.

'Here,' she said. 'Now clear off and let me get on with my business.'

Robbie pushed his cap to the back of his head. 'You see, you're an angel in disguise. It must be a terrible rumour, the

English do have fathers after all.'

The woman lit a match and he drew the smoke down. 'Bloody Scotch,' she said.

Robbie spoke through a cloud of smoke. 'We'd better be making a move. We've come here to deliver a message to Mr Baldwin.'

'Then you can give him one from me,' she said brusquely. 'Tell him he got my vote last time, but I'm buggered if he's going to get it again.'

'You know what my old dad says, voting Conservative is voting for the rich to get richer.'

'Everyone to their own point of view.'

She had folded her arms and looked ready for an argument. Jimmy McGee made his way to the door.

'Thanks again, missus,' he said. 'It was right nice of thee.'

'Aye, it was,' added Robbie. 'I feel like giving you a kiss.'

'You try it and it'll be the last thing you do.'

Robbie followed Jimmy out into the lane and they paced along the street, cigarettes decorating the corners of their mouths, chests thrown out, haughty as the pigeons in Trafalgar Square. They shouldered their way through the ranks as the marchers readied themselves to set off on the last leg of their journey to Downing Street. They found their mates six rows from the front.

'Where have you been?' Jamie Douglas demanded. 'I thought you were going to miss it, and it would have been your own fault if you did.'

'Well, we didn't and we're here,' said Robbie.

'Where'd you get that fag from?'

Robbie stuck the dog end between Jamie's lips. 'From a fat lady who can't abide ginger nuts.'

Jamie puffed down the last few drags. 'You talk a lot of bollocks, you know that, Robbie Gillan.'

Robbie took a deep breath. He felt composed, contented.

He nodded at his comrades as he glanced from face to face. Hamish McDonald was at the end of the line like a rugby prop, solid and stocky. Nat Cohen was next to him. He was a union organiser, well-respected, a Marxist, whatever that meant. Jamie Douglas was bobbing up and down, his red hair surfacing like a buoy above the sea of grey and brown caps. Jimmy was still at his side, the nipped-out half of his cigarette wedged behind his ear.

Flags and banners sailed above. The boom of brass instruments filled the air. The choir provided a festive mood. The government wouldn't listen to their union leaders, but they couldn't fail to hear the raised voices of 10,000 men marching for jobs, not hand-outs; for wages, not the dole; for the chance to feed their families.

As the clocks struck ten, the signal was given and the column set off from Trafalgar Square into Whitehall, a deserted stretch of stone buildings with the Cenotaph at the centre. At this revered spot, where the nation paid tribute to the men who had given their all, a troop of mounted police stretched before them in serried ranks like a black curtain.

'What are they doing?' Robbie asked.

Nat Cohen looked him in the eye. 'The dirty work,' he answered.

The riders gathered speed. Robbie could smell the horses. He could smell unwashed clothes and worn-out boots, and he caught the whiff of something less easy to discern, the coppery waft of sweat and fear. Jimmy pulled at his arm.

'Don't go and get arrested again,' he said.

'I don't think that's what's on their minds.'

His voice was drowned out by the noise. The sound of hooves striking the stone streets was like a thousand hammers on as many anvils. Seconds later, the horsemen charged into the centre of the marchers, forcing a wedge as deep as the line of Scotsmen.

Hamish McDonald deflected the long baton aimed at his head. He reached up, seized the mounted man and landed a punch on his jaw as he pulled him from his horse. Several riders steered their mounts to the rescue.

Robbie stumbled out of the way of the horses to reach Hamish's side. Another rider, leaning forward, truncheon swinging, became an open target. Robbie's fist made contact with his moustachioed face and the copper, acting on instinct, ripped the air with a swift backhand, drawing blood as his weapon glanced across Robbie's cheek. Using his full height, Robbie struck out again, blood for blood, the sound of the crack as his fist met the rider's nose giving him a brief rush of elation.

Robbie and Hamish kept an eye on each other's backs as they retreated. Their friends, bunched up behind them, dodged the downpour of black-oiled truncheons. The flags were scythed down. The bandsmen were silent. It was chaos. Bedlam. Bodies piled up on top of each other. Robbie could hear the whinny of the horses, the litany of oaths in every accent, the hopeless wail of the wounded.

The horsemen were followed by bobbies on foot, big men in the first rank with fierce eyes and medal ribbons from the Great War. They brandished cudgels with poised skill, cracking skulls as they beat the crowd back from Downing Street where Mr Baldwin, the 1st Earl Baldwin of Bewdley, presided over a Cabinet meeting with no intention of receiving the hunger marchers.

Hamish tripped. Robbie pulled him to his feet. Jamie Douglas was down. Blood seeped through his trousers, his curses loud enough to awaken his dead ancestors in County Donegal.

The mounted police moved in single file to the edges of Whitehall, funnelling the marchers back into the confines of Trafalgar Square. Those who dallied were urged on their way with a swipe across the backs of their legs. They sprawled out on the sun-warmed stones. Robbie tried to close the gash on his cheek with pressure from his fingers. Nat Cohen tied his scarf in a tourniquet around Jamie's thigh, stemming the blood oozing from a knee cut to the bone by the iron tip of a horseshoe. Robbie looked from face to face.

'Where's Jimmy?'

'He was next to you last time I saw him,' Jamie said.

'Well, he's not here now, is he.'

Robbie climbed up on the plinth supporting one of the four bronze lions. The fountains were red with blood. A lone bandsman moved on shaky feet towards the National Gallery, face black with tears, a twisted trombone in his arms like a dead child. The remnants of a trade union flag had been ripped from its poles and settled like a rag carpet on the steps. Just about every man in the square looked like Jimmy McGee in shabby clothes and cloth caps.

Nurses arrived in white smocks with broad red crosses and cloaks of navy blue, uniforms that could have been cut from Union Jacks. He heard the slow drum and clatter of horses as the mounted police withdrew. A unit of bobbies under the command of a burly sergeant arrived with barricades stacked on hand carts and erected a cordon across the entrance to Whitehall. Robbie climbed down and went to speak to the sergeant.

'A mate of mine's missing. Where might I find him?'

The policeman looked him up and down, then pointed into the square. 'Out there somewhere, amongst that lot.'

'Aye, and if he's not? If he's hurt?'

Again, the pause. 'Casualties are being taken to St Stephen's in Fulham Road.'

'Is it far?'

'Couple of miles. You'll find it. You found your way here all right.' He pointed over the buildings.

'I'm obliged to you.'

He turned away and the sergeant called him back. 'I'd get a couple of stitches in that cut if I were you.'

'Aye, and if you were me you'd be on this side of the barricade.'

Robbie made his way back to his mates. 'No sign of Jimmy?'

'Not yet,' said Hamish.

'There's a hospital down the road, I'll go and ask.'

'And as like as not you'll find more trouble,' Nat Cohen said. 'I'm going with you.'

The same police sergeant opened the barricade. He directed Robbie and Nat through Admiralty Arch into The Mall. On tall flagpoles all along the wide avenue shaded by trees, Union Jacks lifted on the breeze as if to celebrate a victory. The road ended at Buckingham Palace.

'So that's where they live,' Robbie said.

Nat Cohen hawked up a mouthful of phlegm and spat in the gutter.

They asked for directions again and struck out towards Victoria. People hurried by with flushed faces, men in dusty suits, porters in leather aprons, travellers with trunks on their way to the station. They passed elegant ladies with the voices of songbirds and men in tailored suits who sounded as if they read the news on the wireless.

Chelsea was alive with open-top cars of the sort Robbie had only ever seen in magazines in the waiting room at Glasgow Victoria Infirmary when he took his dad to see the doctor. Da had hurt his back when a crane on the docks came unseated and toppled into the river. He'd been waiting these last nine months for the tribunal's decision on compensation.

Outside the Town Hall in the King's Road, a vendor cried out the headlines from the early edition of *The Evening News*.

'Workers join battle in Barcelona. Read all about it. Battle for Barcelona.'

Nat looked up at Robbie. 'That's the new battleground,

son. Look what the coppers have done to us. If the workers lose Barcelona, we'll lose London and Glasgow.'

'Haven't we lost them already?'

'We will if Oswald Mosley's fascists get into power.'

They squatted down to read the front page of the newspapers stacked on the pavement. Workers and students in Barcelona had organised barricades and repulsed the military's attempt to take the Post Office, main stations and government offices. In the right column below the heading '1936' was a brief timeline.

February 16: Popular Front coalition wins Spanish national elections and forms new Republican government.

July 17: Military uprising begins in Spanish Morocco.

July 18: Insurgents take Seville.

July 19: Insurgents defeated as they attempt to take Barcelona.

July 20: Republic calls for international volunteers.

Nat Cohen pointed his bony finger at the last item. 'That's what I've been saying, laddie. It's one battle. You're either on the side of the fascists and the rich men who support them, or you stand up and fight against them.'

Robbie took off his cap and ran his hand through his dark curls. He felt a tug in his guts, a longing for something, probably a smoke. That's the trouble when you have a fag – it's not long before you want another one. Nat carried on reading and Robbie spoke to the newspaper seller.

'We're on our way to St Stephen's, is it far?'

'You come down with the hunger march?'

'Aye. We've lost one of our mates.'

He pointed. 'It's not far. Go to the top of Sydney Street and turn left on to the Fulham Road.'

*

The casualty department smelled of carbolic soap. It was as big as a railway station with dark walls and a high ceiling. Two guards stood in the doorway. Women with silent children sat in the dim light on wooden benches. The constant clatter of metal instruments in metal dishes was interspersed with the occasional cry of pain as stretcher-bearers rushed through with some poor soul bleeding and dying.

'Hell's waiting room,' Nat Cohen said.

'I'll get in line. Go take a look, see if he's here somewhere.'

A sister with an elaborate headdress like a kite stood at a high desk where a line of people waited for attention. She studied a sheet of paper, then gave it back to the old man before her. 'Wrong date,' she announced and the man wandered off with a crestfallen expression. As they shuffled forward, Robbie noticed the auxiliary nurse at the sister's side. She was all in white like a ray of sunshine. Their eyes met and he looked away. It was 20 minutes before he reached the desk. The sister spotted his gashed cheek and pointed.

'Wrong line. Over there for casualty.'

'No, Sister, it's…'

'Wrong line. Over there.'

He raised his voice. 'There's nowt wrong with me. I'm looking for me mate. His name's Jimmy McGee. Would he be a patient here?'

'Why didn't you say so.' The sister reached for a list containing 20 or so names. 'No, no one by that name.'

'Are you sure? He could be in a ward by now.'

She bristled. 'All the emergency admissions for today are on the list.'

'Unless he had no identification papers on him,' the young nurse suggested.

'Indeed.' The sister adjusted her expression. 'You can enquire at the mortuary.'

Robbie couldn't process the word. Wasn't that a place for

dead people? Jimmy couldn't be dead! He'd never done any harm to anyone. He didn't start fights. He stopped them.

'The nurse will take you. You can't go on your own.'

Robbie noticed Nat sitting by the main entrance reading a newspaper. 'Back in a tick,' he called.

He followed the girl through double doors that led to a staircase where the cold air was a respite from the heat and sweat of the day. They paused for a moment and the nurse studied the cut on his cheek.

'You should have a doctor take a look,' she said.

Her voice was like water bubbling in a stream, clear and confident. She looked directly into his eyes.

'Aye,' he said finally. 'I'd like to find me mate first.'

He followed her down the stairs to the basement. From there, an arched passageway lit by gas lamps led to a green-painted door, the word 'Mortuary' carved into the stone lintel. They entered. Robbie removed his cap. Air shafts gave out a token of light from high-set, barred windows. Lined up in two rows at the far end of the chamber were eight tables. One of them was occupied.

'Miserable place this,' he said.

Their eyes met again. 'Awful,' she replied.

The mortuary attendant made his way towards them. He was tall, a wide-set individual with a grim expression. He held a clipboard.

'We are looking for...' the nurse paused and glanced at Robbie.

'Jimmy McGee,' he said.

'How old is he?'

'About my age, a skinny lad,' he replied and hesitated.

It was hard to recall what Jimmy looked like. He never looked at his mates in the way he looked at the girl, at her green eyes with flecks of gold, at the strands of dark hair escaping from her cap.

'Come and have a look. Don't touch nothing,' the mortuary attendant said.

He led them to the occupied table. As he turned back the sheet, he didn't look at the corpse, he studied his visitor.

Robbie stared down at Jimmy McGee, his body wilted inside blood-stained clothes. His right eye and the whole right side of his face were missing. What was left was just bloody red gore.

'Oh, Jimmy, what have they done to thee?' he said. Tears pricked his eyes.

'So, you know this bloke then? What's his name again?' The attendant had his clipboard ready. He licked the tip of his pencil.

Robbie was unable to answer. His insides were knotted up. It was hard to take in: Jimmy dead. He had never seen a dead person before.

'He's just a lad who walked all the way from Glasgow.'

'From that bloody hunger march, was he?'

Robbie ignored him. He unfurled his cap and placed it on the remains of Jimmy's head.

'Oi, I told you not to touch nothing.'

The man swiped at Robbie's arm with the clipboard.

The nurse stepped forward. 'I say, steady on,' she said.

The attendant went to remove the cap. Robbie clamped his wrist and the man lurched backwards as he released him. He dropped the clipboard and charged forwards. Robbie struck out with a single punch to the gut and the man folded like a closed suitcase as he slipped to the floor. The nurse went down to her knees at his side. He was gasping for breath and looked ready to rise and continue the fight.

'Are you all right?' she asked.

'It takes more than that to keep me down,' he snapped. He glared up at Robbie Gillan. 'Don't think you're going to get away with that.'

The nurse stood. 'You must hurry,' she said. 'They'll arrest you.'

Robbie took one last look at his friend. 'I'm sorry, Jimmy. I should have looked after you.'

He turned and raced towards the door. The nurse followed. As they entered the passage, the mortuary attendant wasn't far behind. He had regained his breath and shouted at the top of his voice.

'Police! Help! Police!'

They chased up the stairs. All eyes were on Robbie as he barged through the double doors into the casualty department. The mortuary attendant's cry for help rose up the stairwell. Nat Cohen rushed across the room.

'What's happened? Have you seen Jimmy?'

'He's down there on a table. The bastards killed him.'

As Nat was about to continue speaking, one of the doormen wrestled him to the floor. Before the second doorman reached them, the nurse pulled at Robbie's sleeve.

'Come,' she said.

The crowd parted as she led him towards a door marked 'Private.' They entered a white-tiled passage, turned and ran along a corridor leading to the rear of the building. They paused to catch their breath. The girl touched her fingers to his cheek.

'You'll be scarred,' she said.

'Then I will never forget this day.'

'What will you do? Where will you go?'

He would look back on this moment and wonder where exactly the words had come from.

'If I had the money, I'd go to Spain.'

Her eyes glowed. They were bright with excitement. He pushed the bar to open the door and she stopped him.

'Wait,' she said.

She took a leather purse from her apron, removed a folded

£5 note and pressed it into his hand. He tried to push it back.

'Don't be mad. I can't take this.'

'Please. I didn't work for it.'

He tried to process what she had said as he looked back into her eyes. Her pink mouth was open. He had a terrible urge to kiss her and would have done so had Jimmy not been lying dead in the mortuary. They heard footsteps racing down the corridor.

'There they are!' a voice cried.

He swung the door open. He took one last look at the girl and kissed her on the cheek.

2

SIMON SHERIDAN PACED the parquet floor with his hands gripped behind his back, a mannerism, Alice realised, that belonged to their father.

'I've never been allowed to make a single decision for myself. Not ever,' he said.

'Tell Daddy what he wants to hear, then do what you want.'

Alice sat in a straight-backed chair, her calm in contrast to her brother's restless journey up and down the library.

'That's all very well for you. You're a girl.'

'I am not a girl. I am a woman. And older than you.'

'I was the afterthought.'

'Oh, poor me!'

'But it is different. Your life is all dancing and fiancés. All you have to do is get married.'

'I'm not going to get married. And I'm not going to get engaged again. There was such a fuss when I broke it off with Pipper Stuart.'

'You must have accepted his ring.'

'Actually, I didn't. He put it on my finger when I wasn't looking, then put an announcement in *The Times*.'

'Is that what you told Father?'

Her eyebrows rose in two arches. 'That happens to be the truth.'

Simon marched on. A muscle vibrated on the left side of his neck as if an insect was burrowing below the surface of the skin.

'Pipper made me laugh. But when I thought about what

it would be like to spend the rest of my life with him...'

Her voice trailed off as her brother retreated into the distance, turned and made his way back again.

'I'm going to do something completely different. I haven't decided what, but when I do, I won't let Daddy stop me.' She stood and took Simon's arm. 'You shouldn't have told him you didn't want to go into the army. You might change your mind next year.'

'There is no chance of that. Everything is changing. Look at Spain. The army's killing its own people because they want human rights.' He paused. 'There was a hunger march today and the mounted police were sent in to break it up.'

A reflex drew her fingertips to her cheek and the memory of running through the corridors at St Stephen's made her heart beat faster.

'I helped some of the injured at the hospital,' she said.

'But it's wrong, Alice. If I take a commission, I'll be a part of all that.'

'Then what will you do?'

He took a breath. 'I'm going to Spain.'

They stopped and Alice looked up into her brother's eyes. 'You're the second person who's said that to me today.'

'The Republic needs volunteers. If we don't stop the fascists in Spain, they'll grow more confident in Italy and Germany. Even here.'

Alice considered her brother's words. The world was changing, splitting along new lines and ideologies. She had drawn her first breath as the country went to war in 1914. A little more than 20 years had passed and the war drums were beating again. She reached up to kiss Simon's cheek as Nanny Fosse appeared in the doorway.

'It's all right, Nanny, we were just going.'

'Thank you, dear.'

She switched on the wall lights and closed the curtains.

It was a task she performed each evening, giving herself a purpose since she no longer had one. Simon held the door and followed Alice into the drawing room where their mother rose from her chair with a worried expression.

'Your father's waiting,' she said, glancing at Simon, then Alice, and back again. 'I really don't understand why everything is so complicated. You don't want to go into the army. Alice has been given the bullet.'

'What?' He turned to his sister. 'Why didn't you tell me?'

'It was the mortician's fault,' Alice said. 'He was absolutely horrible to a young chap whose friend had been killed...'

'In the hunger march?'

She nodded. 'They came to blows. I had to help him escape.'

Simon felt ashamed that in the library they had only spoken of his troubles when Alice had her own. He poured himself a large brandy and drank it down in one.

'Good luck,' she said.

He buttoned his jacket and spoke decisively.

'*All into the valley of death. Rode the six hundred.*'

*

His father was at his desk annotating items in *The Times* when Simon entered his study. The wall lamps emphasised his lean features and put a gloss on the dark wave of his abundant hair, of which Simon suspected he was rather proud. General Sir Richard Sheridan looked younger than his 54 years, broad, six feet two inches with bellicose eyebrows and the rare green eyes he shared with his daughter.

There had, Simon believed, been some unconscionable blunder his father had never been able to understand or completely forgive. Alice had not only raced into the world three minutes before him, she had taken their father's colouring and poise. He was the late arrival, indecisive, artistic, with blue eyes and the pale bronze hair that suited his mother more than it suited him.

'What's happening in Spain, Father?' he asked. 'Isn't the military going against the will of the people?'

'We are not here to speak about Spain, goddam it,' his father replied. He glanced around at the dark-haired, green-eyed ancestors on the walls of the study, then leaned back, knitting his fingers together. 'There have always been Sheridans in the British Army. It is not something over which we have a choice. It is a duty.'

The muscle in Simon's neck gathered speed as he spoke. 'Isn't our first duty to be true to what we believe?'

'When you come down from Oxford, you will go into the regiment. Beliefs are a private matter, something a man must learn to control.'

'Father, this is a vital moment in history. Each one of us must make a personal decision, not one based on family or country.'

'It is not uncommon for a young man to go through this phase. It's like pimples. Something you grow out of. When you do, you'll thank me for not pandering to you.'

'It's not a question of what I want, but what I feel. I have to trust my instincts.'

'You, sir, are the last person to trust in their instincts,' he said.

He paused long enough for Simon to recall the humiliation he had brought down on himself during his first term at Eton. He had clearly been coerced by an older boy who was hastily expelled, but the unpleasant incident had been used as a stick to beat him ever since. His father was stroking the scar below his right eye, a souvenir from the Somme. He had taken the high ground.

'I am pleased that you care about the welfare of others.

It is a crucial quality for an officer. But you are misguided in where you place your passion. This socialist blight spreading across Europe destroys initiative. It makes men lazy and lily-livered when we need the kind of chaps who can reinforce the Empire.'

'The Empire is all but finished,' Simon said and his father guffawed.

'You are being sucked in by the scoundrels who want to destroy our culture. Do you think a handful of bare-arsed Hindus are going to bring down the British Crown?'

General Sheridan took a 12-inch wooden ruler from a drawer, stood and slapped his open hand. He circled the study, tapping the frames holding the portraits of their forebears.

'Your name was listed for your schools the day you were born. The same with the regiment. You are not invited to apply for a commission in the Coldstream Guards unless you come from the best people...'

'People are people. There are no best and no worst.'

'That's socialism.'

'It's Christianity.'

'You are trying to be too clever. When General Gordon was killed by the Mahdi at Khartoum, the officer who led the relief expedition was Colonel Simon Bramston Sheridan, your grandfather. You have the name of a hero,' his father said. 'We are all equal in the eyes of God. Of course. We, you and I, were born in the position to ensure that God's will be done.'

'Is God's will being done in Spain?'

'That's another matter.'

'The army's butchering its own people. They're murdering schoolteachers and intellectuals, even doctors.'

'While the anarchists kill priests and policemen doing their duty.'

'The army and the police should be protecting the Republic the people voted for. That's their duty.' Simon's voice had risen. Always a mistake. 'They may be able to terrorise the people, but in the end, they'll never beat them.'

'Dear boy,' his father said, smiling for a moment. 'The Republic's finished. King Alfonso's arse will be back on the throne in a matter of weeks.'

He spoke in a way that brooked no argument. His father had long since exchanged his uniform for a pin-striped suit and club tie. He called himself a diplomat, but the car that drove him into St James's each morning pulled up at 54 Broadway, described by the sign outside as a fire extinguisher company, the waggish cover for SIS, Britain's Secret Intelligence Service. The general's staff monitored pacifist and labour organisations at home, as well as the political situation in Russia and on the Continent. His agents in Spain would be keeping him informed.

Simon rubbed his fingers over his neck. He should never have drunk the brandy. It had not taken the edge off his nerves. On the contrary, he had broken out in a sweat. Without thinking, he took the keys from the casing in the grandfather clock and passed them through his fingers like worry beads. His father sat, the ruler still in his hands.

'I am pleased that you follow the world situation...'

'Father,' Simon interrupted. 'It doesn't matter what you say. I am not going to apply for a commission. My mind is made up...'

His father stood again. His jacket was on the back of his chair. In his waistcoat and shirtsleeves, he looked ready for a fight.

'You will do my bidding, sir. That is not a request...'

'I will not.'

The ruler gripped in his father's hands snapped under the pressure and a spike of wood stabbed his palm. Blood shot over his shirt cuff. His voice rose to a roar.

'You will accept the King's Commission, or you will leave this house and this family for good.'

Simon was on his feet. The tic below his ear was tapping away like a drum beat. He absently slipped the keys he was holding in his pocket and moved around the desk.

'Father, are you all right?'

'Keep your hands off me. You heard what I said. Now fuck off.'

3

Europe Divisé

It was a concise and accurate assessment. As for the three columns of newsprint below the headline in *L'Humanite* that morning, they were no more than a repetition of all that had been written in the newspapers and debated on the streets during the weeks Simon Sheridan had spent in Paris.

He sat at a table outside a café popular with students on the Quai de la Tournelle. He dipped the claw of his croissant in the froth of a *café au lait* and read once more how the Spanish Civil War had divided Europe.

Germany and Italy had instantly provided weaponry to Spain's military uprising, a Nationalist alliance of generals, royalists, the Church and the old rich. The French and British had opted for a position of non-intervention. They had denied Spain's fledgling democracy arms and medical aid, the policy extended to blocking volunteers setting out to fight for the Republic.

While the French government maintained the travel ban, underground networks were taking recruits through France and over the old smugglers' routes that cross the Pyrenees to Spain. Since he had arrived on the Night Ferry at the Gare du Nord, he had climbed endless flights of stairs to smoky offices where union organisers took one look at him before shaking their heads and echoing the same words: *Pas de papiers, pas d'aller*. No papers, no go.

He marched in noisy demonstrations. He stood on street

corners listening to fiery speeches. There was jazz in the bars at night and the pungent smell of Gauloises clung to his clothes, the perfume of revolution. As he opened his eyes each morning, the same thought entered his mind: disappointment that the battle for Spain was going on without him, assuaged by the pleasure of seeing the light rise over Paris from the attic he had rented in the Boulevard St Michel. Like Harry Houdini, he had escaped from his chains and found in the poetry he covertly wrote something that had always been missing: a sense of rhythm and purpose.

The working people of Spain were facing the guns of their own military and their fellow workers across Europe were mobilising to fight at their sides. To join the ranks, you needed a union card, a history of activity, the coal blue tattoo of the miner. It had been the same in London. After talking to Percy Drew, who had been at Oxford and now worked at the *News Chronicle*, he had made his way to the offices of the Communist Party, the Independent Labour Party, the Fabian Society – all to no avail. They took one look at him with his clear-water gaze and tailored jacket and showed him the door. It clarified in Simon's mind the absurdity of any form of class, race or religious prejudice.

In a moment of self-pity, it occurred to him that if he left Paris now, he could be back in Oxford in time to start the new term. He could finish his degree, endure a stint in the family regiment, then join the Foreign Office. It was a life, and he had to ask himself what was stronger, his determination to go to Spain or his resolve to defy his father.

Alice, after losing her job at St Stephen's, had joined the Red Cross and wrote short, funny letters about life as a student nurse. His poems were laden with metaphor and subtext. Alice's letters, written in green Indian ink, captured life in all its wonder and made him laugh.

Sister McKinley boasts a long nose befitting one of the

witches in Macbeth and has the double vision of one who sees me doing something amiss, even when we're not in the same room. It is fortunate that now I have learned to stitch wounds, I will save a king's ransom with the dressmaker by taking up the hems of my skirts now that it has been decreed by some higher authority that ladies this season should wear them shorter.

He missed Alice. At times, it felt as if they were two halves of one thing, that all the best qualities were in her and he had been forced to set out on this hopeless journey in order to find himself. He missed the lazy days at Oxford, cricket and rowing, the dreaming spires that made the city a living work of art.

Nostalgia is a melancholy flower that opens on long afternoons spent alone.

He closed his notebook, pushed his arms into his jacket and set off for a stroll that ended at the booksellers clustered along the left bank of the Seine. He found, in a box of English books, *The Sun Also Rises*, Ernest Hemingway's novel of a group of expatriates travelling from Paris to Pamplona to take part in the running of the bulls.

He bought the book and made his way back to the quai de la Tournelle. His step was more resolute and he was annoyed that he had earlier allowed any doubts to distract him. He had delayed long enough. He would spend his last night in Paris and leave next day on the overnight train for Perpignan. He would buy some climbing boots and cross the mountains on his own.

When Simon took his meal in his favourite café, he found himself judging the two men at the next table in the same way as the union officials had judged him. He smiled at his own hypocrisy. Is it not the faults in ourselves that we condemn in others? It is the human condition but, still, the two men were oddly out of place. They were older, in dark suits and shiny shoes. The taller of the two had broad shoulders, heavy eyebrows and a pencil moustache. He talked while he was eating, his conversation suffused with murderous loathing for the trade unions and France's socialist government.

'The whole lot of them should be strung up and horse whipped. I'm a monarchist and proud of it.'

'You are right, Michel,' the other man repeated. He had a narrow face and rat eyes that darted about the room. On his head, he wore a black beret with a fleur-de-lis gold badge.

Simon glanced around the bar with its high stools and zinc counter, the bottles lined up against silver-backed mirrors. It was full of students debating the intricacies of revolution, there in that bar because they shared the same views.

He tried to block out the conversation and filled his glass with the fruity red wine stored in barrels stacked against the wall. While his bowl of onion soup cooled, he read an article in *L'Illustration* about Federico García Lorca, the Spanish poet who had been murdered by the Falange, Spain's Fascist Party. The magazine also carried an article about a royalist mob in Pamplona who had celebrated the annual Feast of the Virgin with the customary service at the Cathedral, a fireworks display and, as a finale, 50 Republicans had been marched into the square and shot. The bishop gave the executions his blessing.

It was a coincidence that the book by Hemingway was set in Pamplona, not that it had any significance except that he was suddenly ashamed of being Catholic.

'France is being ruled by the Jews and Bolsheviks,' the man named Michel bellowed.

'Jews and Bolsheviks,' his companion repeated.

Simon leaned closer to their table. 'I suppose if you were Spanish, you would join the Falange?'

Michel threw out his chest. 'I would consider it an honour to serve General Franco. He is driving the communists out of Spain. They,' he paused to make his point, 'are the scum of the earth.'

'*Monsieur*, the scum of the earth is seated at your table,' Simon replied with a politeness the other man found momentarily confusing.

'Filth. Foreigner. Communist,' he then yelled, his eyes growing wild.

His chair fell as he came to his feet. Simon stood and Michel took a swing he had no problem blocking. Simon was six-foot, muscles firm from rowing. He had boxed at Eton.

The man in the beret moved between them. 'Not here,' he hissed.

Several students turned their heads in Simon's direction as he led the way out. The woman lodged behind the *caisse* went to present him with his bill, but the patron threw up his hands and shrugged.

'Here,' Michel said.

He had come to a halt at the entrance to a cobbled passage between high walls. The misty rain was captured in the quivering light of the gas lamp on the corner. As Simon entered the passage, his shadow stretched out long and ungainly before him. He removed his jacket and hung it on a nail poking out conveniently from the wall. He turned to face the men, knees flexed, fists raised.

'Scum of the earth, eh?'

He heard the click of a flick-knife as it flashed into life and gleamed in the hazy light. It was in the hand of the man in the beret. Michel had produced a blackjack, a leather-covered club, a street weapon. Simon felt the sweat on his back turn cold. His mind raced. *They're going to kill me.* The Falange had murdered Lorca because he was assumed to be homosexual. The monarchists shot people for entertainment.

Michel pounced, swinging his weapon. Simon feinted one way, then the other, and stopped the blow before the cosh landed. He released a quick one-two, striking the man's left cheek and right ear. The blows sent him reeling back towards the streetlight.

The other man had moved in at the same time. He slashed out tentatively and cut a zigzag from the air. Simon's long right wiped the grin from his face, but his knife hand swept back in a long arc and the blade sliced into Simon's upper arm. He let out a cry of pain and reached automatically for the wound.

Michel was back on his feet and moved slowly down the passage. He drew back the cosh and paused before bringing it down on Simon's skull.

Dead in an alleyway in Paris. How ignoble. How pointless. He had done nothing. Achieved nothing.

But he had taken a side.

Michel grinned. He paused to savour his moment of triumph, that pause a fraction too long. A hand in the dark gripped the crook of his arm and a knee cannoned into his spine. A figure appeared from the shadows, eyes burning in the spectral light. He elbowed Michel in the neck and punched him on the side of his face with such force Simon heard his cheekbone breaking. The stranger swivelled round, eyes moving from Simon to the man on the ground.

'Don't just stand there, put the boot in.'

Simon still clutched his arm. Blood poured over his fingers. His mind raced on a spinning wheel from death and disaster to elation. The man in the beret was rising, knife outstretched, the wet blade thirsty for more. Simon kicked it from his hand and the man crawled quickly, crab like, to retrieve it.

Michel had levered himself up against the wall like a heavyweight resting on the ropes. He snatched air from the murky night and lurched forward, swinging the blackjack. The stranger stepped to one side, felled him with a blow to the throat and stepped swiftly between the knife and its owner.

Just as the man was about to grab the handle, the stranger scooped it from his grasp and gave him a good kick in the middle of his chest.

The stranger passed the knife from hand to hand. It was like a circus trick. The other man watched, mesmerised. He expected the blade to be plunged into his heart, it's what he would have done, but as he sank back on the cobbles, the new arrival closed the knife and slipped it into his pocket.

He took the linen jacket from the nail on the wall.

'I imagine this is yours?' he said, and Simon nodded. 'In a fight, it's not the taking part that matters.'

Simon's knees were shaking. The cut was deep. The stranger pulled the red scarf from his neck and wrapped it around the top of his arm.

'You saved my life,' Simon gasped, and the stranger looked back into his eyes.

'What do you think you were doing taking on the two of them?'

'I assumed we were going to box. I didn't expect them to be armed.'

The other man shook his head as he finished tying the tourniquet. He grabbed the black beret as they stepped over Michel.

'I've always fancied one of these,' he said, and pulled it down at an angle over his right ear.

They returned to the bar and sat beside the barrels. The patron filled a carafe and placed it on the table with two glasses. He stared at Simon's bloody arm and his languid features trembled with sudden animation.

'Très bien. Compliment de la maison.'

The man who had saved his life studied the beret. It was good quality, edged with a leather band, the hat-maker's label sewn inside.

Simon had caught his breath. 'You ought to take the badge

off. It's what French fascists wear.'

'You know about that sort of thing do you?'

'It's the old symbol of the French monarchy.'

He looked back across the table, weighing Simon up, his sharp features like a Cubist collage of all the union men and party organisers Simon had confronted since his arrival in Paris. The man removed the badge with the fleur-de-lis, placed it on the floor and crushed it beneath the heel of his boot.

Simon's arm was throbbing. 'I was thinking earlier that I hated being a Catholic. Now it seems like a miracle you appearing like that. A perfect stranger.'

'Perfect, maybe. But not entirely a stranger.' Simon looked puzzled. 'I've seen you going in and out of different offices all over the city. And you looked pretty fed up an' all.' He poured two glasses of wine from the carafe and looked up with an expression that was no longer humorous. He had dark perceptive eyes and the scar on his cheek gave him a menacing appearance. 'What are you trying to do?'

'I want to get to Spain...'

The man emptied his glass. 'Now that is a miracle,' he said. 'I might be able to help you.'

Simon pushed his hand across the table to introduce himself.

'Simon Sheridan,' he said, and the other took a firm grip.

'Robbie Gillan,' he replied.

4

SHE DUCKED OUT of the rain into the taxi and made herself comfortable in the moulded leather seat. Percy Drew spoke to the driver and climbed in beside her, his fine hair slicked flat on his head. It had been clear and unseasonably warm when they strolled down Drury Lane to the Theatre Royal. Now rain was bouncing off the pavements.

The taxi raced along Piccadilly. She rubbed mist from the window and watched a man with an inside-out umbrella being pulled along by the wind. Percy held the gloved fingers of her right hand. She would rather have kept her hand to herself, but it seemed to please him.

They turned into Mayfair and splashed to a halt outside a white building with candlelight behind every window. Percy dashed into the rain to open her door and Alice stepped into the steamy warmth of Trattoria Iacomo. A woman took her coat. Waiters moved between the tables as if performing a dance with trays balanced on their fingertips. The restaurant was decked out with red-checked tablecloths and candles in Chianti bottles. Italian food was in vogue, and negotiating plates of wriggling pasta was a trial for diners raised by English nannies obsessed with the correct use of the knife and fork.

With his swept-back black hair and dark eyes, Iacomo was a broad, rugged man aware of his good looks and played his role as maître d' as if he were Don Giovanni in Mozart's opera. As he showed them to their table, he treated Alice as if she were a long-lost member of his own family.

'*Che bella ragazza.* It is always my pleasure.'

Iacomo reeled off the dishes in his singsong Italian which Percy seemed to understand. An elderly waiter brought red wine in a clay carafe.

'You've been here before. I thought it would be a surprise,' Drew said.

'It is a surprise. It is the first time I have been here with you.'

They clinked glasses. 'The play,' he then said. 'What did you think?'

Alice was tempted to merely be polite, but believed honesty was infinitely more practical. They had seen *Careless Rapture*, another new musical by Ivor Novello, the love story set in China with an earthquake and a dance sequence in a Buddhist temple.

'Silly,' she answered. 'Although my toes were tapping to some of the tunes.'

'My thoughts exactly. I don't know how he keeps churning them out.'

'Practise,' she replied.

The restaurant was full of people like them and noisy with sudden bursts of shrill laughter. She received an oblique nod from Cordelia Stuart, Pipper's sister, sitting two tables away. The girl's eyes shifted to Percy and her expression became more animated as she leaned across the table to speak to her companion.

Alice remembered another evening at Trattoria Iacomo when Pipper boasted that he had shot 400 elephants in Kenya in a single day. Her stomach grew queasy as he described 'the torrents of blood' and she had been unable to touch the coils of tomato-reddened spaghetti on her plate. She had left the restaurant without saying goodbye, ending the spurious engagement.

The elderly waiter appeared with bowls of spaghetti carbonara. Alice dug her fork into the mix and lifted a neat coil to her lips.

'You are quite the expert,' Percy remarked.

'It's practising with bandages. Bandages and wandering hands.'

She demonstrated, fluttering her fingers. The shadows from the candle flame skipped over the walls and the melancholy look about her lips turned into a smile. In a high-necked red crepe dress and a matching cloche that hid most of her face, she had the appearance of a pixie.

'What did you learn this week?' Drew asked her.

'Lancing boils and draining fluids,' she replied instantly. 'We are full of the ghastliest things.'

'I don't know how you do it.'

'I have a feeling we can do more than we imagine.'

Alice sipped her wine and stared back over the rim of her glass. She was still getting to know Percival Drew and it was at that precise moment that she decided she liked him. Percy had almost finished his spaghetti.

'Did you ever consider becoming a doctor? A lot of women are now.'

'No, not really. I don't know how to do anything except play the piano and speak French, neither of which I'm terribly good at. I just know I have to do something.'

'So you decided to become a nurse.'

'I decided to go to Spain.'

He went to speak and checked himself. The candle flame reflected two ghosts of light in his eyes. He leaned forward.

'I didn't know you were committed, Alice. Are you a communist?' he asked, and her peals of laughter attracted several people, including Cordelia Stuart, to turn towards their table.

'Good heavens, no,' Alice said, controlling herself. 'I'm

not anything. I don't think it's necessary to put yourself in a pigeonhole.'

'You do know people are dying in the streets. The army's completely ruthless.'

'Better than dying of boredom in your bedroom.' Alice's expression had grown serious and Drew felt as if he were catching a glimpse of the wheels turning in her mind. 'It seems important to take a side. That's what Simon says. We usually end up thinking the same way.'

'Is he in Paris still?'

'I'm not sure. He hasn't written for ages.'

'He probably doesn't want your Papa to know where he is,' he suggested. 'I'm sure you're aware, our government isn't supporting the volunteers.'

Alice raised her glass. 'To Simon,' she toasted, and their glasses rang out as they touched rims. 'Why aren't we supporting the volunteers?' she asked, and Drew shrugged his big shoulders.

'Britain doesn't have permanent friends or enemies. We have permanent interests. That's what Lord Palmerstone said. By standing back and watching, we will be on the winning side no matter who wins.'

'You make it sound as if this is a greedy, nasty little country full of its own self-interest.'

'I didn't mean it like that. Britain and France want to avoid a proxy war with Germany and Italy. But there are business interests behind every political decision.'

Alice sat back reflectively. 'Perfidious Albion,' she said.

'We can blame the French for that.'

'I hate politics.'

'If you do go to Spain, that's a political statement.'

'Or a human statement.'

'Good point.' He paused. 'Do you plan to go with the Red Cross?'

'Ideally,' she replied. 'But there are more people than places. They need ambulances more than volunteers.'

'Then you should raise the money and buy one.'

'Why didn't I think of that?' she said and leaned forward. She kissed a fingertip and touched it to Drew's lips. 'You're a genius, Percy.'

'Not that I want you to go,' he said dramatically. 'The very idea is like a dagger in my heart.'

The waiter appeared. She had eaten two forkfuls of spaghetti and waved the plate away. He returned with a green salad with parmesan shavings and a fresh carafe of wine. It still wasn't certain why Simon had not written, but at least Percy had provided a logical explanation. She had always felt protective towards him. She ran before he could walk. Until the age of ten, she had been taller, quicker. Where she went, he followed. He had shot up and filled out at 14, but still she thought of Simon as her little brother.

The salad was delicious with the nutty parmesan. She watched as Percy ate. She liked his movements. His hands were large but moved gracefully. He had a solid nose and a firm jaw set in a face that was less handsome than memorable.

'Does your father know your plans?' he asked.

'We're not on speaking terms.'

'Then I shall inform on you. He'll have your photograph posted at all the ports: this girl is wanted for activities unbecoming to her class and family.'

'Now you're being silly.'

'But he'll be heartbroken. Losing one twin to the war in Spain is unfortunate. Losing two...'

'He won't be heartbroken, he'll be furious. His only wish for me is that I toddle off and get married.' She paused. 'To the right sort of chap, of course.'

'Would I be considered the right sort of chap?'

His tone was self-mocking but the question made Alice pause

for thought. She shook her head. 'No, of course not,' she answered. 'Daddy would have a file and discover you're a communist.'

*

The rain had stopped. A few stars had broken through the London murk. An empty taxi was waiting outside the restaurant, but Alice wanted to walk and set the pace down Park Lane, her Oxfords resounding like a tin drum on the shiny, wet pavement.

'Alice, can we slow down, I can hardly keep up with you.'

'That's what everybody says.'

She took his arm and hurried him along. They skirted Hyde Park and turned into Lowndes Square.

Entering Percy's rooms was like stepping into the pages of an illustrated magazine. All the dust and detritus of the last century had been replaced with the smooth lines and geometric shapes of Art Deco. The mirror over the mantel was shaped like a fan and there was a painting of a group of women with angular features holding cocktail glasses. On the oval-shaped table was a black figurine of a willowy nude supporting a white globe in her upstretched hands.

'She looks a lot like you,' he said as he switched on the light.

'Is that coincidence or design?'

'Isn't coincidence just fate?'

She looked down at the lines on her palms. 'I don't believe in fate, Percy. I'm much too practical,' she said, and even as she spoke she remembered that just a few hours before Simon told her he was going to Spain, she had run breathlessly through the corridors of St Stephen's with a stranger who had the same dream.

Percy removed a gramophone record from its sleeve, placed it on the turntable and wound the mechanism. She watched as he lifted the arm and placed the needle on the black vinyl disc.

'Vivaldi. '*Cessate omai cessate*',' he said.

He asked if she wanted more wine, or tea? She shook her head. She didn't want anything to drink. She didn't know what she wanted. She stared out at the trees shifting in the black night. Percy turned off the overhead light and the white globe over the lamp shone like a full moon. Vivaldi's strings captured the motions of the sea and she pictured herself on a boat on a warm day with the sun on her back. The singer had a rich, soothing voice that seemed to emerge from the depths of her soul and Alice was vaguely surprised at her own desire as Percy took her in his arms.

Their lips met. His hands moved down her back and rode over the curve of her bottom. She liked the feeling, the thrill of illicit pleasure. It seemed right. Isn't there a right time for everything? He unclasped the row of buttons lying over her spine. The dress slid from her shoulders and fell in a red pool at her feet. He cupped her breast. His hand passed down over her hips. He shrugged out of his jacket, his shirt, his tie. He pulled her warm flesh to his and eased away her slip, her garter belt, her white satin drawers.

Alice viewed the peeling away of her clothes as if she were watching from across the room. She was, at the same time, both present and distant. She wanted to feel the weight of a man's heavy limbs on her. She wanted to give herself spontaneously without considering the implications, as she always did. Percy's fingers brushed over her pubic bone. She felt a dampness that was alarming and marvellous. She wanted it to continue, to go on and on. But some impulse made her open her eyes. As quickly as the desire had come it had gone again. She remained motionless. He pulled back.

'I'm sorry, Percy,' she said.

'No, no, don't say that. It is me who should be sorry. I shouldn't have rushed you.'

'You didn't.'

He looked back into her eyes, his hands clasped around her back. 'Is it because you're Catholic?' he asked with the reporter's regard for explanations where there were none.

'No, Percy. I told you. I don't think I'm anything.'

She lifted her shoulders in a shrug and moved away. She dressed without embarrassment. Percy buttoned the back of her dress. She sat on the edge of an armchair and slipped back into her shoes. Drew dressed.

'I'm sorry,' Alice said again. 'I like you. I like you more than you know.'

'You're afraid, that's all. I imagine you're still...' His words ran out and she gave a high, disconcerted laugh.

'I am, yes. But that has nothing to do with it.'

She rose and went to look out of the window.

'It's really begun to pour,' she said.

Vivaldi had come to an end. She listened to the rain. She was thinking about Simon, the way he had left with his suitcase gripped in his hand like a talisman. She was thinking about the way the boy had kissed her cheek in the corridor at St Stephen's. She was thinking about how she might raise the money to buy an ambulance and her thoughts, her very being, were beyond the room, too distant for Percy Drew to reach. Her naked body that he had held in his arms belonged to a moment that may never have been and would never be repeated.

5

SIMON STARED OUT at the sweep of autumn colours from his window seat on a train heading south. He had been in Paris for eight weeks. His French had improved and so had his writing. At least, he wanted to think so. Thanks to Robbie Gillan's intervention, he had been accepted by the French Workers' International as a volunteer and been made a *responsable* for the journey. His job was to liaise with Alain Beaubien, their guide to the Spanish frontier.

He glanced at Robbie in the seat opposite. He was reading the anthology of Blake, Alice's gift that night at Victoria before he took the Night Ferry to France. Robbie, as Simon's sponsor, had been ordered to watch him and, with a paranoia Simon thought excessive, an Irishman by the name of Paddy O'Hay was watching them both. With them, making a party of 12 men, were Oscar Kuntze, a German; two Dutch steelworkers; José Rosé, a cabaret performer from Cuba, and the five Jones brothers from Wales. There were three units on the train, 35 men in all.

Paris had been damp and overcast when they assembled at daybreak at Gare d'Austerlitz. But the sky cleared as the grey, conical-roofed buildings of the industrial north gave way to the white façades and red tiles of the wine-growing regions of the south. They stopped at country stations with musical names and walls painted with advertisements for Absinthe Robette and Dubonnet.

He turned away from the window as the sun slipped

through a patch of cloud and lit Robbie's face in a way that reminded him of an impressionist portrait – Renoir? Degas? – the fixed lines and luminous eyes capturing something intense and beautiful. Robbie looked up from the book.

'Aye?' he said.

'Don't worry about what it means, just enjoy the flow of the words, the rhythm.' He smiled. 'Reading poetry is like sitting on a train.'

They stopped at a ramshackle station outside Grenoble. Men in berets passed food and wine through the windows. As the train pulled away, they raised clenched fists.

Oscar Kuntze returned the salute. With his fierce side-whiskers and lively green eyes, Kuntze had the fanatical look of the Sheridan ancestors in his father's study. The German had been the leader of the railway workers union in Munich. He was fleeing the Gestapo.

Simon glanced around the carriage. His comrades ate the fat baguettes filled with cheese and ham in the slow way of men who had known hunger. They wiped the tops of the wine bottles with their sleeves before passing them on. Four men across the aisle were playing rummy, the cards slapping the side of his suitcase. Kuntze was next to him with Lloyd Jones opposite, next to Robbie. He had put the book away and spoke to Lloyd as he ate.

'You're quiet today. Still thinking about your birthday present?'

Lloyd's cheeks flushed. He had turned 18 the day before they left Paris and Simon, under Robbie's guiding hand, had made certain provisions with one of the girls on the Quai de la Tournelle sympathetic to the cause.

Dai Jones leaned over from the card game. 'We've decided to call him Jones the Lover Boy,' he announced in his sing-song voice. At 32, Dai was the eldest of the brothers, short and broad with scarred hands and lean cheeks pitted by coal dust.

'Don't, Dai, don't embarrass me now,' Lloyd said.

Dai took no notice. He pointed around the carriage, first at Bowen. 'That's Leonardo Jones, give him a pencil and he'll draw anything...'

''Cept a decent wage packet,' his brother said.

Dai moved on to Glyn. 'This here is Jones the Pigeon. Best breeder in Wales, at least that's what he tells us.' Rhys was next. 'This is Jones the Pole. Look at him, thin as a pit pony, he is. I'm Jones the Voice, for obvious reasons, and now,' he added, throwing out his arms, 'we have Jones the Lover Boy.'

'Ah, shuddup, Dai. I've only done it once.'

The carriage exploded in laughter.

'Well, twice if you must know.'

They laughed even louder.

*

The locomotive let out steam as they halted at another station. A Tricolour, the red end shredded, slapped in the breeze. Dust whirls scurried along the platform. Two men filled the boiler from a water tank. Simon watched Beaubien, their guide, step down from the train. He gazed up and down the platform, then shielded his brow as he stared off into the hills.

As he climbed back up the iron steps, one of the recruits, fortified by the wine, whistled the 'Internationale', the battle hymn of the movement. The train ground its way out of the station and the volunteers began to sing, Dai the Voice with a sonorous bass that filled the carriage as it filled the stone chapel on the banks of the Rhondda Fawr every Sunday. Simon was on his feet conducting the choir when the door burst open.

'It's a trap,' Beaubien screamed. 'They've shunted us off on a side line. We've got to get out.'

Simon translated. There was a pause, panic. Dai Jones

gathered the playing cards. The men grabbed their knapsacks.

'*Sortez. Sortez. Sortez*,' Beaubien repeated. 'Out. Out. Out.'

They pushed down the aisle between the seats. Beaubien opened the door at the end of the carriage and leapt over the ballast on to the raised bank. Oscar Kuntze followed. The Dutchmen, the Cuban, Paddy O'Hay, the Jones brothers, one after the after. Robbie jumped with his beret gripped between his teeth. Simon tossed his suitcase over the bank and braced himself for the fall. He grabbed the case and raced towards the tree-capped knoll at the edge of the fields.

Shots drilled into the dirt, tap, tap, tap, like knuckles on a door. Bowen Jones limped stiffly. Simon threw his arm around his shoulder. The train stopped a mile along the track. Police riflemen poured out from the lead carriage. They propped themselves up along the bank and began to fire. Stray bullets swished through the branches.

Beaubien cursed as he looked around at the damaged men. A Hungarian was dead. Paddy O'Hay had a badly gashed thigh. A Belgian from the same group had a bullet in his shoulder. Jan Janssen, one of the Dutchmen, had a broken leg and shattered ribs.

'We'll have to carry the poor bugger,' Robbie said. Simon translated.

'It is not impossible. All who can walk must move out.' Beaubien swept his hand through the air, urging them on their way. 'Quickly now...'

'We set out together, we'll move on together,' Robbie said.

Alain Beaubien threw up his hands as if ready to concede. Then, in one swift movement, he grabbed Robbie's jacket and pulled him close. 'This place will be crawling with police in ten minutes. They will come with guns. We will all be in jail. Or dead.'

Robbie tensed, ready to headbutt the Frenchman. Simon rushed out the words in English. Robbie stared into Beaubien's eyes. Beaubien stared back. Neither was going to give way. Simon slid his arm between them.

'We are in France, Robbie. We take orders from Beaubien. An army relies on men taking orders.'

Robbie shifted his gaze.

'We follow Beaubien's orders,' he repeated. 'We move out. Now.'

The world stopped for a moment. Simon had that feeling he'd had before in Paris, that Robbie wasn't looking at him, but at the hidden clock that made him tick. He unclenched his fists and looked back at Beaubien.

'Comrade, pardon.'

The dead Hungarian had been forgotten during the confusion. His face, drained of colour, had turned ivory white. Lloyd Jones stepped away and was sick. Paddy O'Hay pressed the lids down over the Hungarian's eyes.

'That's the second dead man I've seen,' Robbie muttered to Simon. He stepped closer and lowered his voice. 'Thanks,' he said. 'I'll remember that.'

Beaubien barked out instructions. The two Dutchmen clasped hands and parted without another word. The injured man would end up in prison. The dead man in a pauper's grave.

'You will be silent. No talking. No singing. No cigarettes.'

Bowen Jones had strapped up his ankle. Paddy O'Hay limped along with his weight on José Rosé. They made their way through turned fields that rose steadily and avoided the network of lanes that joined farms to villages and villages to towns. As the sun dropped behind the hills, they rested outside a tangle of 20 stone houses around a church. Beaubien went on alone.

The mountains were closer, looming up vast and daunting like grimacing teeth. With the moonrise came the chill mistral that carries cold air from the north. Simon pulled an Aran jumper from his case.

'That looks like a nice warm piece of knitwear you've got,'

O'Hay observed. 'I wonder what else you might be carrying in that bag of yours?'

'A radio transmitter and some loaves of bread. Like Hansel and Gretel,' Simon replied.

'It wouldn't surprise me,' O'Hay said and limped off.

'He can be a right pain,' Simon complained.

'He'll be a good man when there's trouble. Paddy won't play by the rules.'

'We're taught to always play by the rules. Otherwise, it's not cricket.'

'I wouldn't know. I've never played cricket.' Robbie peered up at the stars. 'You're going to have to teach me. I don't know nuthin aboot nuthin.'

'That's tosh.'

'I know how to handle myself in a fight. First thing you learn in Glasgow. You've got to fight with your mates to prove you're not soft. You've got to fight to get a job. Then you have to fight the bosses to get your wages. Life's one bliddy great battle from the day you're born.'

'Is that why you volunteered?'

'Why? That's always a good question. And there's always more than one answer. A mate of mine died marching for work. Then I found myself telling some girl if I'd had the money I'd go to Spain. It's hard to believe. She gave me a £5 note, and here I am.'

They were quiet for a moment. The wind blew harder. Robbie rubbed his hands together. Simon buttoned his jacket and gave his jumper to Gillan.

'Here, we can share it.'

Robbie's instinct was to decline the offer, but he remembered something Maw had said as she gave him a shilling that day when he left on the hunger march: it's harder to take than it is to give.

'Don't mind if I do.'

6

ALICE SAT SIPPING a gin and tonic at the Ritz. The Art Deco lamp on the table beside her reminded her of the naked figurine in Percy's rooms and how she had come that night after the theatre to be naked herself. No man except Percy had ever seen her unclothed and it made her feel terribly modern that they had remained friends after failing to become lovers.

The first time Alice had seen a naked man was in the charity hospital where the student nurses went for practical training. She had washed their seeping sores. She bathed infants whose bellies were swollen from hunger. She filled her nurse's bag with liquorice sticks and jelly babies, a momentary cure for crying children whose ailments were the result of poverty and poor hygiene.

Alice had almost completed the seven-week course at Tredegar House. She shared a room with five other girls and had learned to 'flannel-wash' in the crowded bathroom while they gossiped about hairstyles and handsome doctors. She saved no end of time not having to choose her outfits each day and had come to see her white cap and smock as camouflage. In her old world, everyone knew who you were and your annual income to the nearest penny.

The student nurses were called VADs, Voluntary Aid Detachment trainees. They received no pay, but full board and five shillings a week for laundry. Unlike St Stephen's, with its grim wards and grimy corridors, Tredegar House had been built with the panache of a renaissance villa in 1911. It stood out like a beacon among Bow's cobbled alleyways and her heart danced every time she climbed the marble steps to the white-tiled entrance.

Classes were from eight to 12 each morning when the girls gathered like a flock of doves to learn the intricacies of anatomy, bacteriology, hygiene and cooking. VADs were taught how to take temperatures, give inoculations, keep reports, clean and stitch wounds, apply unguents and change dressings.

Alice had learned how to use the X-ray machine from Hugh Tregarth, a volunteer doctor she had met before at a cricket match and who knew her brother. The Sisters tended to be severe and disapproving, the guardians of the gateways of death, as the charity hospitals were called. They were paid from charitable contributions. The doctors made their living in private practice and served the needs of the poor in their free time. The system functioned because of their kind hearts, and Alice had come to agree with Percy Drew that what was needed was a new structure financed to care for everyone.

While the non-intervention policy on Spain persisted and volunteers were stopped at the border, the British government had made an exception for the Red Cross. Hugh Tregarth was raising funds to buy an ambulance and planned to leave for the Republic. He just needed another £300.

Alice finished her drink and signed a chit that would be added to her bill. Hatless and bubbly from the gin and tonic, heads turned as she entered the dining room in a navy-blue suit with brass buttons that gathered the light from the chandeliers. Percy Drew went to greet her.

'You look wonderful,' he said.

'I'm sure I don't.'

'I assure you, you do.' He held her chair for her to sit. The table was set for three. 'Who are we waiting for?'

'You'll see.' She smiled. 'It's been ages. What's happening in the world? I don't even have time to read the newspapers.'

'Oh, you know, everything and nothing.'

'Tell me about the everything?'

'Let me see.' He counted on his fingers. 'The Nationalists made General Franco the Head of State on the 2nd of October. Illegally, of course. The Cockneys in East London came out to help the Jews stop the Blackshirts storming Cable Street. The same day, the 4th I think it was, 100,000 people marched through Paris in support of the Spanish Republic.'

'Very impressive.'

'Oh, yes, and two days later in Berlin, Hitler watched Diana Guinness marry Oswald Mosley.'

'Did she wear black?'

He laughed and she read in his pleasure a hint of misery. She placed her hand over his.

'You are one of my favourite people. We will always be friends.'

The moment passed. Percy came to his feet. Guy Bradwell had appeared in the doorway, a cigarette in a long holder and a red handkerchief spilling like a bloodstain from the breast pocket of a pale grey suit. Guy was Simon's best friend at Oxford, the son of Lord Bradwell, the newspaper peer.

'Darling, how divine,' he said in a loud voice as he approached and bent to kiss Alice on both cheeks.

The men shook hands.

'Hello, Drew. So, you're the mystery guest.'

'I thought you were, Bradwell.'

Guy sat with an amused expression. 'You have the appearance of plotters,' he remarked. 'And to what do we owe this pleasure?'

'Money,' Alice said. 'I need some. Quite a lot. But not too much.'

'Money is not something one talks about. Not on an empty stomach.'

Guy read from the menu: 'Pigs cheeks, grouse, pigeon

pie, duck breast with chicory and potato dauphinoise, lamb shanks, Lancashire hotpot, baked parsley cod...'

'Stop it, Guy, read to yourself. I can't concentrate.'

The waiter came. Guy chose a bottle of French wine. Alice talked about her nursing course, not that he showed the slightest interest.

'I cannot begin to imagine why you are subjecting yourself to this, Alice. It's probably dangerous and utterly pointless.'

'If I'm going to Spain, Guy, I have to be able to do something useful.'

'You're just being bloody-minded. Like Simon. Where the devil is he, anyway?'

Alice leaned forward. 'He spoke to Mama on the telephone. She could hardly hear a thing, but apparently he was leaving Paris by train with some other chaps.'

Percy sipped from his water glass and rested his large hands on the table. 'It's something to be proud of,' he said. 'People talk about doing something for others. Simon's actually doing it. And so are you.' He turned to Alice.

'I just chase beetles around wretched hospitals.'

She was about to continue when the waiter came with their food. He poured the wine. Alice had ordered the fish and just the sight of it on the plate instantly made her lose her appetite.

'When do you finish your course?' Percy asked before tucking into his hotpot.

'I have exams next week. If I pass, I will receive certificates in First Aid and Home Nursing, for which I will have to pay three shillings.'

'Daylight robbery,' said Guy. He heaved some crackling into his mouth. 'You have managed to intrigue us. As always...'

'How's the duck?' she asked

'Just like a duck,' he replied. 'Now, what about the money?'

She glanced from Guy to Percy and back again. 'You probably know this but let me tell you anyway. In 1914, when they knew the war wasn't going to be over by Christmas, *The Times* published an appeal for funds. In three weeks, they raised enough money to buy 500 ambulances.' She rested her cutlery. 'Do you know Hugh Tregarth?'

'He has a bloody good offside spin,' Guy replied.

Drew knew where Alice was leading them. She was a moth to the flame of new ideas. Full suffrage had only been granted in 1928 and Drew saw in Alice the generation of women who would change the world. He sighed. He imagined for the rest of his life he would regret that he had rushed her that night when he held her in the cage of his arms like a precious bird that had slipped away.

'Hugh plans to take an ambulance and medical crew to Spain and needs another £300,' she was saying and held up her hand as Guy went to speak. 'Wouldn't it be super if we put an appeal in the newspapers to raise the money by public donation? A lot of people support the Republican government.'

'My father isn't one of them,' Guy said.

'Tell him it's for me.'

'He may have fallen for your charms, but he is not about to become a socialist.'

'I think it's a brilliant idea,' Drew told her. 'I am sure the *Chronicle* will run something.'

Guy finished his glass of wine and the waiter refilled it.

'Haven't you left it a bit late for grand gestures?' he said. 'Madrid is going to fall to the Nationalists any day.'

'They expected Madrid to fall yesterday,' Drew countered.

'Exactly.'

'And Madrid survived.'

7

A BUGLE SHOOK them from sleep and 600 shabby men assembled in the courtyard grumbling in a dozen languages. As a glimmer of daylight slid along the horizon, the barracks emerged from the dark, colossal, like a ship arriving in port. Simon, in rope-soled alpargatas, stamped his feet to keep warm and turned his back on the icy wind sweeping down across the high plateau from Toledo.

The chatter stopped as eight men filed out from the main doors and took up positions a dozen paces from the wall. They stood at ease, rifles slantwise over their chests. That same moment, three staff cars carrying a group of officers entered the open gates and pulled to a halt. The first to alight was a stocky man wearing an oversized beret and a leather coat like a cape about his shoulders. There was a sporadic round of applause.

'André Marty,' Simon heard a voice whisper.

The dawn ritual was completed by the appearance of the protagonist, a tall man with tied wrists accompanied by two guards and a captain with deep-set eyes and heavy eyebrows. They marched across the courtyard and the prisoner took centre stage facing the ranks.

The guards about-turned. The captain took a length of black cloth from his pocket that he doubled into a blindfold. The prisoner shook his head and raised his bound hands. The officer stared at him as Cain must have stared at Abel, brothers on rival sides of the eternal divide. He then took a knife from his webbing belt and slashed through the rope bindings.

The captain gave the command in French with an English accent. *'Présenter les armes.'*

The squad slid back the hammers on their rifles, left leg forward, sights aligned, fingers pressed against cold, metal triggers.

'Avoir comme but...'

The prisoner's right arm shot up to the heavens as the captain gave the order: 'Fire.'

'Viva Franco,' he cried, his voice drowned out by the roar of eight rifles exploding in unison.

The prisoner briefly remained standing, as if with the will of his cause, then slipped to the ground like an empty sack. Simon felt the colour drain from his face. It was their first day in Albacete. The first execution.

Lloyd Jones, the youngest of the five Jones brothers, broke ranks and rushed to the side of the courtyard to throw up.

The firing squad stood down.

Robbie Gillan released a stream of cold breath. 'There'll be worse,' he remarked, and Simon nodded thoughtfully.

'Before it gets better.'

Robbie stared back at him. 'Don't tell me you've become an optimist all of a sudden,' he said, and turned to Paddy O'Hay. 'You don't happen to have picked up some baccy, by any chance?'

The Irishman slapped his pockets. 'I don't and it's a terrible thing, to be sure. I blame the Almighty for giving us the craving.'

Simon glanced over Bowen Jones's shoulder. He had drafted the scene they had witnessed, the firing squad like a row of shadows, the defiant eyes of the prisoner, the pantomime uniforms of the officers in leather coats and knee boots. Bowen's sketchpad had filled with snapshots from their travels: fleeing the train, following their guide over the Pyrenees to Abaurrea Alta, the first village they had reached in Spain. It was here the men had taken the clothes from their own backs to disguise the volunteers for their onward journey.

He looked away. The sun had slipped free from the horizon. They stood around waiting for orders and complained of hunger, the lack of tobacco, the bane of soldiering. Dai Jones fussed over Lloyd, the last thing he needed. Paddy made the rare offer of a nip from his hipflask, knowing, no doubt, that Lloyd would refuse.

'You may feel queasy today but come tomorrow it'll feel grand when you have your first fascist in your sights.'

'I kill one,' said Oscar Kuntze, jabbing the Irishman's chest. 'In Munich. With a knife.' He stroked his bushy moustache. 'The Gestapo come. I go.'

They fell silent. Talk of killing fascists was one thing. Killing a man with the intimacy of a bare blade was another. Simon rubbed his fingertips over the scar on his arm. Jef Van Portginga, the big steel worker from Rotterdam, took Kuntze in a bear hug.

'You are my hero,' he said, and they laughed.

'What's the joke? I could do with cheering up.'

They turned as the English captain who had directed the firing squad appeared. He stopped, hands gripped behind his back.

'Walt Lewin,' he announced. 'You arrived last night, if I'm not mistaken.' He sneezed and blew his nose on a clean white handkerchief.

'God bless you,' said O'Hay. 'That we did. Now we're ready to shoot a few fascists.'

'You'll get your chance soon enough. Reassemble back in the barracks in two hours. Once you sign on the dotted line, we'll take better care of you than your own mother.' A thin smile crossed his lips. 'Take a stroll into town, get your bearings. It's a free country,' he said and paused. 'At least it will be.'

*

The International Brigade was born on 14 October 1936 with 500 volunteers who had come to Spain to fight for the Republican cause in its battle against the military uprising. André Marty was put in command. The former French navy officer had become a communist hero during the Black Sea Revolt in 1919. The French fleet had been sent to support White Russian forces against Lenin's Red Army. When the sailors rebelled, Marty backed the mutineers and spent time in a French jail.

Unemployment and poverty had spread across the western world in the wake of the Wall Street Crash in 1929. For men stirred by high ideals and a sense of adventure, the war in Spain symbolised the struggle between the past and the future, that ruling-class brand of imperialism Simon believed was personified by his father and the Second Republic the people had voted for. As more volunteers set out for Spain, the Communist Party had shrewdly constructed a framework to funnel recruits across Europe to Albacete, a sleepy rural town in La Mancha.

Marty and his staff officers – union organisers, strike leaders, Marxist intellectuals – occupied rooms in the decaying splendour of the Gran Hotel. The enlisted men were billeted in the former barracks of the despised Guardia Civil. Few were party members. Like those who had boarded the train with Simon in Paris, they were mainly city-bred workers, miners, dockers, printers, factory hands – men who wanted to make a difference in the world. He was the odd man out, the one in 30 from an artistic or privileged background.

That stifling July day when the insurgent troops marched

from their garrisons to invade their own cities, General Franco and his wealthy backers had expected to oust the government before the end of the summer. They had not expected shopgirls and tram drivers to man barricades and defend the Republic with a tenacity that gave the foreign recruits the comfort of knowing that, should they shed their blood on the battlefields of Spain, it would be for a cause worth fighting for.

The mutinous officers from good schools and old families represented the Monarchy, the Church, the Spain of haunting memories, conquistadors, Inca gold and lost empire. The Republican government, a coalition of liberals and socialists with a dozen communist deputies, had come to power promising a more just society: health care, equal rights for women, a minimum wage and the restructuring of an unjust system of land distribution passed down from the Middle Ages. Liberal thinkers all over Europe shared the same ideals, but only in Spain had the government set out to put them into practise.

Change would come. It would come to England, too, he was sure of that, and what Simon found infuriating was that the so-called liberal democracies in Britain, France and the United States had blocked aid to the Republic, while Germany and Italy were shipping out elite troops with the latest weaponry to support General Francisco Franco. It was on Franco's orders in 1934 that his mercenary Army of Africa had slaughtered a thousand miners in Asturias, Moors killing Spaniards on Spanish soil, the poisoned seed that had grown into civil war.

Franco should have been stripped of his commission and imprisoned. But the government, anxious to appease the opposition and continue weaving the fragile strands of its reformist revolution, merely banished him to a command in the Canary Islands where the general and his cohorts bided their time and plotted the *golpe de estado* – the uprising.

Madrid, the capital, the heart of Spain, was the prize the military had in its sights. They say in Madrid: *Nueve meses de invierno, tres meses de infierno.* Nine months of winter, three months of hell. They had survived hell. It was November. Fresh troops were massing on the perimeter and the new boys joining the International Brigade had little time to learn the craft of warfare before the next offensive.

*

Simon watched Leonardo Jones taking it all in like a camera shutter as they strolled into Albacete. He was untutored, observant, gifted and purged his demons by pinning them to his sketchpad. I have to do the same, he thought, smelt and shape words like Wilfred Owen and ring a warning bell. It was the future of civilisation they were fighting for.

His feet had warmed up and he enjoyed the taste of the clean, cold air. The city was waking to a clear sky the same shade of blue as a duck's egg. Clouds gathered around the peaks of the Alcaraz mountains as if in imitation of Franco's troops around Madrid. Banners were looped across the street. Every lamppost and tree held a poster. Military trucks manoeuvred around donkey carts with flatbeds piled with farm produce. Men in work boots passed with raised chins and rifles over their shoulders. A woman wearing bandoliers and a headscarf carried fresh bread in an open basket. The people on the streets looked them in the eye and cried '*buenos días, Viva la República, bienvenidos*' – 'good morning, long live the Republic, welcome.' They were a scruffy gang of 11 men – the football team, Dai called them – but the local people knew why they were there.

The Republic's red, yellow and purple flag crackled over every building. Posters showed girls tilling fields, working at factory benches, carrying rifles. The mantilla had gone.

Birth control centres had opened. Men had cast off collars and ties. The poor in Spain had always been poor. They were still poor. But what Simon witnessed that morning was the spark in the eye that comes with the first taste of freedom.

Albacete was at the heart of a fertile plain bounded by stone villages with whitewashed houses and churches with square towers. Windmills stood on the hillsides like giant insects and Simon understood why Don Quixote had raised his lance to tilt at such unworldly visions. Spain was passionate, poetic, soulful. It drew you into its embrace. When he marched with his companions from Abaurrea Alta dressed in another man's clothes and his hair dyed black by the women of the village, the people had lined the rain-lashed streets with raised fists and tears in their eyes. He turned and grinned at Gillan.

'You're looking pleased with yourself,' Robbie said, and Simon tapped the side of his nose, a gesture borrowed from Paddy O'Hay.

'Look out for a bank.'

'A bank?'

'You do know what a bank is?'

Robbie's eyes narrowed. 'Aye, it's where the thieves keep our money.'

Men in leather aprons sold the daggers and knives for which the city was famous. The shops were busy. A girl with a swagger and red lips crossed the street, catching their eye. She tossed back her mane of blue-black hair and smiled as she passed.

'That's ruined my day,' Robbie groaned.

Simon knew from his tone that he wasn't joking. He felt unsettled by such passions. Simon would still have been a virgin, but just as Robbie had made provisions for Lloyd Jones on Le Quai de la Tournelle, there was a night after an inebriated dinner at the Café Royal when Guy Bradwell had done the same for him. They had gone on to The Windmill to see the nude *tableaux vivant* before Simon found himself in a dark room with an unmade bed where he finally 'dropped his balls.' It was an experience he had barely participated in and scarcely recalled.

Robbie's tone remained dour. 'There's one,' he said, pointing at the Banco de Vizcaya.

Across the square, people braving the cold sat beneath the umbrellas of a street café. Simon lowered his voice. 'Tell the lads to meet us there in ten minutes.'

He did so, then followed Simon into the bank. Robbie watched as Simon unwound the band of hessian from the right leg of his breeches. He produced his wallet and passport. Except for the volume of Blake and the keys to his father's clock, they were the only personal possessions that had survived the journey.

Two tellers sat behind brass grilles set in an ornate wooden cage. They scrutinised the £5 note Simon slid across the counter. They studied his passport and seemed puzzled as they compared the photograph of the clean-shaven man in a collar and tie with the scruffy fellow dressed as a shepherd. Simon explained in a mixture of Spanish and French that he had tinted his hair to avoid the Nationalist patrols in Navarre.

The teller ran his gaze over him one more time, then counted out 124 pesetas. Simon put the coins in his pocket and gave the notes to Robbie.

'*Muchos gracias.*'

'*Gracias a usted,*' the man replied, and his companion raised a clenched fist.

Robbie grinned. 'Finally, I'm rich,' he said as they hurried down the bank steps and crossed the square.

Paddy O'Hay stroked his chin thoughtfully as Robbie dropped into a chair and called the waiter.

*

They marched back to the barracks with cigarettes between their teeth and the military strut of men who have had hot coffee and butter croissants for breakfast. They passed San Juan Bautista, the renaissance cathedral. It was boarded up, the doors coated in posters. Long wooden crates – 'Rifles,' Paddy said – were being unloaded from a truck at the entrance to the Gran Hotel.

A Canadian at the barracks directed them to the gymnasium where there must have been 200 men milling around a line of tables, each with a card denoting the language spoken. They gathered at the English desk where a burly sergeant with a red face and curly brown hair sat over a pile of forms. His arms were filigreed in dull tattoos.

'I'm Doug Sanders, in case anyone's mother has told them not to talk to strangers,' he began. 'Let's have your names and military skills?'

O'Hay stepped forward. 'When do we get our pay?' he asked.

'Pay! You haven't even enlisted yet. Let's start with your name, shall we?'

Paddy puffed up his chest. 'Patrick Fingal Donegal O'Hay. Dungannon Brigade, the Irish Republican Army. Staff officer and explosives expert.'

'That's going to come in handy,' Sanders said. 'I'm a bus driver myself.'

Paddy moved to one side looking pleased with himself. Simon was next.

'Simon Pierce Sheridan,' he said.

'Profession?'

'I was at university.'

'That's not a profession, it's a luxury.

'A luxury paid for by our sweat.'

Sanders sat back and stared at the Irishman. 'That's right,' he said. 'But he's here, same as you. It takes all sorts, even old sods like me.' He turned back to Simon. 'Speak any languages?'

'French.'

'Are you fluent?'

'I think so.'

'We don't have time for false modesty, son. Either you are or you aren't.'

'I am. I can get by in Spanish and Italian.'

'That's what we need. We lost a lot of good men in Madrid. The officers were French and when the English boys weren't sure what to do, they just got their heads down and charged.' He looked Simon up and down. 'Nice outfit.'

'Which reminds me, when do we get our uniforms?'

Sanders shook his head and laughed. 'They went to the early birds, the privilege of saving Madrid.' He hollered out to the sergeant at the next desk where Oscar Kuntze and Jef Van Portinga had joined the German speakers. 'Did you hear that, Franz? This lot have just arrived and they're asking for uniforms.'

'They'll be asking for guns next,' Franz Benedict replied. He was a former teacher from Hamburg with a thick mane of fair hair, sparkling blue eyes and a rare understanding of English humour.

Sanders continued with the Jones brothers. 'Don't they have any other bloody names in Wales?'

'I'm Robbie Gillan,' Robbie said, but you can put me down as Jones.'

'Me, too,' said the man behind him.

'Not with that accent, mate?'

The man grinned. 'I am Constantine Zervos,' he said proudly. He made a circle from his thumb and first finger. 'Best chef in London.'

He was one of a group of Greek Cypriots, George Rossides, Costas, Alexis, Janni, Spiro, Nikos, sailors and hotel porters, men with long names they spelt out and the sergeant from Manchester inscribed on the recruiting forms.

'This is our lucky day,' he said. 'First an explosives expert and finally a decent cook.'

They gripped shoulders, shook hands and O'Hay dipped into the silver cigarette tin Zervos slid from his pocket.

As Sanders continued, the English captain appeared behind the table and glanced through the completed forms.

'Sheridan?' he called.

'That's me.'

'Come,' he beckoned, and took the form with him. Simon followed him up a flight of stairs to a small office. 'Walt Lewin. I look after the English chaps,' he said, offering his hand.

'Simon Sheridan.'

'Where have you come from?'

'Navarre. We crossed the mountains two weeks ago.'

'You've taken your time to get here.'

'There were patrols everywhere. We're jolly lucky to be here at all.'

'I don't know if I'd use the word lucky, but here we are.'

Lewin studied Simon with his fine beard, the sandy roots betraying the hair dye. With the tic on his neck and peasant dress, he had become an odd-looking specimen, but his courteous manner and precise accent were sufficient to place him in the exact pigeonhole.

'Oxford?' Lewin asked.

'Yes, Magdalen,' Simon replied without a trace of surprise.

'I'm a Cambridge man myself.' Lewin drew carelessly on the cigarette he lit as if smoking were a nuisance to him. 'How many British chaps in your group?'

'Eight, sir, if you include the Irishman. An ex-IRA man.'

'Don't bother with the "sir" nonsense, it's not necessary. Either comrade or nothing.' He sat and pointed to a chair. 'What's he like, the Irishman?'

Simon thought before he answered. 'A good man, I imagine.'

'Damning with faint praise?'

'He just has a rather active imagination.'

'I see.' He flicked ash into the ceramic pot, then glanced through Simon's enlistment form. 'You're not any relation to Sir Richard Sheridan, I suppose?'

'He's my father.'

Lewin's grey face became a mask.

'What brings you here?' He waved his arm around the room.

'Disillusion, I think. My father's very sure about everything.'

'And you're unsure?'

'Not anymore. The winds of change are blowing,' he said poetically. 'My father and people like him aren't aware of that.'

'Bloody cold wind, too,' Lewin remarked, and the tension had gone. They were opposites in many ways, but Simon was aware that Lewin considered himself a gentleman, now in the company of another. 'Does your father know you are here?' Lewin added.

'Almost certainly.'

'Then we must be on our guard.' He paused. 'Do you drive?'

'I do, but I don't have a licence.'

Lewin laughed. 'We don't concern ourselves with licences. I'm going to register you as a driver.'

8

ALICE MISSED THE girls at Tredegar House, the daily treks for practical training at hospitals all over London, that feeling of being out in the world. She was a qualified VAD with her three-shilling certificates and two Red Cross uniforms in the closet. She was impatient for the next phase of her plan to unfold and was aware, as in all things, that the unfolding was in her own hands.

She picked at a kipper and watched her mother across the breakfast table slide the letter opener under the flaps of the envelopes containing her morning mail. She scanned the contents, then read one of the letters through to the end. Alice heard her sharp intake of breath.

'Is everything all right, Mummy?'

'Yes, of course, dear.' Mother weighed her words. 'Lady Bradwell is planning a house party at the abbey,' she began. 'She would be delighted if you join us...'

Alice was ready to respond with a polite 'no, thank you' when she felt her pulse race and was struck by a sudden rush of inspiration. 'That's very kind,' she replied.

Her mother's voice brightened. 'You mean you'll come?'

'I can't wait, to be honest.'

Mother read a sentence from the letter as if the words held some subtle nuance. 'Guy has booked a jazz quintet, five Black men from the West Indies, and the house is going to be simply full of young people.'

'How super,' Alice said and hurried back upstairs to her room to dress.

In her closet, she came across the blue suit with brass buttons she had worn that day at The Ritz when she asked Guy and Percy Drew to make an appeal through the newspapers to buy an ambulance for the Red Cross. Guy, in the coming days, became evasive. He claimed it was 'family protocol' not to interfere with the paper's editorial policy. She had rather hoped Percy would have more luck at the *News Chronicle* and was terribly disappointed when the editor rejected the proposal. Hugh Tregarth was still short of the money he needed and Alice was mindful that her best chance of going to Spain as one of his team was to raise the funds herself.

Two nights in the company of Lord Bradwell just might be the answer. His Lordship – Edwin, he'd insisted – was a giant, hairy-handed bear of a man who enjoyed the epithet 'newspaper baron' but was more the old-time robber baron who pinned his flag wherever he cast his eye. He had cast his eye on her, Alice, as a suitable match to bring stability to the life of his wayward younger son by marrying him.

All she had to do was keep a cool head, show interest in Guy, and flatter his father into a corner where refusing her modest request would seem mean spirited. The photographs of factory girls in Madrid building barricades with furniture and old pianos had struck a chord in the country and the opposition had begun to question the government's decision on non-intervention.

*

They rose early on Saturday and Father marched off to the Bluebird Garage to collect his car, a red MG saloon with an engine that boomed like a brass band as he pulled up outside the house. He stepped from the vehicle and Alice watched from the top of the steps as the scene on the pavement unfolded like a sketch from a musical. Armed with umbrellas, Nanny Fosse and Mrs Broom, the housekeeper, fussed around Father like bees while he urged them to stand aside so that he could load the luggage himself. After being in a stale, smoky office all week examining strips of microfilm, or whatever it was he did, he enjoyed using his muscles and having the rain in his hair. He slammed the boot shut and looked up with a rare smile.

'Ready?'

'For ages,' Alice replied.

She kissed him on the cheek before climbing into the back of the car.

'Does that mean we're friends again?' he asked.

'Partially,' she replied. Alice was proud of Simon for defying their father and travelling to Spain, and had still not entirely forgiven him for making it so difficult.

Father held the door for her mother, then settled into the driver's seat. They circled the square and turned into Old Church Street. He sliced through the gears like cheese wire through a wheel of Red Leicester and accelerated past every vehicle that impeded his dash to Oxford.

Alice watched the wipers clear the rain splatters from the windscreen, the steady swishing back and forth vaguely hypnotic. It occurred to her that she should learn to drive and ran all the potential instructors through her mind as they turned on to the London to Fishguard trunk road.

From the turn to Witney, the road became country lanes that rolled and curved through Wychwood Forest. Before reaching Chadlington, he turned on to an unmarked track that passed below a canopy of trees that thinned out into the hills of an undulating park. Elsmere Abbey appeared like a picture-book castle at the end of the long gravel drive.

Guy came out to meet the car and escorted her to her room with the hall boy behind them bent double beneath the weight of her trunk. The room was bright with a four-poster draped in white voile like a ship at sea. Guy stood beside the window while the boy balanced the trunk on the luggage stand. The boy turned to leave.

'Wait a moment,' Alice said, and dug a threepenny bit from her purse.

The lad seized the coin and raced off with a beaming smile.

'There's no need for that,' Guy said. 'He's paid for his job.'

'How much?'

'What?'

'How much is he paid?'

'How the devil should I know?'

'Twenty pounds a year, something like that. People always need a little extra. I know I do.'

Guy turned with a sceptical expression. She went to join him and gazed out at the Italian garden. On a raised bluff surrounded by sycamores stood the boxwood walls of the maze where, at the age of ten, she had found her way to the brass sundial that marked the centre. She recalled marvelling that a mere shadow could imitate the hands of a clock.

'What time is it, Giddy?' she asked.

'I don't know, half past ten. I'm not usually up this early.'

'Let's go for a drive.'

'You're not serious?'

She reached for his hand. 'I'm always serious,' she said, and they hurried down the stone staircase as Guy's father was crossing the hall with a woman wearing a man's suit and smoking.

'My son in a hurry. That's a first,' Lord Bradwell said.

'We're going for a drive before luncheon,' Alice replied and glanced at the woman.

Bradwell made the introduction. 'Rachel Gold. Miss Alice Sheridan.'

The woman looked her up and down in her green tweeds and brown brogues, at her green eyes and boyish hair. She flicked ash on the floor.

'We must have lunch some time,' she said.

'I would like that.'

Guy went to collect the car. Rachel Gold then did something decidedly odd. She ran her fingertips over Alice's cheek before turning and making her way to the library. Lord Bradwell walked out to the drive with Alice.

'Where are you two rushing off to?'

'Guy doesn't know it, but he's going to give me a driving lesson.'

'Good for you. You keep him on his toes.'

'I intend to.'

'Driving's like playing the piano. Let the clutch pedal out slowly and press the accelerator pedal down slowly. You'll get it in five minutes.'

'I hope so. It's taken me a lifetime to learn Bach's 'Prelude' and I'm still positively ghastly.'

He looked at her in the same way as Rachel Gold, although not quite the same way, she realised. Rachel was judging her as a woman. Edwin Bradwell was sizing her up as he might a young filly for sale at auction.

'I'm going for a ride after luncheon. You should join me,' he said.

'Wild horses wouldn't keep me away,' she answered, and he laughed his big laugh as the car pulled up.

Guy opened the door for her. She climbed in the passenger side and slid across to the driver's seat.

'Excuse me,' Guy said.

Alice turned to wave to his father. He mimed playing a piano.

'Steady as she goes,' he called.

Guy clenched his fists. 'You are not driving my car.'

'Don't be beastly. I told your father you were giving me a driving lesson and it would make me out to be a liar if you don't.'

'Alice, you can't always get your own way.'

'You are such a bully.' She looked down into the footwell. 'Which one's the clutch?'

He spoke through gritted teeth. 'I think we should start with the brake.'

He slid reluctantly into the passenger seat. He told her what each of the three pedals were for; she accelerated and the white Morgan bounced like a petrified hare down the drive with Alice clinging to the wheel. They came to an abrupt stop as the motor stalled.

'Out,' he said.

'No. Give me another chance.'

'You are the most awful girl I know.'

She turned, eyes bright as stars. 'This is fun,' she said.

'Go easy on the damned accelerator.'

They waited for another vehicle to pass. Alice set off again with less of a bounce and felt confident that she would turn into a far better driver than a pianist.

*

She dressed that evening in a strapless white gown, swept her hair across her brow and regretted for a moment that it was so straight at a time when curls were in fashion. The wind biting her cheeks as she rode through the estate had given her a healthy glow and she was sure she looked her best when she took her seat at the table in the dining room.

They were 20 people seated below chandeliers suspended on chains from the pointed roof. An audience of abbots gazed down at them from the varnished portraits on the walls. Lord Bradwell sat at the head of the table with the 'elders' in the group – Lady Bradwell, a 'society beauty,' a reflection of Edwin's power and prestige; Alice's parents; the American Ambassador, Edgar Gold, and his wife, Rachel; the Stuarts and James A Arnold, the famous wit with his wife, a former ballet dancer.

The 'young people' were at the foot of the table, Guy and his brother Jasper, Pipper Stuart and his sisters, Cordelia – named from *King Lear* – and Portia – *The Merchant of Venice*; girls with sour faces and sturdy legs. There were two other girls whose names she had yet to learn and a handsome lieutenant named Peter Greves with his young wife, Daphne. The girl was in her fourth month of pregnancy and, at 20, a reminder to Alice that she had not been reared to drive cars and tend the sick, but to play the piano and breed like the prized herd of Aberdeen Angus on the family farm.

She ate rare roast beef with horseradish sauce and three of the cook's celebrated roast potatoes cooked in duck fat. She finished every scrap of her apple pie with cornflour custard. She sipped wine, not too much, just enough to take the edge off her nerves, and admired Cordelia's black silk gown with cap sleeves and a plunging neck. The one small compliment was all it took for her to forget Alice's cruelty to poor Pipper, who had studiously ignored her all day. Young men have egos made of straw.

Cordelia looked cosy beside Jasper Bradwell. Like his father, he was tall with thick waves of dark hair, but lacked his father's energy and humour. The Quincy Quintet must have arrived. She could hear a clarinet practising in the music room. The footmen, regal in blue livery with gold piping, cleared plates and filled glasses. The chatter flowed around the table like waves sliding into shore. The men said things considered amusing and the girls giggled even if they didn't get the twist or the witticism. Simon was omnipresent in that his name was never mentioned.

She noticed her father deep in conversation with Rachel Gold, her shiny black hair loose over her shoulders. Their eyes met as she glanced across the table.

Father raised his glass. He was proud that she could ride as well as a man. Minor achievements mattered to him. But it was a double-edged sword. He admired her independent spirit without being able to modify his belief that his children were born with preordained roles. Simon had been raised to be a soldier. Her responsibility was to play by the rules, be comely, intelligent, but not too intelligent, and to marry well within their own circle. Pipper Stuart was just the ticket.

Goodwin, the butler, appeared with a trolley containing cigars in wooden boxes and decanters storing old cognacs and ports. Lady Bradwell came elegantly to her feet, the men stood and the ladies fluttered their way to the drawing room like a flock of myna birds.

'I'm going to try one of those cigars, if you don't mind,' Rachel Gold said.

Lord Bradwell chuckled. 'I like a woman who doesn't bend to conventions,' he acknowledged. 'I have a box of Partagas, just arrived from Havana.'

'*Perfecto*,' she replied and Lord Bradwell turned, noticing Alice was still at the table.

Alice smiled. '*Et moi, s'il vous plait.*' She wasn't sure why she had replied in French, but the men found it amusing.

The footman gave her 'a small' port. She lit a cheroot, coughed until she was red in the face, proof that smoking was a male preserve, and dried her eyes on the handkerchief given to her by the handsome lieutenant.

The men guillotined the ends from their cigars and lit up. Once more, the conversation moved like a tide around the table. Edward VIII was finally free to marry Wallis Simpson – 'that woman' – now she had divorced her second husband. Lord Bradwell welcomed plans at the BBC to broadcast a regular news programme, not that it 'would ever replace the written word.' Guy said he had reserved two tickets for Terence Rattigan's new play, *French Without Tears*, and Lord

Bradwell glanced at Alice.

'There's a chance to improve your French,' he said.

'If I'm invited,' she replied. 'And if I'm still here, of course.'

He laughed. 'Where else would you be?'

'I intend to go to Spain.'

The laughter stopped. The men stared back at her. Had she stood and removed her clothes, it would have been no more shocking.

'Alice, if you please. That's not funny,' her father said.

'Father, I am deadly serious.' She turned to Lord Bradwell. 'In fact, I was rather hoping to persuade you to make an appeal through the newspaper...'

'Alice, you heard what I said.'

Bradwell held up his hand. 'Richard, it's all right. Let the girl have her say.'

'Hugh Tregarth, he's a doctor, you probably know him,' she resumed. 'He's a member of the Spanish Medical Aid Committee. He's raising funds to buy an ambulance for the Red Cross to take to Spain...'

The Earl, Pipper's father, interrupted. 'There's a treaty. We're not allowing aid to Spain.'

'You are right, of course. The government has made an exception for the Red Cross.'

They were quiet for a moment. That a young woman had remained at the table and was expressing thoughts they did not share, or that she should have thoughts at all, was unconventional bordering on the eccentric. Rachel Gold broke the silence.

'And you'd like to see an appeal in the newspapers to buy that ambulance, is that right?' she asked.

'That's exactly right. We just need to raise £300.'

Lord Bradwell readjusted his weight in the chair. 'Alice, this is a foreign quarrel. It's up to the Spaniards to sort out their own mess.'

'There are those who believe it's a war of principle. Principles don't have boundaries.' She took a breath. 'The people in Spain voted for the Republican government. Not once, but twice.'

'My dear young lady, from where do you get your information?' It was Edgar Gold, the American, 20 or more years older than his wife, a man with a slow Southern drawl and a boot-string tie gathered in a turquoise clip.

'The newspapers, the wireless, from working as a nurse,' she answered. 'When you see hungry children with no shoes, it becomes obvious that we have to do better, we have to do more.'

James Arnold let out a cloud of smoke. 'When the barefoot boy gets a pair of shoes, he forgets that time when he went barefoot.'

The comment was met with nods of agreement.

'That may be Darwinian, but surely we have evolved to a point where the fittest are obliged to ensure the weak survive?' Alice said. 'The whole world sees the danger of what's happening in Germany and Italy...'

Her father brought the flat of his hand down on the table. 'You mustn't be misled by your brother. He's got himself mixed up with those damned Reds at Oxford.'

'That's simply not true, Father. Simon is an idealist. He believes the world could be a better place. He believes we should support Spain because it is the right thing to do.'

The lieutenant sat stiffly in his seat as if waiting for orders. Guy, Jasper and Pipper gazed blankly into the distance. They were like cut out figures, all the same and, she realised, that she had always been merely decorative, the female version of that empty stare.

'My dear girl,' Bradwell now said with affection. 'You speak as if everyone agrees with your ideas. You are the minority.'

'It is a growing minority. People are waking up and seeing

that the world is unjust. They don't want to see people going hungry in a land where there really is enough for everyone.'

Lord Bradwell tapped his hand on the table as men do playing billiards when the opponent makes a good shot. 'That's well put, Alice. But you must see, an appeal for the Republican cause would not sit well with my readers.'

'But it's for an ambulance. If English boys are being blown apart, surely it makes sense that English nurses are there to put them back together again?'

'My dear Miss Sheridan,' the Ambassador drawled. 'I should remind you that war is not woman's work.'

'Is killing women and children man's work?'

As Alice spoke, the howl of a trumpet left the music room and bounced around the walls. Lord Bradwell raised his voice.

'Guy, for God's sake, go and tell those damned people to stop making such a bloody racket.'

'It's only £300,' Alice continued. 'If everyone at this table were to give me £30, you wouldn't really miss it.'

'I can give you a cheque right here and now,' Rachel Gold said, but her voice was drowned out.

'That's enough!' her father exclaimed.

Again, Sheridan brought his hand down on the table, harder this time, and knocked one glass against another. They shattered as they fell and a red stain spread across the white cloth. The trumpet was silent.

'Stop this nonsense this instant,' her father added. He stood. 'You are going home.'

'Father, I am going to Spain.'

He trembled like a volcano about to explode. 'Out. Out. Go to your room.'

Alice came to her feet and the lieutenant rushed to hold her chair. She left the table and was surprised to see her mother standing in the doorway. She wore an expression impossible to read and suddenly looked old and sad.

9

BY DECEMBER 1936, more than 500 Brits had reached Spain. This first wave of volunteers formed the British Battalion under the flag of the xvth International Brigade. The additional battalions were the American Abraham Lincolns, the Dimitrovs, from Yugoslavia and the Balkans, and the '6th of February,' from France and Belgium, 2,000 men with ancillary and medical staff.

General Sheridan had been unequivocally wrong. Madrid had not fallen and the king's arse was not back on the throne.

The British were posted to Madrigueras, 20 miles from Albacete, where the recruits spent long, bone-chilling hours on what was grandly described on the orders sheet as 'Manoeuvres' – chasing over fields in slanting rain armed with broom handles.

After the initial outbreak of vandalism by the local people, the church of San Pedro y San Pablo had been smartened up and the men gathered inside the thick stone walls to scoff down their rations. They rolled cigarettes and settled back to listen to the daily discourse from Reggie Foster, the Political Commissar, a towering Yorkshireman with a Stalin moustache and quick, clever eyes. No one doubted the sincerity of those who had enlisted in the cause, and it was assumed that a grounding in Marxist theory would turn them into an indomitable fighting force. The lecture was followed by first aid lessons and weapons training.

The rain had stopped. Shafts of light seeped through

the boarded-up windows and the men gathered in a circle around Sergeant Jimmy 'Mac' McVicar as he showed them the intricacies of the machine gun using a museum-quality Maxim. A runner arrived while he was in mid-flow, swung back the door and called in broad Cockney from the threshold.

'Anyone 'ere seen Comrade Sheridan?'

'That's me.'

'Orders from the co. Report straightaway.' He took a long hard sniff. 'And get a move on. Sommink's 'appening.'

'About bloody time,' one of the lads shouted and the others laughed.

Simon crossed Plaza Ramón to a three-storey building with stone terraces and a gabled roof. It was the home of El Conde, the local lord of the manor, ensconced now in Burgos where Franco had formed his illegal government. Lewin had set up his office in the parlour at the back of the house with windows facing a walled garden. He sat at a table in his greatcoat.

'Sheridan, dear chap,' He waved his arm. 'How's everything?'

'One can't complain.'

'I can't see why not, there's plenty to complain about. Sit, sit for heaven's sake.'

'Thank you, sir.'

He pointed at the ceiling as if to God. 'Marty prefers comrade. It's like "*monsieur*" in French, always appropriate.' Lewin sneezed. 'Bloody weather.' He wiped his long nose. 'How's the training coming along?'

'I think we're getting better.'

'Good, good. How's our Commissar? Does he get on all right with the men?'

'Yes, I think so.'

There was some friction between Lewin and Foster; the old soldier and the idealogue: war before revolution or revolution before war. But if the CO was digging for tittle-tattle, he wasn't going to get any from Simon.

Lewin nodded his head thoughtfully as he removed a biscuit tin from the drawer. 'We have, by all accounts, received a consignment of uniforms from France. It's waiting in the Gran Hotel.'

Simon's face lit up. He had acquired clothes to replace the odd costume he had worn on the journey from Abaurrea Alta, but the battalion in civvies looked more like men in a soup line than a fighting force. Lewin opened the tin and removed some peseta notes.

'Buy some eggs while you're about it, as many as you can get.'

'The rumours must be true.'

'Rumours are more interesting than facts. Take Gillan with you. He'll know what to do if the Americans get there first.'

Simon buttoned the money into his pocket and returned to the church. Dai Jones was sitting, legs spread, behind the Maxim.

'I have to take Robbie Gillan with me to Albacete,' Simon announced.

'Oh, aye? It must be like a busman's holiday for you drivers,' McVicar said. He peered back over the top of his glasses. McVicar was exacting, bald as a billiard ball and a veteran of the Argyll and Sutherland Highlanders.

'We have to buy some eggs,' Simon replied in an even tone. 'And we have to collect a shipment of...' he broke off into a long pause...

'Well, come on them, shipment of bliddy what?'

'Uniforms.'

A cheer went up.

'We'll be at the front before the week's out,' came the booming voice of Andrew McBride, a choirmaster from Stonehaven.

Dai Jones stood. He swung his arm around McBride, a baritone who had found a tenor.

'If you happen to see anything my size, you know, it would be nice.' It was Rory Laing, another Scot, six and a half feet tall with trousers half-mast.

'First thing I'm going to do, lad,' said Robbie Gillan. 'So we don't have to keep looking at your hairy white legs,'

The lads laughed and Robbie's smile faded as he followed Simon out of the church. They made their way down the road to the motor pool, where they collected a grumbling old Renault from Johnny Aldous, the mechanic.

'Don't drive like a maniac,' he said. 'Treat the gear stick the way you treat your girlfriend, nice and easy, little touch here, little touch there.'

Robbie turned to Simon. 'I don't think you've got a girlfriend, have you?' he asked, and Simon replied in the same vein.

'Not one that I'd introduce to you.'

Aldous, a ship's engineer from Dover, looked from one to the other.

'Now then, you've got enough petrol to get you safely to Albacete and back. If she overheats, just let her have a rest for ten minutes and put some more water in the rad. There's a jerry can in the back.'

Simon settled in the driver's seat and fired the engine. First turn. Good omen. The village was behind them in a few moments and the landscape spread out, stark and colourless.

Robbie took out his tobacco. It came in packages containing 20 small packets, each with enough brown shag for one cigarette. Simon enjoyed watching the way Robbie shook out the contents and made sure every speck of tobacco was accounted for. He rolled the paper between the thumbs and fingers of his long hands, then poked out his tongue to lick one side and seal the paper in a neat cylinder. He lit up and blew smoke in the air.

'Careful,' he cried out and straightened the steering wheel.

'Watch the bliddy road, you're going to kill us at this rate.'

'Sorry, I was distracted.'

'That's your bliddy problem, mon.'

'I don't have a problem.'

Robbie took a long draw on his cigarette. 'I just think you should make a commitment.'

'Jesus Christ, Robbie, I'm here.'

'You've made a stand against your father, not a stand for the movement.'

'I spent two years thinking about joining the goddam party. Something held me back. I don't want to see the struggle in Spain going the same way as the revolution in Russia.'

'I cannae see the conflict?'

'When you take away one set of oppressors, another always replaces them.' Simon paused for breath. 'Stalin once took a chicken into a meeting of the Politburo and proceeded to rip out the feathers in front of the other members. When he'd finished, he stood the chicken on the floor. The creature didn't run off, petrified. On the contrary. It clung to Stalin's leg. That, he said, is how we must treat the people.'

Robbie stabbed out his cigarette. 'That's just propaganda.'

'Everything's propaganda. The party doesn't believe in justice. It believes the ends justify the means. Nothing is good nor bad unless it advances the revolution.'

'Towards a better future for everyone. For the last, the least, the lost, the looked over. For the homeless and the hungry.'

'Mr Foster's words.'

'That doesn't make them less true. Every working-class movement in Italy and Germany has been crushed. Their leaders are in prison. Or dead. Workers in Britain live in fear of the bosses, the dole, that their families are going to starve. The party may not be perfect, but that's what we have, and it's about time you realised it.'

Simon grabbed his sleeve. 'We have the same dreams,' he said. 'We are looking at the same coin from different sides.'

Robbie shrugged away. 'Aye, and the coin's still in your pocket.'

Simon had felt elated when Lewin gave him his orders. Now a depression like a black worm had crawled into his head. Instead of uniting the battalion, the lectures on class conflict had divided them into believers and agnostics, those who had joined the Communist Party and those over whom there was a cloud of doubt because they had not done so. Communist and anarchist militias in Barcelona disagreed on how best to organise society *after* the battle was won and had turned their guns from the Nationalists to fire on each other.

He had tried to tell Robbie that splits on the Left played into the hands of the Right, but his friend had embraced his faith in the party as men embrace their sweethearts when they come home from war. The arguments achieved nothing except to cleave them apart.

Simon wiped condensation from the window with his sleeve. He could see his image in the glass. His hair had been cut prison-short to get rid of the dye. Clean shaven, he could have been mistaken for an inmate at an asylum. They were silent for the remainder of the journey.

Albacete was cheerful with the shops open and people out in the street. There were fewer farm carts and more military vehicles. Along the front of the Gran Hotel, a dozen light field guns stood in a row. He parked at the far end beside an olive green ambulance, a new Talbot, and noticed the wordy inscription below the red cross on the door: British Committee for the Relief of the Victims of Fascism.

As Simon stepped down from the truck, he heard a girl talking and thought for a moment his mind was playing tricks on him. The voice was crystal clear, silvery in tone, spirited, yet authoritative. He turned towards the hotel as she came to a stop.

'Oh my God, what have you done to your hair?'

'I don't believe it…'

'And where's Daddy's keys?'

He smiled. Alice was leaving the hotel entrance with a group of medics who looked down from the steps at Simon and Robbie as if confronting a pair of tramps.

Alice took a step closer, then hesitated. Her eyes fell on Robbie and her entire countenance changed.

'You made it,' she said.

'Did you doubt that I would?'

She shook her head. 'Not for one second.'

Alice's smile had gone. Robbie seemed uncomfortable, unsure of himself. Simon was confused.

'You know each other?' he asked.

'It's a long story,' Robbie replied, and Simon suddenly understood.

'The girl with the £5 note?' he said, and Robbie looked back at Alice.

'I'll pay you back as soon as I can,' he told her, but she didn't appear to hear him.

'I did say you needed a stitch in that cut. It's left a scar.'

'It doesnae matter.' He looked down, avoiding her eyes, then glanced at Simon. 'I'd better go and find those uniforms.'

But he didn't budge. They remained rooted to the spot like old trees. Simon looked back at Alice. She was dressed for action in a beige jacket, trousers tucked into knee boots, the ends of her tartan scarf tossed over her shoulders. Her hair was hidden by a green beret and her green eyes lit her face.

Robbie finally woke from his daze. He hurried past Alice and vanished into the hotel. The rest of the medics gathered around them and the scene that had just taken place remained in Simon's mind like a list of questions from a crossword. Answer one, and he would have the answers to them all. Alice took his arm.

'Simon, my brother, although it doesn't look like him at all.' She turned to Hugh Tregarth. 'Hugh, you know.'

'Small world,' Hugh said. They shook hands. Simon noticed Hugh studying him in that way doctors have when confronted by a patient with an incurable disease.

'How did you manage to get through the frontier?' Simon asked him.

'We sailed from Southampton to Bilbao. It's firmly Republican,' he replied. 'Medical supplies don't have much problem coming through France. It's armaments they're trying to keep out.'

'Damned hypocrites.'

The speaker was Graham Webster, another doctor. He gritted his teeth and his round face topped by a prematurely bald pate seemed to deflate like a punctured ball. Two more nurses completed the team. Matilda Griffiths had a soft West Country accent, mousy hair and melancholy eyes. Ivy Button was her opposite, a petite blonde with a line of dark roots, a curvy figure and a South London accent.

They all shook hands and climbed into the ambulance ready to drive out to Madrigueras and join the battalion. Alice delayed a moment.

'It must have been a butcher who cut your hair,' she said.

'Actually, it was Robbie.' He took her arms. He kissed her cheeks. 'What are you doing here?'

'What are you doing here?' she repeated and they laughed.

'I've missed you,' Simon said.

'Why do you think I came?'

'I suppose I'm never going to get rid of you...' They laughed again. 'I'd better go and find Robbie.'

Her expression changed. 'He seems...' she broke off. 'He seems distracted?'

'It's this place. He joined the bloody party. How stupid is that?'

'I wouldn't know.'

'It's unbelievable that you're here.'

'Not really. Hugh was raising funds to buy the ambulance. Mummy made a donation.'

'My God, she hasn't become a socialist?'

Alice laughed, that clear-as-a-bell laugh he so loved. 'She knew I was going to come and find you. She thought I'd be safer travelling with Hugh than going on my own. She's very practical.'

'How is she? How's Father?'

'Mummy's coping. As for Daddy, he's hopping mad.' She leaned closer and lowered her voice. 'Percy Drew says he'll have agents tracking our every move.'

'They can join the queue. There are agents here to watch other agents, and other agents are watching them.' He looked into her eyes. 'And how's Percy?'

'I'm sure he's fine. We are friends, nothing more.'

He smiled. 'Unbelievable.' He shook his head. 'I have to go.'

He kissed her cheeks and her voice stopped him as he ran up the steps.

'What about the keys?'

He opened his shirt collar. They were hanging on a leather thong like a talisman around his neck.

10

THE ONLY UNIFORM aspect of the uniforms was a khaki beret, not that Robbie Gillan gave up his prize headgear from Paris. The cotton jackets and trousers came in various shades of beige, taupe and tan, many perforated with bullet holes, and inadequate for the cold *sierra* winds. The ensemble was held together by a belt, cross-straps with two ammunition boxes and a bayonet frog without a bayonet or rifle to attach it to. It was topped off by a cape that flapped in the wind and gave them the appearance of bedraggled pigeons.

But it was a uniform. They were soldiers and they set out that night with a military swagger to celebrate at the Casa del Pueblo, a social club set up by the Spanish trade unions with a bar selling brandy and anisette. The walls were decked out in revolutionary posters. The men invented new words to old songs to stage revues. The eggs Robbie Gillan had scrounged up in Albacete had been put into the hands of Constantine Zervos, who cooked omelettes with powdered onions on a makeshift stove.

The medical team had settled into an empty house in Plaza Ramón, close to the co. Alice, knowing that her name assumed certain implications, went to introduce herself to Captain Lewin. He gave her the same advice he had given her brother: to keep her head down and avoid the press. The war had dug in and a number of journalists who had journeyed to Madrigueras had painted an erroneous picture of a rebel army of artists and aristocrats.

Lewin counted off on his fingers some of the well-known figures who had made it to Spain. Eric Blair, better known as George Orwell, had volunteered immediately after the publication of his new novel, *Keep the Aspidistra Flying*. Esmond Romilly, Winston Churchill's nephew, had fought with one of the first units to defend Madrid. Julian Bell was an ambulance driver. Lewis Clive, who had won a gold medal at the 1932 Olympics, was serving in the ranks, as were the sculptor Jason Gurney and poet John Cornford, great-grandson of Charles Darwin. Working with one of the medical crews was Jessica Mitford, a human rights activist as far to the Left as her elder sister, Diana Mosley, was on the Right.

'Imagine the arguments in that family.'

'Much like my own,' Alice replied, and Lewin lit a cigarette.

'Having celebrities in the ranks does no harm in the propaganda battle, but 95 per cent of the volunteers are ordinary workers,' he said. 'We don't need more poets. We need two more battalions of chaps who can sleep on their feet and march on empty stomachs.'

Alice stiffened. It seemed like a direct attack on Simon. 'I imagine poets can do that as well, sir.'

He went to correct her but changed his mind. She was sitting in the same chair where her brother had sat that morning with her hands in her lap, fresh as something just made, a glimpse of another world, the past always vaguely present, a girl he had admired at Cambridge and who had never returned his affection.

'My father is a very private man,' Alice continued. 'I am sure he shares your anxiety that his name does not appear in the newspapers.' She stood. 'There was one more thing, where would I find Simon?'

'All the chaps are at the social club. He'll be there, I imagine. I'll show you.' He walked her to the door and pointed at the lights on the far corner of the square. 'La Casa del Pueblo. That's where they are.'

*

When Alice entered the club, the group of men singing bawdy songs stopped and there was a moment's silence that would have been embarrassing had Robbie not approached her.

'Hello,' she said. 'I was looking for Simon. Isn't he here?'

'He's back at the hoose. He doesn't fraternise with the likes of us.'

'I'm sure that's not true.'

'I'm not in the habit of telling lies.'

'I didn't say you were. It's all a matter of perception.'

'I can see you're as smart as he is.'

'But not as smart as you.'

She looked him up and down. Clean shaven, moustache trimmed, Robbie looked like a young subaltern in his uniform with polished boots and his beret flush against his dark eyebrows.

'Very swank.'

'There you see, as canny as a box of tricks.'

She was thrown off balance for a moment. 'If that sounded unkind, it wasn't meant to be.' She paused. 'Let's start again. I'm Alice Sheridan. How do you do?'

'Not as good as you, that's for certain.' He bowed and smiled without humour. 'Robbie Gillan, at your service.'

The card players had resumed their game. The singers had started up again. Alice looked around at the posters, men with heroic faces and raised fists, girls driving tractors. She turned back to Robbie.

'If you could give me directions to the house, that would be awfully kind.'

'I could, but you won't find it.' He hesitated. 'All tiny

streets. I'd better show you.'

She wrapped her blue cape about her as they entered the cold night.

'I had a feeling I would see you again,' she finally said.

'Why's that?'

'I don't know.'

'I wouldn't be here if it wasn't for you.'

She was going to say 'me neither,' but the thought was fleeting and she kept it to herself. 'Perhaps the time will come when you don't thank me for that.'

'That's nae ganna happen. I didnae know nuthin' aboot nuthin'. Now, if anything happens, I won't die a complete idiot.'

They turned a corner and entered a narrow lane. Alice remembered the way Robbie had put his cap over his friend's head to hide the wound. She hadn't really thought about anyone dying until that moment. A shudder went through her. Everything that had been hypothetical was suddenly chilling and very real.

They had reached a stone house in a row of houses, most shuttered and in darkness. Robbie pushed the door open and she found Simon sitting beside the fire reading in the glow of an oil lamp.

'I'll be off then,' Robbie said and closed the door.

Alice threw up her arms. 'I'm not sure what I said.'

'It's not what you said. It's who you are.'

They hugged and Simon's world was back on course. When they were apart, it felt as if a piece of himself was missing. He had a need to be a part of something bigger than himself, not in an abstract sense, as in being a member of the rowing team, or joining the Brigade, but on a personal level. Alice completed him. He had transferred that need to Robbie Gillan and had felt rejected since his friend joined the Communist Party.

Alice brushed down his uniform blouse and straightened the lapels.

'This has seen better days.'

'There was a free-for-all when we opened the bundles. It was the cleanest one I could find.'

'I remember someone who didn't want to be a soldier.'

He made tea. They sat close to the fire. Simon added another couple of logs and they watched the flames as he talked about training without rifles, the mud, the cold. The strain of waiting for something to happen.

'I would say the waiting's probably over,' Alice surmised.

'The problem is there are shortages of everything. Everything that matters...'

'Except volunteers. Aren't there 15 brigades?'

Simon smiled. 'No,' he said. 'They started numbering from 11 to fool the Nationalists.'

'Will it?'

'What do you think?'

'It's strange seeing him again.' She gazed into the fire. 'He seems different. His friend died on a hunger march and the way he reacted was so tender, so sensitive.'

'He is sensitive. Actually, he's quite amazing.'

She caught the look of loss in Simon's expression as she turned from the fire. His blue eyes were bright in the firelight, the whites very white. He ran his fingertips over the tic on his neck.

'It's the pressure of this place, the politics,' he said. 'The men are warned that people of wealth and privilege lack commitment.'

'And he's blaming us?'

'Marx said the state is a device for the exploitation of the masses by a dominant class. Robbie has just learned that. When he looks around, who does he see?'

THE CONTINUAL BARRAGE of enemy guns rattled the windows where Simon stood looking out over Chinchón. He was on the fourth floor of one of the pastel-painted houses that circled the perimeter of the bullring. His hair was back to its normal length and he had pressed his uniform with a flat iron. He was aware of the futility of his efforts, but there is something theatrical about war. You dress for the occasion.

Rain fell gently, untiringly. He watched Johnny Aldous working under the bonnet of a farm truck with a sagging canvas roof, one of two dozen vehicles parked in the churned quagmire of yellow mud at the centre of the ring. The battalion was hunkered down in the church of Nuestra Señora de la Asunción, 600 men with almost as many rifles.

Walt Lewin was seated at a table opposite Doug Sanders, the Manchester bus driver, two men with thinning hair and worn faces, veterans of the Great War. Sanders showed Lewin his packet as he lit a cigarette.

'Only one left, comrade. I'd like to save it.'

'Always too much waiting…'

'…and never enough tobacco,' said Sanders, completing the axiom.

Simon's thoughts were interrupted by the ringing telephone. He crossed the room and lifted the receiver. He spoke in French.

'Comrade Sheridan for Captain Lewin. British Battalion Headquarters.'

He wrote down the orders from Albacete and replaced the

receiver in its cradle. Lewin blew his nose on a clean white handkerchief, then turned to Sanders.

'You can give the command, comrade. Good luck both of you.'

*

The heat generated by 600 British riflemen, machine gunners, cooks, stretcher-bearers, drivers, doctors, nurses and political advisers had warmed the cold stones of the church and boredom had replaced anxiety.

Dai Jones began to sing, 'Why are we waiting…' only to be hushed by his brother Glyn.

'That's enough of that, boyo,' he said. He pointed at the stripes on his brother's sleeve. 'You're supposed to be setting an example.'

Dai had been made a corporal, something his brothers poked fun at. They had laboured together in the pits and underground there are no leaders, only workers.

'A man in your position should know better,' said Rhys.

'…a man of your age,' added Glyn.

'Now you listen here, I didn't get these stripes for my age. I got them for my brains.'

'Or your binoculars,' Bowen suggested. The brothers laughed and Leonardo Jones continued sketching the scene in the church.

'Come on, Lover Boy, let's have a smile,' Dai said to Lloyd.

'I'll smile when I feel like it.'

*

Robbie Gillan was reading *Moby Dick* when he became aware of someone peering over his shoulder.

'I didn't think you read novels,' Alice said. 'It must be a relief from Marx.'

He replied without taking his eyes from the page. 'How would you know? You've never read Marx.'

'You have no idea what I've read.' She moved away and Robbie glanced up as she turned back again. 'I would like to know why you are always so unpleasant. I don't actually care. I would just like to know why.'

He closed the book with his finger marking the page. 'You don't have to talk to me, you know. There's more than a few blokes here who want you to talk to them. Talk and a lot more than talk...'

'When all else fails we stoop to vulgarity.'

'What else would you expect from someone of my class?' He glanced around the church. 'Look at 'em all. Then take a good look at yourself. I don't know why you think you're so special because you're not.'

Alice's lips tightened and her green eyes glowed with annoyance. She tossed her scarf over her shoulder.

'You,' she said, 'are beneath contempt.'

As Robbie stood, the church doors swung open, and Alice walked rapidly away. Doug Sanders entered with Simon, both dripping wet.

'Can we have a bit of hush, gentlemen,' Sanders shouted. 'We have received orders from Albacete...'

A cheer went up and he waved for silence.

'If I may? We are moving out... and you know where to.'

Now they did cheer and their war cries rattled the stained-glass windows.

'Leave in sections,' Sanders ordered. 'Don't run. And for Gawd sake, don't leave your bloody weapon behind.'

They laughed. They pinched out cigarettes. They grabbed their gear and shouldered their way up the aisle in tin helmets and capes, rifles like periscopes above the undulating waves of green and khaki. Someone had found the bell ropes and the bells rang out as they squeezed through the doors and made their way to the bullring.

Simon spotted Robbie. They gripped arms. 'Don't do anything rash,' Simon said.

'Och, mon, nowt's going to happen to me.'

The machine gunners passed, Rory Laing, Andrew McBride, Stuart Finch, Ray Carney, all Scots; Sydney Long, who had been an actor, Bruce Seattle, the Australian, Dave Cooper, the tin miner from Cornwall. Sergeant McVicar, stern as ever, glanced back at Robbie.

'Come on lad, or you'll get left behind.'

'Aye, keep your hair on,' he replied, and grinned as McVicar reached for his bald scalp.

'Ya wee bastard,' he spat.

It was a flash of the old Robbie Gillan. As he pulled on his beret, Simon gave him his helmet.

'Here, I won't be needing it.'

'Are you joking? This is my lucky hat,' he said. 'And you, you take care. They're shooting toffs as well as the workers. You've got nowt to prove.'

'One more thing,' Robbie added. 'When you see your sister, tell her I didn't mean what I said.'

'I imagine she didn't mean what she said, either.'

They remained motionless like a boulder in the stream of volunteers. Then Robbie did something which came as a complete surprise. He kissed Simon on both cheeks, Spanish style, and vanished into the crush of mismatched uniforms.

*

Simon found Alice buckling her medical bag. She was dressed in her Red Cross uniform, blue cape buttoned at the throat. Her brown hair formed a fringe beneath her cap and her teeth seemed extremely white behind her pink lips.

'I'm awfully proud of you,' he said.

'I should jolly well hope so.'

Simon walked with Alice and the medical team through the cobblestone streets to the bullring.

'Are you wearing lipstick?' he asked her, and her shoulders went back.

'Once you let your standards slip, there's no telling where it might lead,' she replied.

'I have a message for you from Robbie. He didn't mean whatever it was he said.'

'I can't even remember. He was just plain rude.' Her features softened. 'Now don't do anything stupid. If anything happens to you, Mummy will never forgive me.'

Simon glanced around the bullring with its tiers of rickety benches and faded flags. In the summer, a band with blaring trumpets would escort the matador into the ring and there, armed with a thin sword and swirling pink cape, he would do battle with 1,500lbs of charging bull. There would be laughter in the cafés, flamenco guitars and girls dancing beneath an enamel sky lit by the eye of the sun.

It was a different sort of chaos that morning as he watched the rank and file of the British Battalion pat shoulders and tramp through the mud to find their units. Franco's troops, professional soldiers armed to the gunwales, had mounted a fresh assault on Madrid and those scarcely trained men in sodden boots were going to stop them.

Alice turned, her face full of light. 'I don't think anyone would believe us,' she said, and it wasn't clear what she meant, but he understood.

Drivers climbed up into the trucks. They muttered a prayer as they turned the key and tested the motors. The wooden balconies around the bullring were filled with people, old men in berets, old women in shawls, thin children with earnest faces. They raised their fists in the loyalist salute.

'Viva España! Viva los Ingleses!'

'*Viva la República!*' the volunteers cried.

'*Viva la República!*' the people returned.

They had found enough flour to bake 600 tiny, three-cornered loaves of bread and enough eggs and Spanish sausage to send the foreign soldiers off to battle with full stomachs. That day, and for many days after, the people of Chinchón would go hungry.

Johnny Aldous was at the wheel of another old truck. He was pulling at the choke while Dai Jones turned the cranking handle. Once, twice...

'Bloody English. Call yourself a mechanic...'

Finally, spitting and farting, the engine fired and Johnny looked like a man who had been delivered from some terrible ailment. No one wanted to be left behind. Dai stowed the cranking handle in the engine cavity and caught sight of Simon as he closed the bonnet.

'Nice weather for it, boyo,' he said. 'Typical wet Monday.'

'Trouble is it's Friday.'

Simon shook hands with the rest of the Jones boys over the tailgate, then ran to the front of the convoy and slid into the driver's seat of a camouflaged Citroën Traction Avant.

'Nice of you to join us, comrade,' Captain Lewin said.

'Shall I?' Simon asked and started the ignition.

Lewin was in the front passenger seat with a scout's hand-drawn map spread out on the lid of the glove compartment and the orders from HQ in his bony fingers. Reggie Foster sat in the back beside Mike Marples, a reporter from the *Daily Worker*. He wore a pistol buckled in a case over a blue leather jacket and an expression that reminded Simon of an exam invigilator.

It was 12 February 1937. Marples was there to witness the British Battalion going into action for the first time.

12

CHINCHÓN WAS 40 miles from Madrid on the La Mancha plateau connected by a sequence of S-bends that descended to the plain. The wipers swept over the windscreen and the car filled with cigar smoke that coiled in spirals from the back seat.

Lewin scanned the landscape for orientation points. The road signs had been removed and at every crossroad it was like playing the three-shell game choosing whether to go left, right or straight on. Twenty minutes after their departure, the boom of gunfire came as a relief and Lewin decided to follow the old maxim: march towards the sound of enemy guns.

'Take the next right, see where the hell it leads us.'

Immediately after the turn, they saw in the distance a straggling file of refugees fleeing from their villages with flocks of goats and bundles piled on farm carts.

'Pull over. Find out if we're going the right way.'

Simon slowed to a halt and glanced at the name of their destination on the orders from Albacete. He stepped out of the car and spoke to an old man at the head of his family.

'Señor, are we on the right road to Morata de Tajuña?'

The man removed his hat and held it to his chest as he looked down the line of vehicles. 'This is correct. Just follow the road to the river.' He bowed from the waist. His face was wet with tears and rain.

'Thank you, señor. Thank you. *Muchos gracias.*'

Simon climbed back into the vehicle. As he pulled away, he noticed the reporter scribbling in his notebook in the rearview mirror and wondered what tone his article would take: the capacity of British workers to smile on through adversity, or that they had no reliable charts; no grenades, essential in trench warfare; the ammo was old and insufficient and the last men to arrive in Madrigueras had no rifles?

The roar of battle grew louder as they reached Morata de Tajuña, a small rural town with empty squares and shuttered houses. Lewin set up his HQ in a farmhouse on the highway. From there, the road rose for a mile to low hills carpeted in olive trees, before plunging down to the River Jarama.

During the previous night, General José Varela had crossed the river with 25,000 men including Spanish Legionnaires and Moroccan *regulares* from the Army of Africa. With tanks and artillery support, their objective was to break the Republic's hold on the Valencia–Madrid highway and create a corridor for a fresh attempt to enter the capital.

Russian tanks had countered the offensive. The northern side of the Jarama river had been contained, protecting the road to Madrid. The Nationalists had seized the high ground, rested for the night, and shifted the main thrust of their attack towards the crossroads at Morata de Tajuña. Artillery was softening the defences before General Varela drove his infantry down into the valley from the heights of Pingarrón, then up the ragged slopes where the British Battalion had been ordered to hold the ridge and protect the highway.

To the south of the British, on their right flank, was the '6th of February,' the name taken from the date of the Paris riots in 1934, with 800 French and Belgians. On the left, the Dimitrovs fielded 800 men from the Balkans. The Abraham Lincoln Battalion, 600 recruits from the

United States, Canada, Cuba and Ireland, was being held in reserve.

*

The vehicles passed through mature olive groves and entered a sunken road that created a ready-made trench deep enough to hide the convoy beneath the overhanging trees. The sunken road had formed over centuries by mule and oxcarts that ground the earth surface to dust in the sun and washed it away in the winter rains.

The troops stepped down from the vehicles. The back-slapping and handshakes were more subdued. The majority of the British volunteers had never fired a gun in anger and there were some who had never fired a gun at all. They discovered, as they scaled the chest-high walls of the road, that war is a noisy affair and stinks like rotten eggs. The hosing from enemy machine guns was interspersed by salvos from 75mm field guns and the brassy ping and ricochet of bullets. The air smelled of cordite, saltpetre, burning trees and human fear.

The big guns roared. They could see the sparks of rifle fire pinpricking the hills as Dai Jones led his riflemen out from the trees and across the open space towards a ridge of cover. Johnny Aldous ran along at his side, fingers black with oil, a grin on his thin lips.

'You managed to get us here,' Dai said. 'Hope that bloody truck's going to get us home again.'

He never managed to reply. A piece of shrapnel sank like a guillotine into his neck and Johnny Aldous was instantly decapitated. His body spun in a pirouette and the blood from the wound, as if thrown from a bucket, drenched the soldier chasing along behind him.

Lloyd Jones stopped and stared down at Johnny's head. There was an astonished look in the mechanic's eyes, a grim smile on his grey lips. Lloyd screamed one long, piercing scream. He threw down his helmet and rifle, his cape and ammunition boxes and ran back to the sunken road.

Dai would have followed, but Bowen held him back.

'Johnny didn't have a chance,' Dai said. 'The bastards...'

'Remember why we're here, Dai.'

'What about Lloyd? He's just a kid...'

'He'll be all right. He's better off wherever he's going.' Bowen glanced up at the ridge. 'Come on, boyo.'

They set off behind their comrades as they spread out in a thin line, 100 men, the ranks depleting as they scratched out foxholes and found cover in shell craters that instantly filled with water. Dai Jones began to sing.

> *Guide me, O thou great Jehovah*
> *Pilgrims through this barren land*
> *I am weak, but Thou art mighty,*
> *Hold me with Thy pow'rful hand.*
> *Bread of heaven, Bread of heaven,*
> *Feed me till I want no more;*
> *Feed me till I want no more.*

Leonardo, Glyn and Rhys Jones joined in and they heard the voice of Andrew McBride, the Stonehaven choirmaster, roaring through the chorus from beyond the curve of the hill.

McVicar's company of machine gunners had dug into protective points on the lee of the incline where they could set up a crossfire. The Maxims were heavy, water-cooled beasts on iron wheels with two legs that supported the wide barrel. The cartridge belts came in wooden crates that needed all a man's strength to move. They had stored them below an overhanging escarpment of rock, ripped them open and rushed the belts out to their positions facing the enemy.

Robbie Gillan was McVicar's number two. His job was

to feed the belt through the firing mechanism in an even flow and change belts when the cartridges were spent. They had practised for weeks. Robbie knew the drill. But the damn things just wouldn't fit. McVicar shook his fist.

'Give it here. What the hell do you think you're doing?'

He pulled the ammunition belt from Robbie and tried to force it into place himself. His wet fingers moved frantically. Then he stopped and stared back with a look of horror.

'They're the wrong ones. This bugger won't fit.'

Robbie raced along the line, then crawled down to the supply dump. They were all the same. Useless. He made his way back to McVicar.

'Get the information to the CO,' he ordered. He shouted to Laing, manning the next gun in the line. 'Go with Gillan. Make sure one of you gets through.'

Robbie didn't move. 'Wait,' he said. 'If we've got the wrong ammo, these belts are needed some place else.'

McVicar's old, blue eyes turned misty as he let the words sink in. The noise roared all around them. The rain kept falling. A rattle of bullets stung the air and a row of holes perforated Rory Laing's chest. He fell, his long legs twisted beneath him. McVicar stared down at the dead boy and still couldn't speak.

'We have to take the ammo back,' Robbie said and shook McVicar by the lapels.

'The stupid kid stood up.'

'Mac, you're not listening to me.'

'He's too bliddy tall to stand up. He got himself killed.'

'We're all going to get ourselves killed before the day's out, Sergeant.'

McVicar turned away from Laing and brushed Robbie's hands from his jacket. 'Aye, laddie, you're right,' he said and motioned for him to follow. 'Come on, we've still got to put up a fight.'

They led a dozen men back down the hill lugging the unusable cartridge belts. One of the crates received a direct hit. A thousand shells exploded at once and Ian McNaughton vanished into pieces too small for the stretcher-bearers to find and carry away.

The medical team had moved up to the sunken road and set up a field dressing station under a canvas awning between the trees. The wounded were laid out in a line with severed limbs and torn bodies, their pain muffled by the momentary bliss of morphine. Robbie saw Alice bandaging a boy's bleeding leg and his eyes filled with tears. He put the ammunition box down. He waited for her to finish before he approached.

'I'm sorry, Alice. I'm so sorry. I didn't mean what I said.'

She moved closer and her palm, as she touched his scarred cheek, felt warm and healing.

'I know,' she said, and continued with her work.

Robbie had witnessed his share of suffering when he took his dad to the Victoria Infirmary in Glasgow. He had seen Jimmy McGee laid out with a tag on his toe. But what he saw that day in the dressing station was different. Numbing. Overwhelming. Impossible to believe, to process. All along the sunken road from the canvas shelter to the open air were 30 or more young men at the beginning of their lives and their lives were draining out of them. Their wounds were hideous. The smell of death made him gag. There weren't enough stretcher-bearers to move the dead away to some place more dignified – and that dignified place didn't exist.

What surprised him was that the damaged men didn't cry out. There were no dramas. No hysteria. Some moaned softly. Others gazed up with stunned expressions at the clouds crossing the sky.

'Have you got a fag, mate?' he heard.

Robbie had rolled a few skinny smokes before going into action. He lit up and placed the cigarette in the man's dry lips.

'Ah, that's better.'

He reached for Robbie's hand.

'I'm dying, aren't I?' he said. Robbie nodded and the man was able to let go. 'That's all right. I did my bit.'

His fingers lost their grip and his hand turned cold. Robbie gazed along the line of men and remembered the photograph of the fusilier in uniform standing in a wooden frame in his parents' bedroom. His uncle, Robert Ian Gillan, whose name he bore, had died aged 18 in the first days of the war to end all wars. It is the young they send to be sacrificed. Death, when it comes, is cruel and random. When it came for him he wanted it to be quick and final.

He turned. His heart drummed behind his ribcage as he watched Alice. She gave a morphine shot to a lad and started to ease the wriggling coils of his guts back into a bloody wound open from his throat to his groin. He had said to Alice in the church that morning that she wasn't special. But of course she was. She was there.

*

Lewin received the information that the machine gunners had the wrong ammunition like a punch-drunk boxer receiving another blow. McVicar had found him in a hollow at the far end of the sunken road poring over a hand-drawn map, coat off, tie straight, face drawn.

'The positions are crumbling before we can even get them established,' McVicar told him. 'We're up there without a weapon between us. It's bliddy suicide.'

Lewin's expression didn't change. 'That's what they're calling it, Suicide Hill,' he replied. He inspected the cartridge belts. 'They belong with the French if I'm not mistaken. That was good thinking to bring them down.'

'Don't thank me,' McVicar said and pointed. 'It was Gillan who kept his head when it mattered.'

The captain studied Robbie as he made his way towards them with the last of the ammunition cases and what he saw was the composed look that comes to men when they have come to terms with death. It was the warrior face, features relaxed, eyes with an unnatural glow. When the whistle blew, they were the first to go over the top.

'Don't put the box down, the armourer will be looking for it,' Captain Lewin said.

They exchanged glances and Lewin led the gunners back up the sunken road to a truck lit by hurricane lamps. It was where Wilf 'the Rocket' Tooley, a former jockey, five feet in his socks and scrupulous with odds and numbers, had set up his stockroom. Some antique weaponry had arrived from Albacete 30 minutes after the battalion climbed the hillside. The armourer showed McVicar's gunners his collection of Russian Mosin-Nagants, a rifle constructed almost entirely of wood with a long bayonet. He held one up.

'The Tsar himself had one of these, so you look after them. They won't jam. I've cleaned every one of these buggers myself.'

He made a note in a dog-eared exercise book, then passed out six dozen rifles wrapped in oilcloth.

*

As Robbie trudged up to the ridge with his bundle of rifles, he saw one of the stretcher-bearers begging a weeping boy to make his way back to the sunken road. He had thought of the orderlies as fence-sitters and shirkers. He was wrong. Two hours on Suicide Hill and he realised he had been wrong about a lot of things. While the Nationalist artillery pounded the hillside, the stretcher-men worked tirelessly in the open to bring the wounded to safety. Pacifists, intellectuals, artists, they wouldn't bear arms but were willing to die for what they believed in.

Robbie distributed the guns along the line and dug in beside McVicar. No one had come for Rory Laing. His mouth had unlocked and filled with rain. Robbie closed his eyes and straightened his limbs.

Bullets hummed through the air like mechanical insects.

When they came close, he kept his head down and put his fingers in his ears. The shells from the big guns thudded into the rock face and snatched up handfuls of debris. He was bathed in a shower of powder and sludge. The thin orange mud was slowly coating their uniforms so that they no longer looked like soldiers but troglodytes, fashioned from the earth into which they would return.

He poked his rifle through a fissure in the rock and stared down the barrel. The expanse of no man's land on either side of the river was an empty moonscape pock-marked in craters. On the right of his position was a cluster of stone buildings that had been demolished by enemy target practice first thing that morning. He let go with three short blasts aimed across the gorge at the blue flashes, then dropped down, waiting for the response. It came instantly, tenfold, snapping and spitting around his shelter.

His focus was drawn back to Rory Laing. Only one bullet in 10,000 kills a man. That's what they said. Rory had taken that bullet. He had taken three of them. The big lad was from the Gorbals, not far from where Robbie had grown up. Ian McNaughton, killed going down with the useless cartridge belts, was from Dundee. Danny Wilkinson, who had been blown to bits on the way back up, was from Aberdeen. He'd heard it said that in proportion to its population, there were more volunteers from Scotland in the International Brigade than from anywhere else in the world.

Why was that? What made them volunteer? Was life so harsh in Scotland a muddy hill outside Madrid was better? He didn't know. He wasn't sure. He wasn't sure about anything. He was thinking about Glasgow. But it seemed like a place he had visited once and was slipping from his memory. His brain was scrambled and it was Alice Sheridan who kept pressing into his mind.

The dry hiss of mortar shells passed overhead and detonated behind the line. They were getting closer. The air smelled of tobacco from the saltpetre in the explosives and he lit his last roll-up. There didn't seem much point in saving it.

13

A FLIGHT OF RUSSIAN Polikarpov 1-16s swooped low over the sierras and raked the enemy gunners dug in on Pingarrón. They peeled off one at a time like the pages of a book being turned, and Simon felt inexplicably jubilant seeing the Nationalists being showered with lead.

As the fighters passed overhead, the riflemen raised their guns and the last craft in the formation did a victory roll before vanishing into the clouds. They cheered. They were dying up there on the ridge, picked off one at a time. But they weren't alone.

The rain that had fallen without pause since daybreak suddenly stopped. The sky turned blue and the sun was so brilliant steam billowed along the ridge of Suicide Hill.

Running in short bursts from cover to cover, it took Simon 30 minutes to reach Reggie Foster's beleaguered company, and the only thing he could do was turn around and go back down again. Foster had taken Mike Marples up the hill to see the action first hand and the reporter from the *Daily Worker* had remained on the line.

'Tell the captain, I've got no idea what they're waiting for. There's sod all there,' Foster said. He indicated a sheltered escarpment above the ridge. 'Not a gun, not a tank, not a bloody hope in hell.'

Simon slithered up between the fissures of rock and gazed down into the valley. The greenery along the banks of the Jarama glistened in the sun. He could hear the river surging down from the peaks, the respite from artillery and rifle fire more ominous than comforting. Beyond the British line, the left flank was entirely exposed.

He glanced back at Foster and the two men exchanged nods of respect, overdue on Simon's part. With his pep talks and propaganda films, the Political Commissar was a bore, but a front-line bore. 'First into battle. Last to retreat.' That's what he had said and he was as good as his word.

Simon dropped back from the ridge. The riflemen were using their tin helmets to rake out the rocky soil and deepen their shallow trench. Dai and Bowen had joined Foster.

'The Dimitrovs should be there,' Simon said, pointing to the left.

'Well, they bloody well ain't,' said Foster. 'If the fascists make one sweep on their right flank, the battalion will be surrounded.'

'It's worse than the captain imagined,' Simon told them, and Foster repeated the closing word.

'Imagined? You mean our runner didn't get through?'

'No, no one from this section.'

'What about GHQ? Are you telling me they haven't been informed?'

'The trouble is, we can't see a thing. It's cleared up now, but visibility's been down to a hundred feet.'

'Jesus H. What's wrong with the man, doesn't he have a pair of field glasses?'

Simon shook his head. 'No glasses, no grenades and the machine gunners ended up with the wrong ammunition belts. A truck carrying medicines was hit, so we're running out of morphine...'

Bowen cast a glance at his brother and Dai slipped his bird-watching binoculars from around his neck.

Simon gasped. 'These are more precious than gold,' he said. 'You are going to make the CO a happy man. He needs cheering up.'

'We all do,' Dai replied and took a grip on Simon's arm. 'Have you seen Lloyd?'

'I haven't. There are several shell-shocked chaps back at the farm. He's probably there.'

'I shouldn't have let him come. It's my fault...'

'It's no one's fault, Dai,' Bowen assured him. 'He's a man. He made his own decision. He'll be just fine.'

Dai glanced back at Simon. 'Bloody optimists, they really get my pip.'

They laughed. They were on the train again steaming out of Paris and Simon thought, how superb and resilient the human spirit. How the lunacy of war leaves you detached and more than a little mad.

The battle's lull ended with the grinding roar of aircraft and nothing Simon had seen that day was more chilling than what he saw now through Dai's binoculars. Messerschmitt fighters flew low across the valley, strafing the hilltops where they were dug in. They were followed by Heinkel bombers dropping their loads in a criss-crossing pattern down the ribbed slopes leading to the sunken road. Rocks and rubble rose into the air as the riflemen threw themselves face down into the dirt.

This show of force by the Condor Legion, German pilots flying German planes, was both demoralising and tactical. As the dust settled, Simon raised his head and adjusted the field of vision on the binoculars. The dark dots of countless men were swarming down into the valley from heights of Pingarrón. He passed the glasses to Foster.

'They're coming,' he said. 'Thousands of them.'

The escarpment, with its wide view of the valley, rose from their position like the prow of a ship and what Foster saw when he settled his bulk behind the rocks was the gleam of bayonets flickering over the landscape like flashes of sunlight on the sea.

'They're testing our fire power with the Africans,' he said and passed the glasses back to Simon.

'Poor blighters.'

'Save your sympathy. Our riflemen lost their officer before he got to the top of the hill.' Foster took a grip on Simon's shoulder. 'Take care, boy. Tell the captain, we're going to hold this hill. But I don't know for how long.'

A line of shells about ten yards apart dropped behind them and Simon used the brief pause that followed each volley to take off down the hillside. He had learned a maxim for retreating under fire. Run as fast as you can.

Lewin's expression didn't change when Simon gave him the field glasses and delivered his report. He followed the CO up through the olive grove to a high point where he could see the deployment of his troops.

'Do you know what time it is?' Lewin asked without waiting for a reply. 'It's 12:30. The attack started at the stroke of noon.'

'German advisers,' Simon remarked.

Lewin carried on scanning the landscape like a sailor sighting land for the first time.

*

From out of the mud and miasma of yellow smoke, an enemy fighter leapt screaming over the hilltop and landed on McVicar.

In one swift action, Robbie ran him through with a bayonet, thrusting and lifting the way he had been taught, only it was human flesh, not a sack filled with sawdust and straw.

McVicar struggled out from below the body of the dead soldier. 'That was a close one,' he shouted. You had to shout, the enemy guns were loud and constant.

Robbie relieved the dead boy of his bolt action Mauser and a pouch with three grenades. He slid back into position and stared down into the valley.

The Moroccans kept coming. They held each salient and laid down a carpet of fire for the next section to dash up the slopes from the river to the strung-out line of rifles along the ridge. Some forgot their orders and kept going, charging over the peak to be skewered on the British bayonets. There was no shortage of rifles now.

Robbie fired the Mauser's five rounds, replenished the chamber and kept firing until his hands blistered and burned. He reloaded his gun and used the last of the grenades to take out a boy closing in fast. The grenade exploded with a dull thud and he screeched like a bird as he flew backwards from the force of the blast.

Still, they kept coming. Like locusts in a swarm. Like the morning rain. In the middle of the afternoon, three Red Army tanks appeared from the north, lobbed a few salvos into the arena, then scuttled off to where the '6th of February' had been forced to retreat. The British were now vulnerable on both flanks. The ridge where they were dug in was at the apex of an isosceles triangle, a finger of land like a seaside pier that jutted into the stormy midst of a Nationalist division.

This was Suicide Hill, the last obstacle blocking the enemy's advance to Morata de Tajuña and the highway from Valencia to Madrid.

*

Shortly after the show of muscle by the Russian cavalry, the ammunition for the Maxims arrived at the sunken road. It was hauled up to the gunners by Captain Lewin, Simon Sheridan, Doug Sanders and the walking wounded, men in pairs who had lost the use of their rifle arms and swung the wooden boxes on rods across their shoulders.

Simon spotted Robbie in his Paris beret. As he lugged the case of belts to his position, his friend watched as if he were seeing a mirage. His vision was blurred. His eyes were dead. They gripped hands and Robbie didn't seem to want to let go.

'You're okay?' Simon asked and Robbie slowly nodded.

'I'm alive.'

'You're blacker than Othello.'

Robbie's features, stretched like drum skin, slowly relaxed. His eyes came back into focus.

'You're a grand fellow, Simon.'

'You're not so bad yourself.'

'No.' Robbie shook his head. 'I'm not. I'm not that.'

They were interrupted by 'Mac' McVicar. 'When you two have finished chinwagging, there's a fucking war going on.'

McVicar's weapon was already loaded. Sanders fed the belt through the breech into the chamber, the bolt firing pin clipped the cartridge, igniting the primer, and the first spray of Maxim bullets roared into the field of battle.

Simon tore open the case. He had trained with the gunners. He knew the drill. In 20 seconds, Robbie Gillan sent a hail of hot lead into the fading twilight. The gun's roar echoed along the ridge as Sergeant McVicar's band of survivors raised a wall of crossfire that routed the Nationalists' last concerted charge of the day.

The British left flank remained undefended. The Dimitrovs had covered another section of the Jarama. Enemy spotter planes must have observed the gap. But General Varela's battle plan was to cut the Valencia–Madrid Highway by frontal assault and generals don't like to change their plans.

The line should have broken.

It had not broken.

14

THROUGH THE LONG, dark night, the stretcher-bearers brought in the wounded and the dead. When all who could be accounted for were back in camp, they worked on, bringing down guns, grenades and the enemy injured left out to die by their own officers.

Captain Lewin wandered like a ghost among the exhausted men spread out on their groundsheets. The practicalities of battle were often lost in the folly of Brigade politics, but the boys who had come down from Suicide Hill still had confidence in their commanding officer. He gripped arms and shook hands. 'Well done,' he said. 'Well done.' The Nationalists had set out that day to overrun Morata de Tajuña and the little speck of a town with whitewashed houses and shuttered windows was still in the Republic.

Robbie had found a dry patch in the olive grove. The silence of the guns was eerie, like a clock that had suddenly stopped ticking. The wind stirred the trees and brought the cold down from the mountains. He had taken the lives of other men that day. He was afraid to close his eyes and see what hell may lie behind them. Simon dropped down at his side and gave him an envelope containing ten loosely packed cigarettes.

'Jesus, mon, I didn't know the shops were open.'

'I confiscated them from one of the Moors. He had a full packet. I left half.'

'You're a wee saint, you know that. But when it comes to baccy, next time, leave him five.'

Robbie lit up. Simon heaved himself up on one elbow.

'He was wearing a crucifix. Their officers told them if they wore crosses the red bullets wouldn't hit them.'

'Aye?'

'The thing is, they're Muslims,' he continued, and Robbie realised Simon was focusing on small things to avoid thinking about the battle that day. You had to find a way. This was his way. 'It's remarkable how a culture can go into decline. Muslims kept the quest for knowledge alive in the Middle Ages. The Moors conquered Spain. Now Morocco's just a Spanish colony.'

Robbie took a long draw on the cigarette and picked a piece of tobacco from his lip. 'Did you learn anything useful?'

'Not much. Few of them spoke any French. They are not even sure who they're fighting.'

'Do they know why?'

'That they do. Their wages feed their families.'

'Now they're prisoners, the money will stop,' Robbie said. He drank from his water bottle. 'They were bliddy good soldiers. We lost a lot of good blokes today.'

Simon knew how many and Robbie let the figures wash over him as the smoke from his cigarette filled all his empty spaces. Of the 600 men who had left from the bullring in Chinchón, 550 had gone into action. Three hundred and forty had remained on the ridge at sundown. The remainder were dead, wounded or missing.

Robbie had avoided asking after Alice. In the quiet moment the words spilled out of him.

'Simon, how's your sister?'

'Frazzled. Tired. Coping.'

*

They crawled under blankets, backs pressed together for body warmth, boots on, clothes damp, and slept through their nightmares until the boys from the cook house woke them at sunrise with hot coffee and rolls stuffed with ham and wedges of cheese. Across the camp, the volunteers rose in capes and tin helmets like phantoms in the half-light, raw recruits turned veterans through the longest day they had ever lived.

As they checked their ammunition boxes and stretched sore limbs, they listened to the Nationalist artillery dug in on Pingarrón. The boom of 75mm shells exploded across the valley. The rat-a-tat tat of the machine guns was louder, closer, like a drill on a stubborn piece of steel. In a brief pause while the guns reloaded, they heard the familiar voice of Dai Jones. It made men smile. It gave them hope.

> *They were summoned from the hillside*
> *They were called in from the glen,*
> *And the country found them ready*
> *At the stirring call for men.*

'Somebody's woken up cheerful,' Robbie said.
'He saw Lloyd back at the farm.'
'He's all right?'
Simon shrugged. 'He's alive.'
Dai's brothers and others joined in the singing and the choir drowned out the sound of the enemy guns.

> *Let no tears add to their hardships*
> *As the soldiers pass along,*
> *And although your heart is breaking*
> *Make it sing this cheery song.*

Robbie pulled on his beret, straightened the line and tucked the right side down towards his ear. His eyes became glassy.

'I remember something Blake wrote in that book of poems. He said it was easier to forgive an enemy than to forgive a friend.' He broke off and lowered his eyes. 'I've been a bit of a bastard, Simon. Will you forgive me?'

Simon shook his head. 'No. I won't forgive you because there's nothing to forgive.'

He had to fight the urge to take Robbie in his arms, hold him tight, tell him how he felt. There was so much Simon wanted to say, but it wasn't the right time. It would never be the right time.

'Just keep yer bliddy 'ead doon,' Simon said in his best Scottish accent.

Robbie turned away and joined the gunners climbing the ammunition boxes stacked up as steps along the side of the sunken road. Bruce Seattle carried a Maxim. Robbie took the barrel from him and steadied it across his shoulder. They spread out. The gunners sang as they made their way through the olive trees. They emerged on the other side and their voices didn't weaken, they grew louder as they gave full voice to Ivor Novello's hymn.

> *Keep the Home Fires Burning,*
> *While your hearts are yearning,*
> *Though your lads are far away*
> *They dream of home.*
> *There's a silver lining*
> *Through the dark clouds shining,*
> *Turn the dark cloud inside out*
> *'Til the boys come home.*

Reggie Foster wandered among the ranks with words of encouragement. He stopped beside Simon and they watched the bedraggled army plot its course through the enemy shelling. One man, leg missing from the knee down, was on crutches. His companion carried a rifle over each shoulder.

'You know something, I don't think I've ever met better

people in my life,' Foster said.

'Nor I,' Simon replied.

They turned towards each other at the same time and you didn't have to be a mind-reader to know what the Political Commissar was thinking. Simon was thinking the same. Unless there were reinforcements, few of those men singing as they marched up to the ridge would be marching back down again at sunset.

Foster glanced past Simon and his expression changed. 'There's a sight for sore eyes. Who kicked you out of bed?'

It was Doug Sanders in cape and helmet, rifle over his arm.

'Not much point running the office when there's no bloody office,' he said. 'Some bloody Russian's turned up.'

'Probably a commie,' Simon remarked and the two older men laughed.

Sanders turned to Simon. 'It's been nice knowing you, you're a good lad.' He spoke with a resigned air and Simon felt tears pressing into his eyes as he shook the old sergeant's hand.

He climbed the steps. Foster followed and the two figures vanished into the swirling grey mist as if they had become their own ghosts.

Simon walked back along the sunken road and found Lewin in his outdoor office with Anatoly Sokolov, André Marty's aide-de-camp, a tall Russian with sharp features like an actor dressed for the role in knee-boots and a leather flying jacket. Sokolov spoke heavily accented French in a staccato rhythm.

'Comrade Sheridan. You must speak with Comrade Marty,' he said. 'The first reinforcements have arrived.'

Simon glanced at the co who shrugged. 'No idea,' Lewin said. 'Just be…' he searched for the word. 'Circumspect.'

Beside the desk stood a motorcycle. Sokolov pulled on his leather helmet and goggles. He stamped down on the kick start and the engine grumbled to life. Simon climbed on the pillion. He gripped the pannier and enjoyed the feel of cold air as they accelerated along the sunken road to Morata de Tajuña, deserted except for two old men on cane chairs sitting amidst the rubble outside the church.

Two miles beyond the town, Sokolov slowed as he negotiated a dirt track that curled down to a stone quarry. This was the field headquarters where Marty directed the defence of the eastern approaches to the highway from the Mediterranean to Madrid. After 20 times trying, Simon had spoken to him briefly the previous day about the need for reinforcements.

Sokolov swerved to a halt beside a row of a dozen T-35s, a heavy-duty tank with a pair of 37mm cannons, machine guns and side skirts over the tracks. The Russian pulled up his goggles and threw out his arm.

'Beautiful, no?'

'Certainly very clean,' Simon replied.

The tanks had five-man crews whose chief occupation appeared to be polishing the armour plating. Simon waited for a response from Sokolov, but none came. Russians of the Red Army variety didn't seem to have a sense of humour and he saw little value in asking why the tanks were lined up under camouflage netting, not taking part on this crucial second day of the battle.

Clean-cut officers with red flashes on their lapels gripped attaché cases as they hurried smartly through the compound. He followed Sokolov towards a canvas awning where six translators sat over telephones shouting orders in a babel of languages. Comrade Marty stood to one side, feet apart, his ample beard giving him a sagely aura. He approached as they came into view.

'Ah, this must be Mr Sheridan,' he said in good English. 'I wanted to ask you something, comrade. Is it true what George Bernard Shaw says, that it is impossible for an Englishman to open his mouth without making some other Englishman despise him?'

'There is some truth in it, yes.'

'It must be terrible to live that way. I pity you.'

'That's awfully kind, thank you.'

Marty glanced at his aide. 'There you see, English civility.' He turned back to Simon. 'That is why you despise each other. You never say what you think or do what you say.' He paused. 'He was a good socialist, Mr Shaw.'

'As are the Englishmen spread out across the hills.'

Marty brushed the comment aside. 'The British kept their position without fresh troops. Imagine what you can do today with reinforcements.' He took a long piercing look at Simon, then switched to French as he spoke to Sokolov. 'Give the workmen their orders,' he said, and turned away.

They made their way back past the T-35s to a group of Spaniards who gathered around as the Russian removed a square of paper that he unfolded and spread out on the bonnet of their truck. It had an irregular edge on one side and must have been torn from an atlas containing a geological survey of the Guadarramas, the mountain range that arcs like a crooked spine across 50 miles of craggy sierras from Ávila to Madrid. The map had no road markings or distinctive features except the handwritten addition of a line in blue ink drawn between the concentric circles denoting two peaks above the Jarama. At each end of the blue line was a single word in Cyrillic script, to which he pointed and translated.

'*Británicos. Franceses.*'

One of the Spaniards stabbed the blue line. '*Españoles*,' he guessed, and the rest punched the air in unison.

'*Viva la República*,' they cried, and the energy in their faces was suddenly uplifting in the oppressive air of the quarry.

'*Viva la República*,' Simon repeated, and they cheered.

Simon was taller than the young militiamen, terribly

English with his blue eyes and fair hair, but they judged him neither by his looks nor the tone of his voice. With every encounter, he had experienced a universal acceptance of the stranger, the foreigner. Spaniards were emotional, spontaneous and it wasn't unusual for someone to plant a kiss on both his cheeks the moment they met. They were a race of primary colours. Those who believed in the Republic were utopians unable to comprehend the opposition's blind faith in Franco and, in consequence, the civil war.

The Spaniards comprised a platoon of Milicias Antifascistas Obreras y Campesinas – a workers' militia with basic training that had been effective in securing key positions during the initial assault on Madrid. Their role in the defence of the highway was to construct trenches, barriers and booby traps in the valley between the ridges held by the British and French in preparation for the deployment of the Líster Brigade, professional soldiers led by officers loyal to the Republic.

To Simon, the task the platoon had been set was unrealistic. The Nationalists were already advancing. But when he translated the orders, the militiamen cheered and threw their forage caps in the air. They clambered into the high-sided truck, a Hispano-Suiza, the figurehead a stork in flight. The 50 or so men squashed together among the crates and tools: shovels with long handles, pickaxes, metal stanchions, coils of wire, a bundle of ancient rifles and boxes of explosives stamped with the skull and crossbones.

The platoon leader latched the tailgate and it was only when he climbed into the passenger seat that Simon realised he was expected to drive as well as guide the Spaniards to their location. He wasn't sure why he had been selected for this particular detail unless André Marty had wanted to see with his own eyes the son of Britain's despised General Sheridan.

He shoved the gear stick into first and the truck growled up the incline to the open road. His companion was a man his own age with a thick moustache and slicked-back black hair like a matador. He stuck his hand across the cab.

'Eloy Ferrer,' he said, introducing himself.

'Simon Sheridan.'

'*Inglés?*'

'*Sí.*'

'*Gracias, camarada, gracias.*'

He spoke with unreserved sincerity, and Simon remembered the old man with tears in his eyes as he directed the convoy towards the Jarama Valley. A little more than 24 hours had passed and it felt like another lifetime.

Their destination was clear on the geological survey, but there were no road markings, only the far-off sound of gunfire to guide them. They headed from Morata towards San Martín de la Vega, then wove a path over a series of unsurfaced roads that took them beyond the British position on Suicide Hill.

They reached an unmarked intersection and Simon stopped to take a closer look. They stepped down from the cab to study the landscape. From along the range of crests and summits, two peaks stood out as likely strongholds. The militiamen started climbing out of the truck and Ferrer had to shout over their war cries to urge them back in again.

'They are eager to get to work,' he said as Simon started the motor.

He took the right fork and headed towards the twin peaks. The track rose through juniper groves and pastures carpeted in wildflowers. They saw a herd of ibex with long, curving horns feeding on broom shrubs ablaze with yellow buds. The track curved on to a meadow with scatterings of cork oaks planted for shade beside houses with red roofs and square windows. Dry stone walls marked boundaries. He saw a pair of white horses watching the vehicle pass, signs of everyday lives the people had lived and had been obliged to abandon.

He dropped down into second gear as the ascent grew

steeper. He was able to pick out what he was now certain were the peaks held by the British to his right, the French to his left. He leaned forward to get a better view and it was lucky that he did.

From out of the canopy of blue sky, he saw a Messerschmitt in flames diving at them through the gap between the hills. The pilot opened fire, the burst of shells zipping along the track towards them. Fountains of mud rose up, blocking his view. He swerved to avoid a direct hit and the truck rolled on its side, taking a spray of bullets as it slid 200 feet back down the incline like a giant sleigh before coming to a halt.

The combination of sounds was deafening, the hail of bullets from close range, the scraping of the steel side of the truck against the stony terrain, his head knocking against the windscreen. There was an almighty explosion. A blur of blood blinded his eyes, then there was nothing.

15

ALICE WAS PICKING shrapnel from the face of a soldier when the room darkened and a strange chill ran down her spine. She stopped what she was doing and gazed out the narrow window at the clouds passing over the sun.

'Are you all right?' the soldier asked. 'You're shaking.'

'I just shivered for some reason.' Her dry lips turned into a smile. 'I'm not hurting too much, am I?'

'No, I can't feel a thing.' The man had been sealed in his own thoughts; it wasn't unusual when they left the hill and engaged with her for the first time. 'You're Simon's sister, if I'm not mistaken?'

'Yes, Alice.'

'We came down together from Paris. I don't think we'd have made it without him.'

'That's kind. I'll tell him that.'

He lowered his eyes, then looked back at her again. 'You don't happen to know my brother, Lloyd Jones? I thought he was here.'

'They've gone now. He was taken with the other chaps to Albacete. They're being looked after.'

Bowen Jones had a brief look of relief that faded as he glanced down at the ball of gauze held in a sling around his neck. An unexploded grenade that had landed in his foxhole detonated as he tossed it back. The back blast had severed his hand and sprayed iron shavings over the right side of his face. The doctors had sculpted the flaps of skin into a stump. Alice had dressed the amputation and stared through a magnifying glass as she picked out the fragments from his cheek with a pair of tweezers.

They were by the window in the farmhouse outside Morata in the large room immediately entered from the main door. Kerosene lamps hung from the low beams over the table where Hugh Tregarth and Graham Webster in blood-blackened aprons laboured over an endless chain of men with wounds they would never have imagined the human body could survive.

The nurses at the dressing station on the sunken road treated the lightly injured. After a cup of hot, sweet tea and a few minutes to catch their breath, they checked their weapons and set out again on swollen feet back up Suicide Hill. Those too badly wounded to return were laid out on the stone floor in the farmhouse among piles of discarded boots and bloody uniforms reeking of gangrene and pus.

Alice brushed Bowen's hair from his brow. Sliver by sliver, she cleaned his face while he stared out at the changing light on the mountains as if to fix the scene in his memory.

Beyond Bowen's view, along the length of the River Jarama, the Moors scratched their way up the rock face to the patchy line of defences. Field guns shelled the lee side of the long descent to the sunken road. Above, against swirls of tail smoke, snub-nosed Polikarpovs with the hammer and sickle on their tail fins circled in a death dance with Luftwaffe Messerschmitts, their guns spewing out shells that showered the landscape.

Robbie rubbed his burning palms in the dust while Ron Yates fed a new belt through the cartridge guides. His number two was an unprepossessing railway clerk from some small town, stoop-shouldered with yellow teeth and grey eyes behind spectacles that constantly required cleaning. Robbie barely knew him and had learned from their first day on the front that it was better not to get to know him now.

McVicar's company had dug in on the crest of the hill with eight Maxims in a criss-crossing pattern covering the assault. The riflemen manned their flanks on each side of the triangular escarpment.

Robbie gazed up as pairs of aircraft cartwheeled in a dogfight across the sky, each pilot trying to outmanoeuvre the other. They climbed into the clouds, vanished from view, then dived back into the fray, guns pounding, the roar continuous like a train hammering endlessly into a station. He adjusted his gun sights and stared down 4,000 feet of slate grey hills. Three regiments of Moors were climbing the slopes, but what with the smoke and dust, if you saw them at all, what you saw appeared to be clusters of giant moths in flapping ponchos that fluttered into view then dissolved again into the scrub.

It was odd that he hadn't seen Simon dashing along the line. When he thought about Simon, Alice came into his mind and it struck him how small the world is sometimes, how life appears to have a shape that drives you along a defined, if unseen, path. It had to be more than coincidence that her gift of £5 had brought them together in Spain. If this was destiny, it had a cruel sense of humour.

*

One hundred yards below the riflemen was a fold of rock like a petrified wave where the Moors had gathered to reload and catch their breath. Those who had made it to this point knew how to time their runs. They would have counted the number of rifles and grasped that this was the soft spot with few grenades and no artillery. If the Moors could smash a hole through the defences, they would squeeze the British in a vice.

Dai knew it wouldn't be long before they came. He peered

up as a flight of German bombers dropped through the clouds and sewed their thousand-pound payloads along the ridge. He was showered in fragments that drummed his tin helmet and Doug Sanders copped a slice of shrapnel that tore across his chest like a pick into a seam of coal. Dai waved his fist.

'Fucking bastards.'

He dashed along the trench and the old sergeant grinned up at him as he spoke his dying words.

'I wouldn't want to be anywhere else in the world Dai, not anywhere.'

On cue, the Army of Africa rose from the rocks with spitting rifles. Dai closed Sanders's blue eyes and peered over the dugout. All along the line his comrades stood with their weapon butts nestled in their shoulders. When death grows familiar, a time comes when a man feels free, without material ties or ambitions to achieve or prove anything. That time had come. They stood their ground.

The first wave of Moors was cut to shreds and Dai Jones would have leapt from the trench to pursue them had Glyn not dragged him back by the flap of his cape.

'Not so fast, boyo,' he said and pointed.

A row of six T-35s had mounted the hill with Red Army commanders in leather coats and fur caps stationed behind the long barrels. Reggie Foster had got his hands on the battalion flag and waved it for all he was worth as he raced down the hill to direct the tanks towards their line of defence. The tanks divided into two groups of three, settled below the crest and sent their shells in a continuous barrage that drove the Moroccans back down the incline they had spent half the day climbing.

Foster planted the flag in the rocks. The riflemen hunkered down out of the wind to roll their tobacco and not much in life had tasted better than those cigarettes. They watched as the armoured vehicles reversed, the dust settled and they set off on their grinding caterpillar tracks across the defiles and bomb craters to provide a show of muscle for the '6th of February.'

*

In the valley, two miles away as the crow flies, Simon's eyes flickered open. There was a throbbing ache in his temples and in his mouth the coppery taste of blood. A body was pressing down on him, their arms and legs entwined like wrestlers. It occurred to him after a moment that it was the Spanish officer. He was cold, rigid as a board and had that musty smell that comes to the dead.

As he turned to take the weight from his shoulder, he caught a glimpse of the sky and a sequence of images spooled through his mind. The aircraft in flames, the burst of gunfire, the screech of steel as the truck flipped on its side and careened down the rocky slope. He took deep breaths. He jammed his feet against the door and twisted at an angle until he was able to stretch out and grab the metal frame around the passenger seat. Pushing down from his toes and pulling up with his right hand, he sloughed off Ferrer's body and manoeuvred his way through the shattered windscreen to the ground.

Except for the pain in his shoulder and the drums playing in his head, he had no obvious injuries. For half a second, he thought he might be deaf, but the faint ringing in his ears ceased and he was mindful of the buzz of insects, the murmur of the wind, the relentless distant rumble of artillery. He spat on his fingers and rubbed the grime from his watch face. The hands had frozen at 10:20. He had no idea how long he had been unconscious.

The scene had turned from the bucolic coming of spring to something surreal and incongruous. The foothills formed a viridian carpet dotted with wildflowers and militiamen in pools of their own blood. He went from one to the next. All were dead. Scattered around him were digging tools, spools of fuse wire, cases of explosives. It was extraordinary that none of them had ignited.

Simon turned away and leaned back through the windscreen. Ferrer had taken a single shell that had entered his right temple and blasted a hole the size of a fist through the back of his head. He found his papers in a wallet with a picture of a girl wearing a bandolier stuffed with cartridges.

He levered himself up on to the side of the truck and turned in a circle to study the landscape. Off to his left, a house stood at the edge of an olive grove against the background of slowly rising peaks. Coils of smoke drifted from the crashed Messerschmitt, the explanation for the bloodbath suddenly clear in his mind. Other planes must have followed to see if their comrade had bailed out and maximized their flight-time gunning down the militiamen as they fled.

He intended to gather the papers of the dead men, but the moment he began, he saw too many tunics to undo, too much blood and gore to deal with. What he did find in an outer pocket of the first man he searched was half a dozen dried dates that he ate immediately. He went on to the next man and the next. He found a chunk of bread, a block of cheese with mould on top, some olives, a bag of almonds, the thick end of a blood sausage.

He was disturbed by the leathery flap of wings and looked up, shading his eyes. Twenty or more vultures circled the killing fields. Wolves and rats would follow. The dead were dead. If he had a responsibility to those men, it was to get word to the Líster Brigade that the entire platoon had been wiped out and the valley was undefended.

With his hoard of food jammed in his pockets, he made his way up a dirt path to the farmhouse. He hauled water from the well and plunged his face in the wooden bucket. He couldn't remember the last time he had washed with hot water. That's what he needed to clean the blood from his skin. He walked around the building to the barn. He found a spade that he used to prise open the shutters. He then ran his knife blade in the gap between the windows and slipped the latch.

The house was neat and orderly inside, with plates lining a high shelf and a row of saucepans along the back of a scrubbed wooden counter. Everything was old, cared for, precious. The people had raised pigs or cows or goats. They made their own cheese and picked their own olives that they would have taken by cart into Morata to be pressed into oil and exchanged for small sums to buy those things they couldn't grow or make for themselves.

He opened the shutters to let the light in and lit a fire in the range. He let himself out with the key he found hanging on the back of the door and felt inexplicably happy to find the two white horses he vaguely recalled seeing on the hillside. They were pushing their muzzles into the bucket he had left beside the well. They stood aside as he hauled up more water and filled the trough with which they were obviously familiar.

He took pails of water back into the kitchen and filled a steel tub. While the water heated, he searched through the house with its wooden furniture and modest adornments, a few photographs in frames, a standard lamp with a frilly shade. He found a pair of high-waisted wool trousers, a work shirt with patched elbows, a sheepskin-lined canvas jacket, undergarments smelling of mothballs, towels, some soap, shaving gear, a hairbrush and a small round mirror in which he saw reflected the thin, haunted face of a stranger.

When the water was warm enough, it needed all of his strength to lift the tub down to the floor. He removed his uniform. He shaved, then stood in the tub to scrub himself clean. The water had turned a muddy shade of red by the time he had finished. He strode out to the courtyard naked, pulled up another pail of water and tipped it over his head to rinse off. The horses watched and he laughed at himself in spite of the cold.

The trousers were short but the jacket was warm and a good fit. He combed back his hair. After emptying the filthy water in the courtyard, he washed out the tub and put it back where he had found it. The larder was empty except for a few coffee beans in a hessian sack that he ground in the hand mill he found in a drawer. He sat at the table with his pauper's banquet and a terracotta jug of steaming coffee.

Could he have avoided the crash? He shook his head. You ask yourself such questions when you know there's no answer. Every decision in extremis is split-second. You do what you think is right, then face the consequences. He ate slowly, savouring the flavours, and his heart beat slower.

He washed up and stared out of the window into the valley. He ran his fingers over the tender spot on the left side of his head. He had probably suffered a mild concussion. It had passed. The feeling of shock had passed. He found a pencil and paper. He wrote a note apologising to the owner of the house for taking what he had taken. He left his discarded clothes in a pile by the door. He had some pesetas in his pocket, but a money gift would have been inappropriate. He signed the note with the words 'Soldado de las Brigadas Internacionales.'

Simon closed the shutters, locked up, slipped the key under the door and whistled to catch the attention of the two white horses.

'¡Vengan! ¡Vengan!' he called.

16

ALICE LEFT THE farmhouse to help treat the wounded as they stumbled back down the hill to the sunken road. Her lips had narrowed. Her face was drawn.

Robbie hurried towards her. His throat was chafed with cordite and his voice came out in a whisper.

'Have you seen Simon?'

She stared back as if he were a carving cleaved from the landscape. He was grimy, skin encrusted in debris, a laceration on his cheek, the whites of his eyes unusually white. She wanted to cry.

'Not since this morning.' She swallowed hard and composed herself. 'Are you all right?'

He slowly nodded. 'Aye...' he said, and of course he wasn't.

The second day of the Battle of Jarama had ground to a halt at nightfall. General Varela had expected to seize the highway, and the boys of the British Battalion considered it a victory that the Nationalist troops, after 15 hours of frontal assault, were still bogged down across the river. Fresh recruits with two weeks' training had arrived from Albacete and Spanish regulars loyal to the Republic had clashed that day with regiments whose officers had staked their futures on Franco. They had dug the trenches deeper. Thousands had died. The lines had not shifted an inch.

The stars were out on a clear sky. They could hear the clamour of friends finding each other, the clatter of spoons in tin pannikins. There was plenty of food, cigarettes, some casks of wine. Alice looked at the tangle of damaged flesh on Robbie's cheek.

'That needs treating,' she said.

She sat him down on an empty crate under the glow of an oil lamp. She bathed the wound with a saline solution and he looked up at her as if at the light through a stained-glass window.

'Brace yourself. It's going to hurt,' she said.

She willed her hand to remain still and he watched as she threaded a needle. He tilted his head to one side, gritted his teeth and, stitch by stitch, Alice closed the gash on his cheekbone. When she leaned forward to examine her work, their faces were so close he could feel the warmth of her breath.

He tried to speak but his tongue was swollen in his mouth and he wasn't sure what he wanted to say. Her eyes turned glassy like pools and filled with tears. She sobbed against his chest and he was grateful to have finally taken her in his arms.

'I'm sorry,' she said, when they broke away. 'I don't usually cry.'

'He's out there. I know it.'

She reached for the undamaged side of his face. 'You love him, don't you?'

'It's not a word I would have used but, aye, I reckon.'

She rubbed the tears from the corners of her eyes with her fingertips and took his two hands. 'Love's a funny thing,' she said.

'You're right there. I'm in stitches,' he responded, and her lips turned briefly in a smile.

She covered the suture with a dressing and buckled her bag. The noise around them seemed to have grown silent but it returned again, the retort of rifle bolts as weapons were cleaned, the chatter of men who needed to talk. Two stretcher-bearers on their last legs came in with an injured man and Alice slipped away to lend her assistance.

Robbie joined the gunners sprawled out around a log fire. Bruce Seattle, the Australian, filled a tin cup with wine and before he had taken a sip they were interrupted by the unlikely sound of cheering coming up the road from the direction of the farmhouse.

'Don't tell me they've surrendered?' Seattle said.

Robbie gulped back the wine and hastened down the slope. A crowd had gathered around the dressing station. He pushed his way through and a grin stretched across his face, pulling at the stitches. He saw Alice and shouldered his way towards her. She grabbed his arm like someone drowning and they watched as two figures backlit by the moon clip-clopped their way along the sunken road on a pair of white horses.

'You should have seen him as Sir Lancelot in his school play,' Alice said. 'He's quite the little showman.'

Simon hitched the horses to the back of a truck while Captain Lewin climbed awkwardly down from the saddle. He raised his arms for silence.

'Gentlemen,' he announced. 'The post has come.'

There was more cheering, then a hush descended as the absurd miracle of the mail's arrival from Albacete reminded them of the comrades they had lost those last two days. Simon and the captain unloaded mailbags from the horses. They dipped in and read the names on the envelopes, a roll call of the living and the dead. The brigaders wandered off, clutching their letters like flowers. Simon slid the rest back into one of the bags.

There were two letters for Robbie, four for Alice. The Jones boys had one communication between them, from an uncle, Dai said. Simon joined them and it was like old times, except Lloyd was missing and Bowen had the vacant stare of those for whom life would never be the same again.

An unease arises when comrades find each other after battle. There's nothing to say because there's nothing you can say, and what you try to say comes out wrong. They shook hands. They clutched shoulders. They noted as they looked at each other how the months had aged them by years and they knew without a mirror they looked the same.

Lanterns rocked back and forth below the canvas awning like lights at sea. Alice watched Wilf Tooley, the armourer, the former jockey, lead the horses away, and turned to Simon.

'Where did you find them? They're beautiful.'

'I borrowed them, if you must know.'

'Who saddled them for you?'

'I did it myself.'

'That's a first,' she said.

He glanced at Robbie. 'Alice is always Alice.'

'That's why we love her,' Robbie said and the words sounded strange as they left his mouth.

Simon laughed. They looked at her at the same time. There was light in her eyes and the tension had gone from her face.

'I'm glad you both find me so amusing,' she said, and turned on her heels.

She took a lamp and they followed her up into the olive grove. Robbie felt a stab of jealousy as she hugged her brother. She admired his neat hair and new clothes. They sat. Alice rested her head on Simon's shoulder. Robbie opened his letters. They were from his mother and younger sister, little notes so earnest his dusty eyes grew wet again.

'My sister's going to have a bairn,' he said, and the thought of a new baby coming into the world struck him as miraculous and unthinkable.

'Is it her first?' asked Simon.

'Second. If it's a boy she's going to name him Robert.'

'That's lovely,' Alice said.

'If I know Rosalind, she's got some ulterior motive.'

'Don't be unkind, Robbie...'

'You don't know my sister.'

Simon began to tell them about his strange day and was interrupted by the sound of a motorcycle screaming up from the farm. He knew by the machine's timbre who it was and the coincidence that Anatoly Sokolov should appear now seemed cruel and perverse. Robbie and Alice followed him down to the road where they found the driver lifting his goggles from his face.

'*Bonsoir*,' he said with a sharp nod towards Alice. He jerked the bike on to its stand and removed his helmet.

They spoke for a long time in French, raising their voices. Simon shrugged and kept shaking his head. Robbie noticed the spasm vibrate on his neck and felt inadequate that he understood nothing. Simon's shoulders finally sagged.

'I have to report to Comrade Marty,' he said and brushed Alice's cheeks with his own. He took Robbie's hand. 'Look after each other,' he added, and was about to straddle the pillion when Alice stopped him.

'Wait, wait a moment.' She took a pair of scissors from her bag and proceeded to cut her tartan scarf in two equal lengths. She folded the first half around Simon's neck, the second around Robbie's, tucking it into his jacket. 'There,' she added with the air of a job well done.

'Very nice. Good evening,' Sokolov pronounced in English.

He started the bike and Simon climbed aboard. Alice and Robbie watched the machine race down the sunken road and it seemed unnaturally calm as the noise faded and disappeared. They remained motionless and Robbie in the months ahead would think often of that moment standing in silence, as if some inexplicable force was gathering momentum. Alice took his hand.

'Who was that?' Robbie asked her.

'He's Russian.'

Before he continued, Alice sealed his lips with the tip of her finger and he felt as if his heart was about to explode. They climbed the embankment and made their way up through a low gradient of evenly spaced trees that cast shadows like a labyrinth. Alice turned left and right. She remembered finding the sundial at the heart of the maze at Elsmere Abbey when she was a child and how happy the discovery had made her.

She stopped on the far edge of the grove where the trees formed a canopy over a bed of leaves. Their lips joined. Her hands had trembled before she stitched the wound on Robbie's face, but her fingers now, as they unclasped his buttons, were sure and steady. He did the same, releasing her ties and clasps in a rush as if the world might end at any second. Their bodies touched. They weren't cold. They were burning. They made love beneath the olive trees in the glow of the icy moon. It was the right thing to do. The only thing to do. There was just that moment and they knew that it would make every moment of the days to come more terrifying.

17

SHELLS SAILED OVER the ridge and exploded, showering them in shards of rock. The rain fell diagonally, wind-driven and icy. Yellow mist stinking of sulphur glided through the ravines.

A wave of Moors in billowing capes rose from their burrows and charged into the arcs of blazing machine guns. The cartridge belts screeched through the guides like knives being sharpened. The African boys were fast. They were brave. He could see the whites of their eyes in their dark faces.

The gunners had learned to change belts as fast as the human hand can do this numbing work. Their palms were wet and blistered. The water-cooled guns steamed. When they ran out of water, they filled the chamber with their own piss. It was the third day on Suicide Hill. General Varela was a mile from his goal. He had waited long enough.

They fired their guns and the enemy kept coming up the hill to the ridge until McVicar yelled the order and the gunners yielded their position before they were overwhelmed. They laid down covering fire and stumbled under the weight of the Maxims into the slit trench dug with depressing foresight further down the incline.

The line was shrinking, shredding, breaking apart. Robbie carried the barrel, George the iron wheels and ammo. They set up with Bruce Seattle and his number two on the left, McVicar at the point. Andy McBride was on the right flank supported by Reggie Foster and the tattered rump of the Third Rifles.

George locked a fresh belt into place and stuck his thumb up in a gesture of desperate optimism. A hotel porter with scant English and a constant smile that was alternatively uplifting and irritating, George Rossides was one of the dozen Cypriots who had signed on with the battalion in Albacete.

Mortars thudded into the hillside without detonating and a cheer ran along the ranks. Some of the shells were faulty. Others contained sand instead of explosives and notes signed by fellow travellers in the armament factories in Italy. They were not alone. But they were alone. And they were dying, plucked one at a time like low-hanging fruit from a tree. Robbie had expected to die on those hills. He'd prepared for it. But that was yesterday.

*

There were now more than 40,000 Italian combatants on the Spanish peninsula sent with pomp and news cameras by Benito Mussolini. A regiment of Dio lo Vuole armed with M91 carbines had crossed the Jarama and were climbing to the peak behind the Moors. Robbie had never been clear what the word 'fascism' meant until Simon explained that the movement should really, according to Mussolini, be defined as corporatism: the merger of state and corporate power. As for 'Dio lo Vuole', it meant 'What God Wants', and Robbie wondered what kind of God it was they believed in.

The noise was constant, like a brass band playing as the musicians careened off a cliff. Planes thundered overhead. Russian tanks lobbed their payloads into the arena. He could hear small arms fire hiss above his head. The Italians used high-expansion bullets packed into nickel jackets that exploded on impact and left grisly wounds few would survive.

George gave Robbie a shake and he glanced over at McVicar. His thumb was pointing back down the gradient.

It was time to move again. They dismantled the gun, listened for a moment as if the battle contained omens or messages, then set off towards an escarpment fringed with trees. The Nationalists had taken the ridge. Robbie looked down the long gradient towards the sunken road and wondered what she was doing at that moment.

*

He had shaved and shined his boots. He wore a brown tie and peaked cap, a wide belt with a diagonal cross strap and a Webley pistol. Walter Lewin had endured the assault on Passchendaele in 1917. The Battle of Jarama, 20 years on, may have been smaller in scale, not in passion or intensity, not in the quotient of the damaged and the dead. In his blouse, he carried a letter written to his parents to tell them he loved them and that he had no regrets, which parents of dead sons want to hear, and wasn't entirely true. You get one life, in his experience, one gift, and his regret was that he had chosen the dubious merits of the legal profession over his dream to become an architect.

Lewin stood on a box observing the rout through field glasses. The line had gone. Not broken. It had evaporated. The battalion was a smashed vase of scattered pieces. They had hung on for six hours and for every two men he had sent up the hill, one would not be coming down again. A lump came to his throat as he watched Reg Foster stumble through the olive grove with a handful of riflemen. The Political Commissar slid over the earth bank and landed on his knees.

'Jesus Christ, what have I done?' Foster moaned. 'There were hundreds of them, hundreds. I couldn't help it. I just didn't… I couldn't…' He was shaking, middle-aged, exhausted, a union organiser, a workers' leader. First into battle. Last to retreat. 'I've let the side down. I've let everyone down.'

Streaked in oil and mud, dead eyes like fish, the Jones

brothers, Dai, Glyn and Rhys, staggered in with the last of the Third Rifles, 30 men, 40 at most.

Alice Sheridan and Matilda Griffiths, uniforms black from neck to hem, moved along the line of bodies that stretched the length of the sunken road. The morphine had run out. Some of the wounded wept in agony. Others bit down on chunks of wood. Bowen Jones carried a pan of coffee with his one good hand and wore a bandolier of tin mugs slantwise across his chest.

Lewin showed no anger. It was what he had expected. The men out on the hill were losing their nerve. He had to keep his.

'It's all right, Reg. You take some time out,' he told Foster.

'There were hundreds of them. I didn't think we could hang on.'

'I know. It's been a long day. Reinforcements are coming. I'll send someone up with the lads. We'll plug the gap,' Lewin said.

Foster shook his head. He squared his shoulders and glanced back at the rest of his company drinking coffee. The veins on his neck rose up, blue and swollen as he took a breath and saluted.

'No, comrade. That won't be necessary. I'm all right now. Retreating like that was a bloody stupid thing to do, but it's not too late.'

As he was speaking, they heard the rumble of a motorcycle approaching up the sunken road. It did a half turn as it skidded to a halt. Simon Sheridan climbed off the pillion and the driver accelerated back towards the farmhouse. The riflemen rose from where they had been resting and approached Lewin to listen while Sheridan gave his report.

Enrique Líster had positioned his brigade between the hills occupied by the French and British. He didn't say that he had led them there at daybreak, but Lewin knew that. Simon then announced that El Campesino's troops were stationed across the peaks on the Nationalist's left flank, supporting the 800 volunteers of the Abraham Lincoln Battalion.

The riflemen had felt drained and defeated, but the way Simon gave his account gave them heart. He looked fresh, well groomed, his tartan scarf adding some colour in the field of khaki. Dai raised his clenched fist.

'*Viva la República*,' he cried, and Lewin lifted the binoculars Dai had given him high above his head.

'*Viva la República*,' he repeated.

Not everyone knew who El Campesino was. Walt Lewin did. So did Dai Jones. Valentín González was a miner like himself who had established one of the first militia units to defend against Franco's assault on Madrid. He was a hero.

Wilf Tooley, the armourer, rattled up pushing a trolley laden with rifles, ammunition, German grenades shiny as fresh fruit. The riflemen dug in. They weren't waiting for Lewin's orders. They knew what they had to do.

Alice hurried along the road towards them. Simon moved away to meet her. He glanced over her shoulder, back at the gruesome scene on the sunken road.

'Have you seen Robbie?' he asked her.

Her eyes shifted to the mountains. 'He's still up there,' she replied. 'There's just a few stragglers.'

'I'm going up.'

'I know. I won't tell you to take care, you never listen to a word I say.'

Simon slid the strap of a Mauser over his shoulder. He carried a webbing pouch containing envelopes with confiscated tobacco. He fitted six grenades in the available space and slung the pouch across his chest.

'Have you forgotten anything?' she asked and he kissed her cheeks.

'I don't think so,' he replied and buckled his helmet.

He climbed the weapon crate steps and followed the riflemen through the olive grove back to the hill.

18

McVICAR'S GUNNERS HAD withdrawn another 500 yards back down Suicide Hill and settled on a platform of rock with good sightlines back up to the ridge.

As the 40 riflemen spread out along the left flank, Simon hurried along the line with cigarettes tucked in envelopes and intel that gave them the lift they needed. El Campesino was leading his force of Madrid veterans up the far slopes of the Guadarramas to General Varela's eyrie on Pingarrón. At the same time, Enrique Líster, a stone mason in another life, was advancing with 3,000 militiamen on key crossing points on the Jarama between the French and British positions.

The gunners lit their smokes and threaded the ammunition belts through the guides. It was impossible for Simon to distinguish who was who. They were bloodied and bandaged, faces caked in gun oil. McVicar and his number two were at the end of the line.

'Where's Gillan?' he asked. McVicar lifted his chin in an upwards direction.

'Still up there. Silly bugger. He covered the retreat.'

'On his own?'

'The lad he was with copped it.'

As Simon stretched out from the escarpment, McVicar pulled at his cape.

'There's no going back, son. No heroics. We hold the line.'

Simon stared into the old Scotsman's eyes. 'I'm sorry, Sergeant, it is something I have to do,' he said.

McVicar loosened his grip. 'None of us are going to come off this hill, you known that, don't you?'

Simon nodded. 'Yes, Sergeant, I know.'

Mac adjusted his helmet and pointed to a lone tree beside a crude dolman.

'If he's alive, that's where you'll find him.'

'Thank you. Good luck, Mac.'

He slid out from McVicar's position and set off, sprinting on a zigzagging course towards the advancing guns. He passed corpses in shallow trenches dug and abandoned. There were weapons everywhere, tin helmets, a pair of boots with no one in them. The air smelled of death.

He slowed as the dolman came into view.

'Robbie. Robbie,' Simon hissed. 'It's me.'

A pair of brown eyes in a black face below a worn French beret looked back at him down the sights of a rifle.

Simon squeezed into the hollow beneath the dolman's stone cap just as a formation of Panzers crested the summit and shelled the hillside. The tank commanders pumped out their payloads, the boom, boom, boom resounding over the hard surface of the rock face. Then there was silence, sudden and sharp, like when a telephone stops ringing.

Robbie put his finger to his lips. They heard a cry for help off in the distance to the right of their position.

'That sounds like an English voice.'

'Welsh,' Simon corrected.

As the dust settled, an Italian infantry company crossed the ridge behind the German tanks in a show of confidence. They trotted at a steady pace in neat uniforms.

'We're cut off,' Simon said.

As he spoke, they heard the same cry for help.

'Stay low. Follow me,' Robbie whispered.

Simon ducked down and, in Robbie's shadow, they descended from their position and followed the contour of the hills away from the advance. Smoke filled the air. Mature cactuses like frozen statues stood randomly among the broken pines that had taken root in the thin soil lodged in the volcanic rock. Every sound bouncing off the hard surface was either muted or magnified.

They began to climb again as the voice grew closer and stopped to take cover as a building in a spinney of trees came into view at the narrow end of a long, triangular delta. An artillery shell had caved in the roof and the broken windows stared over a pasture where yellow broom had sprung up through the undergrowth. It was quiet now, except for the fading cries of a man in his death throes.

Robbie led the way around the delta. They stopped in the scrub adjacent to the building. One wall had been sliced away to create what looked like a doll's house, a depiction of Spanish life suspended in time like an exhibit at a museum. The beds were made up with patchwork quilts and lacy pillows. The cupboard doors had been flung open by the blast to reveal dresses and coats. There was a picture of the Virgin on the wall above a chest of drawers where a blue glass vase lay shattered. The pieces glimmered where they caught the light. Most of the ground floor was hidden behind piles of fallen masonry.

'Cover me,' Robbie instructed and dashed across the open space.

Simon waited two minutes, then followed. He scaled the rubble and the blood drained from his face. Glyn Jones had been castrated. His genitals lay on his chest. Franco's dog soldiers raped women and butchered the men to exact retribution, not only from their victims, but their families, the clan. It was a weapon of war as old as time and time was going backwards.

Rhys, Jones the Pole, was at Glyn's side, suffocated by his own testicles.

Robbie knelt. 'Glyn, it's me, Robbie.'

Glyn's eyes slowly focused. He panted for breath. 'You can't leave me like this.'

Robbie made a vague gesture, as if he'd been struck by paralysis. His knees were wet with Glyn's blood. Glyn saw Simon behind him and smiled. They always smile.

'Bless you, Simon...'

A shot rang out, resounding off the walls. Simon dropped his rifle and turned to vomit up the bile from his empty stomach.

'They're animals,' Robbie said. 'Fockin animals.' He stared down at Glyn, Jones the Pigeon. The bullet had turned his head to mush.

'I've done everything, Robbie. I've even killed a friend,' Simon murmured.

'Aye, you did it for me as well as Glyn. I know that.'

Simon trembled uncontrollably and only calmed as Robbie took him in an embrace.

'What can we do?' he said.

'Make sure we stay alive.'

They joined hands and made one fist. Simon glanced back at their dead comrades and a line of poetry came to his mind.

'Red lips are not so red as the stained stones kissed by the English dead.'

'Is that a prayer?'

'It's Wilfred Owen. He was Welsh.'

Simon found their papers and pushed them into his pouch. He grabbed his rifle. As he climbed the rubble, Robbie, too, glanced back at the dead brothers and that split-second pause saved his life. Two quick rounds rang out and Simon tumbled like a sack down the pile of masonry.

Robbie's instinct was to leap forward. His muscles tensed and he needed every ounce of self-discipline to remain in the shadows. The shot Simon had fired must have attracted the attention of some deserters, almost certainly the same butchers who had cut up the Jones boys. What were they doing there in that bombed out house? Men had fled the advance in every direction and where you landed was just chance, from the inferno to the unpredictable. War is madness. Nothing makes sense except the present moment, perhaps the last moment. One thing war does teach you, he thought, is patience.

A rock thrown from the distance landed on Simon's motionless body. Then another. Robbie kept his vision trained down the barrel of his rifle as two men in ponchos emerged from the trees. They loped across the clearing, keeping low. Robbie breathed slowly. His firing finger rested on the trigger. When the two men were a pace from Simon, he squeezed, shifted the angle and aimed at each man's chest, the widest part of the target. Robbie controlled the urge for haste and counted the seconds until he guessed two minutes had passed. He slid out from the building and studied the pasture below the house. Nothing moved.

The tic drummed on Simon's neck. One bullet had shattered his left arm below the shoulder. The other had hit him above the heart. Robbie opened the buttons on his jacket, below which he wore an army blouse, a jumper and a cotton shirt. The keys to his father's clock hung around his neck on a thong. Robbie unbuttoned the blouse, slit the jumper down from the V and located a bullet lodged against his chest. It had bruised, without breaking, the skin.

He slipped the bullet into one of Simon's blouse pockets and found in the other the anthology of Blake's verses bored through with a perfectly defined hole. On the first page was the inscription in green ink he'd first read on a train racing through France: 'Be safe. Be well. Be happy. But most of all, be yourself.'

Robbie closed his eyes. He felt as if he were drowning, but it wasn't his whole life that flashed before him. What he saw was Alice beneath the olive trees in the moonlight and the tears he'd been holding back ran down his cheeks.

Half the men who had died on the hill had bled out before the stretcher-bearers reached them. He brushed at his wet cheeks and tried to remember their first aid training. He could feel Alice's presence, the way his heart had erupted when she kissed him, the way she tensed and bit her lips when he entered her body. He had a pain across his chest and had to shake himself to shake away the memory, the beautiful, tragic, hopelessness of it all.

Apply pressure. Stop the haemorrhaging. Don't hurry. He pulled Simon's shirt from his trousers and cut off a strip of material that he wrapped around the wound. He used his half of the tartan scarf to cover the dressing and hold the damaged area together. He stripped the belt from one of the dead Moors to use as a tourniquet. As he tightened it just below the shoulder joint, the flow of blood slowed and began to clot.

Robbie swung Simon's pouch with the grenades across his chest and shortened the strap to keep his rifle firm against his side. He lifted him in a fireman's carry and crossed the delta on a course away from the sound of gunfire. He stopped for a break in a hollow beneath a line of trees and Simon's eyes fluttered open.

'I'm wounded?' he said.

'Oh, aye, you are that.'

'I shot Glyn?'

'It was a brave thing to do.'

Simon thought about that and nodded. 'Is there any water?'

Robbie held his water bottle to Simon's lips. After taking a few sips, his eyes closed again and Robbie hefted him back across his shoulders. The hillside was littered with corpses, Moors, Spaniards, Italians, Scots and English, their differences gone in the regiment of the dead. The rain had stopped falling and the hazy light created the illusion that the bodies were floating above the ground, unwilling to enter the embrace of the Spanish soil.

Fighter planes soared in and out of the clouds, guns clacking. A rainbow arched incongruously over the hills. Robbie rested against the side of a rock and took a few breaths. His legs felt like lead. He could just make out the olive trees in the distance. He left his rifle and set off on the last stretch like a tortoise with Simon on his back.

The camp was in chaos. Brigaders were staggering in from what had been termed the front-line. There was no line. Just a rain-swept avenue of retreat to Morata and Madrid. The wounded were lying all over the place.

He eased Simon down to the ground at the first aid post and Alice ran towards them. Her mouth was slightly open and her hair was loose about her cheeks. She looked into his eyes and Robbie had that feeling of drowning again. She cupped his face and he felt like weeping. She kneeled to deal with Simon.

'His arm took a bullet and there's a bruise on his chest.'

Her fingers worked swiftly. She released the tourniquet, then cut away the remains of Simon's jumper and shirt. She cleaned and cauterised the wound, then applied a fresh dressing. The bruise was like a target, a red bull's eye surrounded by a ring of claret, then navy blue. She looked up, holding the leather belt he had used as a tourniquet.

'You saved his life,' she said.

He retrieved the anthology from Simon's blouse. 'You did,' he told her, and gave her the book.

'Robbie...'

Whatever she was going to say didn't come out. Hugh Tregarth appeared. He took Simon's pulse and called to a team of stretcher-bearers.

'One more,' he shouted.

'Hugh,' Alice began, and Tregarth held up his hand to stop her.

'He'll bat for England. It's a clean wound.'

Simon's eyes opened. He looked from Alice to Robbie and back again. Then he was whisked away on to the floor of the ambulance leaving for the farmhouse. Hugh moved on to another man.

'They're evacuating the wounded. I'm not sure where to,' Alice said. She drew closer. 'Robbie, thank you. Thank you. I've been looking for you...'

She was rambling. There were things she wanted to say, there were things he wanted to say, feelings hard to put into words, but those things didn't belong there, now, on the sunken road.

Robbie saw Dai Jones approaching and the moment passed. He shook his head.

'They didn't make it.'

'You're sure, Robbie? They got cut off...'

'I'm sorry, Dai.'

'Glyn?'

'Aye.'

'And Rhys? Both of them?'

'They were together.'

Dai nodded. His teeth locked. His face compressed inwards like a punctured balloon. 'They came for me, Robbie. Now they're dead and I'm still here.'

'They came because that's what good men do.'

Dai shrank away to deal with his grief.

Alice took Robbie's hand. Their fingers meshed.

Men struggled in with black faces, expressions on the edge of madness. They shouted in Spanish and French and English as they pushed along the sunken road. Robbie and Alice joined them as six old men carrying ancient shotguns clattered towards them on donkeys. They dismounted, went down on their knees and kissed the ground.

Captain Lewin emerged from the opposite direction

waving his revolver. He was screaming above the noise. It was a few seconds before they could make out what he was saying. 'Another hour. Just another hour.'

The old men stood with raised fists. '*Viva la República!*' they exclaimed, and the cry was repeated along the ranks.

'*Viva la República!*'

'Robbie, Robbie.'

McVicar made his way towards him with the surviving gunners, lads he didn't know and would never know, lads bandaged like mummies back from the infirmary, lads from Brigade headquarters. The remnants of a Spanish company had appeared, a platoon of French and Belgians, a half dozen Italians who would meet their own countrymen on Suicide Hill. Men babbled in different tongues as they gripped hands and seized weapons from the cart Wilf Tooley wheeled among them.

'We're going back up, Robbie,' McVicar said. He glanced down at Robbie and Alice's joined hands. 'She'll wait for thee.'

Alice squeezed Robbie's fingers as she turned to look up at him. 'I will,' she said.

Before he could speak, their attention was drawn to the extraordinary sight of what looked like a company of Great War doughboys in campaign hats and puttees marching three abreast from the direction of San Martín de la Vega. Leading them, with chevrons of sergeant stripes on his sleeve, was Paddy O'Hay, a German semi-automatic over his shoulder, a fag between his teeth. Like most of the Irish lads, O'Hay had joined the International Brigade as a step towards getting the British out of Ireland. They felt more at home alongside the Americans in the Abraham Lincoln Brigade.

'General Gillan as I live and breathe.' O'Hay stopped and the Americans gathered around him. 'Looks like you need a helping hand.'

'You're late,' Robbie replied. The two men sized each other up. 'You wouldn't happen to have a spare cigarette?'

O'Hay slapped his pockets. 'Last one, you should have asked me yesterday.'

One of the Americans gave Robbie a fag and he stuck it behind his ear.

'I thought the Lincolns were up on the hill,' Robbie said and pointed.

'We are. Our truck broke down, we're lucky to get here.'

'Dead lucky,' Robbie replied.

Captain Lewin paced towards them. He carried two Italian light machine guns, better than any weapon the men in the battalion had seen. He tossed one of them to Gillan.

'Make every one count,' he said.

Tooley followed with the appropriate ammunition belts. Robbie threw as many as he could carry over his shoulder.

He turned to Alice.

'I've never prayed before,' she said. 'It seems rather silly and selfish, as if God has time for your prayers.'

They gripped fingers for a second. He turned away and she watched as the men in their bloodied and filthy uniforms climbed the earth embankment and marched once more up Suicide Hill.

19

DAI JONES BEGAN to sing the 'Internationale'. The men at his side joined in and the song grew louder as it moved along the line. Bent shoulders straightened. Weary limbs lost their fatigue. The wounded staggering in from the last line of dugouts watched the advancing column and raised their voices as they climbed back up the hill.

> This is the final struggle
> Let us group together, and tomorrow
> The Internationale
> Will be the human race.

The Spanish sang, the Belgians, the Italians, the French.

> C'est la lutte finale
> Groupons-nous, et demain
> L'Internationale
> Sera le genre humain.

The French and Spanish peeled off to the east, to form a right flank with a Spanish sergeant in the lead, their voices creating an Esperanto echo that rang out across the valley. The cry 'olé olé' punctuated the singing and a Spanish boy fired shots into the gathering twilight to warn General Varela that he was coming.

Captain Lewin formed a left flank with Reggie Foster,

Dai Jones and the survivors from three rifle companies, their numbers swelled by the American Lincolns commanded by Paddy O'Hay. Mac McVicar led the machine gunners into shallow trenches swimming in mud 1,000ft below the ridge occupied by German Panzers, the Italian Dio lo Vuole and the Army of Africa.

The Brigada Líster was closing in on the banks of the Jarama. The militia led by El Campesino was within mortar distance of the heights of Pingarrón. General Varela had to smash his way through the last line of defence on the Valencia–Madrid highway at Morata de Tajuña before daybreak. He was throwing everything he had into the battle. The tip of the spear was aimed at the weakest point, the International Brigade on Suicide Hill.

On 12 February, 600 volunteers from the British Battalion had been deployed to defend the road. Fewer than 100 remained on the third day of combat, with 200 Internationals from a dozen nations in support.

The air was infested with bullets, canon shells, the acrid smell of cordite. Visibility was down to a few yards and the roar of 300 men singing as they emerged through the mist was so sudden it startled the Nationalist infantry.

The men of the International Brigade climbed the hill knowing this was the last battle to protect the highway and prevent the Nationalists marching on Madrid. They knew with each step the odds of coming down were small. But their fear had gone. No longer content to hold the hill, they began to counterattack. There were no sections, no platoons, no orders. Individuals took it upon themselves to move forward. They danced from shelter to shelter, into bomb craters and behind trees where they set up their guns and made the way safe for the next wave of comrades.

Enemy soldiers trapped in the unexpected offensive scattered in disarray and were slaughtered in the withering crossfire. The Internationals had been on retreat for three days. As they pressed on into the path of the German tanks, it occurred to Gillan that, for the first time in its short history, the battalion was advancing, not withdrawing.

As that thought entered his head, the charge came to a halt. They had waded through a sea of dead Moors, Spanish Legionnaires, Italians. Each step along the way they had left their own men sprawled out in the mud: Bruce Seattle behind the Maxim he kept immaculate; John Egan, the billiard player; Roger Gollick, who had started the offensive as a stretcher-bearer. They went in ones and twos. Ten were dead. Then 20. Then 40.

They had no strength to support the challenge. They dug in and fired their weapons until their hands blistered and the 'Internationale' died in their throats. The Nationalists rallied. Tanks followed the infantry, cannon blasting shells that pulverised the rocks and coated the volunteers in sparkling specks of grit. Freddie Amos fell. Keith Dolan. Ali Ashraf, the Egyptian deck-hand, was run through with a Moroccan bayonet and bled to death mumbling words from the Qur'an.

Mac McVicar slumped over, guts sliced open by shrapnel. Robbie went to his side. The old Scotsman was smiling. He had never seen him smile before.

'We nearly did it, lad,' he said in a voice that had lost its brittle edge.

Robbie was expressionless like a statue. His moustache, silvery with dust, and three-day beard made his features appear as if they had been hewn from the rock of the hill.

Dead men still holding their weapons stretched out to his left and right. He stared in one direction, then the other. Like the wind, battles pause, draw breath. He lit the Lucky Strike the American had given him. He remembered the march for jobs, Jimmy McGee discarded like old rags in the mortuary, the £5 note. His heart thumped like a trapped animal behind his rib cage. What would happen to her when the Moroccan boys overran the hill and reached the sunken road?

He slid the last cartridge belt into the Italian gun. He lifted his lone fist into the dying day and bore down on the enemy, spraying lead in a steady sweeping motion. His action coincided with the appearance of Captain Lewin, Dai Jones, Paddy O'Hay and two dozen doughboys who had come through the barrage and charged the Nationalist infantrymen at the very moment that he opened up with his burst of gunfire.

The enemy front line turned straight into the blazing guns of the mixed company of Spanish, French and Belgians. They met in a bayonet charge that left scores dead in the enemy ranks and wiped the Internationals out, virtually to a man. Political Commissar Foster was the first to charge, the first to fall.

The German cavalry maintained its course and would have kept coming, but Paddy O'Hay, with his sniper eye, put a bullet through the head of the German major commanding the lead tank. Robbie tossed a grenade into the open hatchway. The tank erupted in a ball of fire and the entire formation was momentarily startled. The second tank swerved into the path of the third. They collided and the rest panicked.

The attacking infantry still outnumbered the defenders by ten to one, but an entire regiment had been decimated and the sight of their tanks pulling back appeared to leave them with no alternative other than to retreat. The manoeuvre disintegrated into a rout as Lewin's handful of survivors slashed at them from a clump of wind-bent pines.

Robbie leapt into a shell hole. He replaced his empty gun with another. The retreating soldiers in billowing capes appeared, in the light of the burning tank, to be flying and fell like shot birds as the rounds pumped down his gun barrel. He wasn't sure if Lewin had seen this spontaneous action, but the captain emerged from cover and paid the price. A

Moroccan in a head-cloth winged him in the shoulder and took off, sprinting behind the scurrying tanks.

Dai Jones had followed the captain from the trees. He charged after the shooter and ran him through with his bayonet, lunging downwards, lifting upwards. He had the wind in his sails. He ran on and, as he ran, he began to sing again, his voice a cry of rage that chimed over the rocks of Suicide Hill. He forged on up the incline until he vanished from view.

Robbie didn't think, he just followed Dai up to the crest and chased him down the far slope into the no man's land they had never entered. Dai must have run out of bullets. He abandoned his rifle, his helmet. He was no longer a soldier, he was a pitman with a voice and he kept singing until an enemy marksman took the time to turnabout and silence him. Robbie ducked from cover to cover until he reached Dai's side.

Jones the Voice gazed up at the sky. The stars shone in his dead eyes.

'We beat them, lad,' Robbie whispered. 'They're on the run.'

The sound of the tanks faded as they slid like rats back to the river. The Moors, with crosses about their necks, and the Italians, with Mussolini's false promises in their hearts, were in total disarray. In a remarkably short time, little more than an hour, the battalion had regained all the ground it had lost. Three hundred men had climbed Suicide Hill and at eight o'clock on the third day, Robbie Gillan could not see a living soul.

The half-moon had risen over the mountains east of the river shedding a ghostly light. He could see the glint on shell cases, the white sergeant stripes on the uniforms of the dead. He shivered. The night was cold and silent. He closed Dai's eyes.

'Bye, then, lad,' he said. 'Time I was going home.'

He grabbed his gun and glanced around like a man setting

out on a journey from a familiar place he knows he will never see again.

*

The turban of white muslin Captain Lewin wore around his head covered the ricochet that had crossed his skull. Hugh Tregarth had removed a bullet from his shoulder. Alice was dressing the wound when a motorcycle slid to a halt on the sunken road. The driver carried a dispatch from Albacete.

'From André Marty,' the messenger said.

Lewin read the message as the motorbike roared back in the direction from which it had come. He spoke without emotion.

'Enrique Líster's brigade has reached the Jarama. General Verela has quit Pingarrón. Forty Russian tanks are defending the road at Morata de Tajuña.'

'So we won,' Tregarth said flatly. The young doctor was pale, drawn, fatigued to the point of collapse.

Alice glanced from Tregarth to the captain. She completed the dressing and fixed the bandage with tape. Her eyes wandered constantly to the steps down to the sunken road where two stretcher-bearers were bringing in another man, his face hidden beneath a field dressing. Bowen Jones stood beside the steps with a saucepan of coffee and his bandolier of enamel mugs. Their eyes met and Bowen shook his head.

*

The mist had lifted. Stars flickered to life and the moon lit the way as Robbie tramped down Suicide Hill. His head was cloudy, as if he had had too much to drink. He caught sight of the olive trees. When he stepped down into the sunken road, someone called his name and in this world of the dead it seemed strange that he had a name and someone should be calling it.

'Robbie.' She ran towards him. Tears washed over her cheeks. 'I knew you'd come back. I always knew.'

Bowen Jones approached, the coffee mugs rattling.

Robbie shook his head. 'He's up there with the dead.'

Captain Lewin stood as Robbie approached. Robbie laid his rifle at his feet.

'Bloody good show,' Lewin said. 'You did a good job.'

Robbie opened his mouth to speak, but nothing came out.

The captain turned to Alice. 'I could do with a cigarette. There's some in my jacket.'

She found the packet.

'Fancy a smoke?' he said to Robbie and Robbie shook his head.

When he spoke, his voice was hollow, distant, like a voice on a telephone. 'I don't think I do.'

Alice put a cigarette in the captain's mouth and lit a match.

A soldier nearby screamed in pain.

'We've just received a communiqué from HQ.' Lewin turned his head to blow out the smoke. 'We held the road. Russian tanks are occupying Morata.'

'I'm glad,' Robbie said.

Alice took his arm. 'Are you going to be all right?' she asked and he looked back at her with incomprehension.

'I'm going home,' he said.

'Home?' Alice repeated.

'Aye. I want to go home now.'

'You can't do that, Gillan,' Lewin said. 'You know that.'

Robbie looked back at Alice. 'I walked all the way to London and I walked across Spain with Simon. I've walked halfway across the world.'

'I know,' she said and held on more tightly. 'I'll look after you.'

'You know, when I saw you that day in the hospital, I thought you was an angel.'

'I thought the same about you.'

He looked puzzled. 'I've got to go now.'

Captain Lewin raised his voice. 'That's desertion. You're not the type.'

'It's just a word, Captain. I signed on to kill a few fascists. I've done that.'

His voice trailed off. He could feel Alice's body close to him, the sudden warmth, the connection, another link in the chain of confusion.

'Listen to me a moment,' Lewin said. 'The brigade needs you. I'd already decided, I'm making you a lieutenant in the field. Right now. I want you to go to the training school. You'll make a fine officer.'

Robbie shook his head. 'I didn't come here for all that. I told Dai Jones I was going home and that's what I'm going to do.'

'He's dead?'

'Aye, Captain Lewin. They're all dead,' Robbie turned away and looked closely at Alice for the first time. 'Simon, he's all right?'

'Yes,' she replied.

Robbie untangled their arms. Tears rolled down her cheeks. As Robbie moved away, Lewin shrugged the blanket from his shoulders and reached for his Webley.

'You are making a mistake Gillan. You think about this till morning.'

Robbie took off his beret and wiped his face. 'There's been too much killing, comrade.'

He put his beret back on, straightened the line, and made his way along the road towards Chinchón.

Alice would have run after Robbie, but Hugh Tregarth held her back. She would never forgive him.

20

A TRUCK LURCHED to a halt outside a house in the main square of Morata de Tajuña. The driver left the engine running while he lowered the tailgate and reached for the two pieces of luggage: a suitcase with leather straps and a portable typewriter in a case. He stood them beside the doorway as Guy Bradwell stepped out of the vehicle into an oozing puddle of yellow mud.

'Captain Lewin's office, comrade. He'll put you right.'

'Thank you so much,' said Guy.

He looked down at his shoes as the truck pulled away and wondered for a moment whether he should have tipped the man. Spain was a strange place. Normal rules didn't apply. Not that the driver was Spanish, he was from Deal, on the Kent coast, but just as strange in that he had behaved on the journey from the railhead a lot like some of the staff at Magdalen, like railway porters and shopgirls, servile with hostile undercurrents.

The truck turned a corner, the engine noise faded and the stillness carried that sense of waiting that warns of a storm. He couldn't for the life of him remember why he had brought the typewriter. He didn't even know how to use the damn thing.

Guy looked up at the house with its panoply of flags. The date '1816' was carved into the lintel above an arched door with iron studs and a bull's head with a ring through its nose. He lifted the ring and landed three firm knocks. There was no response. He tried again before turning the handle. The lock clicked back and he made his way into a hallway in darkness except for the glow coming from an open door at the end of the corridor.

'Hello, is anyone there?' he called. He entered a furnished parlour where he was surprised to see a man wearing a sling on his left arm seated at a desk smoking.

'Captain Lewin, I presume. Guy Bradwell...'

Lewin pushed back his chair, crossed the few feet of space between them and punched him on the nose.

'Look, I say...'

'This way. Come along,' Lewin said, and led him back to the entrance.

'Now listen here, what the hell do you think you're doing?'

Lewin pointed. 'See the cottage across there?' he said. 'Count three down from the church. That's where you'll find Mr Sheridan. Good night.'

He shuffled Guy out and closed the door.

Guy dropped his cases. He reached for his handkerchief as the enormity of what had happened sank in. He was tempted to go back and box the man's ears. Perhaps he should have a drink in the bar, he needed one, but couldn't face the incomprehensible hissing and spitting that comprised the language. Then there was his luggage to contend with. He'd packed an evening suit, for goodness' sake. He turned up the collar on his raincoat, snatched his bags and marched across the square to the third house from the church. The door was opened as soon as he knocked.

'My God. What's happened?'

'Your CO assaulted me.'

'I don't believe it...'

Guy waved his bloody handkerchief.

'Sit, sit. Let me take a look.'

Simon produced a bottle of surgical spirit. Guy winced and pulled away as he ran a dressing around the wound.

'Ouch!' he yelled. 'Let me do it.' He snatched the wad of cotton wool and clenched his teeth as he cleaned the cut. 'The fellow should be locked up.'

'You must have said something.'

'I didn't get the chance. British officer! He's a damn ruffian.'

Simon took Guy's damp coat and hung it on the back of the door. 'He was at Cambridge,' he said darkly.

'He looks like the actor we saw in the *Merchant of Venice*, what's his name?' Guy continued. 'Is he a Jew?'

'An atheist, as far as I know.'

'They absolutely destroyed the German economy, Jews and communists.'

Simon had heard all this before. 'How was the journey?'

'Excruciating.' Guy removed a cigarette from a gold case. 'And another thing. Why is it so bloody cold here?'

He was wearing, Simon noted, a fashionable summer suit with two-tone dark and light brown brogues coated in mud.

'Let me make a fire, Guy. That'll warm you up.'

'That's very considerate of you, Corporal,' he said with a salute. He lit his cigarette. 'Where's Alice? I didn't expect a brass band...'

Simon held Guy by his two forearms and studied him more closely. 'Aside from the red nose, you look absolutely marvellous. You never change.'

'I'll take that as a compliment. What about that fire?'

Simon stacked some kindling in the hearth. He added logs from a basket and touched a match to a balled-up sheet of newspaper. He glanced back.

'How's the rowing coming along?'

'I'm done with all that. I only took it up to keep you company.' He paused. 'We used to be best friends.'

'We still are.'

Guy flicked ash into the fire and gazed around the room as if he had just registered at a foreign hotel where nothing was quite up to standard. There was a table with a jar of yellow flowers on the scrubbed surface, four chairs with cane seats, a cabinet with earthenware dishes, a solitary armchair. The space was lit by a paraffin lamp that cast a cold glow over whitewashed walls.

'Do you live here with Alice?' he asked.

'No, I share with another chap, Graham Webster. He's a doctor. They came out together.'

'It's certainly tidy. I thought you might have a maid.'

Simon laughed.

The door opened as Guy was about to continue. He turned and wasn't immediately sure the girl dressed as a Red Cross nurse was Alice Sheridan. She pointed at her cheek.

'You finally arrived,' she said, her voice unmistakeable.

'Be careful, I'm injured,' he replied, and pecked her cheeks. 'The Grim Reaper punched me on the nose.'

'Who?'

'Your so-called CO.'

'You must have been poking your nose where it doesn't belong.' Alice examined the wound, turning his head from side to side. 'It's nothing.'

'You look positively awful. Are you sick?'

'Yes, she is,' Simon answered.

'No, I am not.'

'You are not a girl who looks well in uniform,' Guy announced, as if he were an arbiter of such things. 'You're as thin as a shadow.'

Alice threw up her hands. 'That's enough,' she said, and drew out a paper package from her apron. 'Would you like some cocoa?'

'Cocoa?'

'Or would you prefer a glass of Chablis?' asked Simon. He cast his eyes about the room. 'There's a case around here somewhere.'

'Thank you, Alice,' Guy said. 'I would adore a cup of cocoa. It will remind me of the nursery.'

Simon set a fresh log on the fire. Alice handed them steaming enamel mugs. She drew the armchair closer to the grate and warmed her feet.

'Captain Lewin hates your father's newspapers,' she said matter-of-factly.

Guy stiffened. 'I can't see why. We gave you a bloody good write up on the Jarama battle. The thin red line of British heroes...'

'...however misled and misguided they may be,' said Simon, continuing the quote. 'You applaud the volunteers and damn the cause we stand for.'

'Don't blame me, it's the editor who writes the leader columns.'

'Employed by your father to express his point of view,' said Alice.

'I do recall a rather presumptuous young lady importuning my father to buy her an ambulance.' He shook his head. 'You ought to see a doctor. You must have lost a stone.'

'Oh, do shut up, Guy.'

His brow fluted. 'That's better,' he said and she laughed, a tiny tinkling bell of a laugh, and they rattled their mugs together in a toast.

Guy was right, Simon thought. You don't notice the changes in people when you see them every day. Alice was working to keep busy, even when there was nothing to do. They had buried the dead. The wounded were in hospital in Albacete or, like Simon, recuperating back with the battalion.

He had taken on the functions of Doug Sanders, the old bus driver from Manchester. He translated dispatches from

HQ, managed the accounts and ran a class for men brave enough to admit they had never learned to read. He had been made a corporal which, he was aware, Guy found demeaning.

A clap of artillery shook the ceiling. Guy flinched.

'Do you get this every night?' he asked.

'Mostly. It's not serious. They're just letting us know they're still there.'

Guy leaned forward to warm his hands over the fire. 'Franco isn't fighting a war,' he said. 'It's a crusade. He believes communism and atheism are the same thing. He's never going to give up.'

'We know that,' Simon said and the cine reel of Suicide Hill span through his mind. 'And we will never give up.'

The Battle of Jarama had ended with 15,000 dead on both sides. It had been the bloodiest confrontation of the war and had obliged the Nationalists to open a new front to attack Madrid. The British Battalion was rebuilding with volunteers who had travelled on no-passport round trips from London on the ferry to Paris and were smuggled across France.

Guy leaned towards Alice. He smiled teasingly and used his thumb and first finger to stroke his moustache, a pale tress of gold barely noticeable on his top lip.

'I did hear it was your mother who acquired the ambulance that brought you here,' he said.

'Did you confirm your sources?'

'My sources, my dear, are impeccable.'

She waved away the subject and Simon noticed that in Guy's presence, Alice was more her old self. They sparked off each other. Guy snapped open his gold case and fired the Dunhill lighter he kept in the ticket pocket of his jacket.

'Have you seen our parents?' Simon asked.

'We collided at Christmas. Lady Southley was having one of her ghastly soirées. She served this absolutely dreadful marmalade she claimed was caviar.' Guy took a sip of cocoa and pulled a face. 'This tastes like vinegar.'

'We're out of sugar,' Alice told him. She placed her empty mug on the mantel. 'I'm happy to see you. I'm sorry if I'm so beastly.'

He stood. 'You are always beastly. That's why I love you.'

She swung her cape about her shoulders and stepped into the cold night.

The door closed and smoke billowed from the fire. 'I have never seen such a change in a person. That girl is not the Alice I know.'

The pulse in Simon's neck had picked up speed. He always told the truth. It was his greatest failing. But he knew if he told Guy the reason for Alice's malaise, he would regret it.

'Look,' he said, and came to his feet.

Simon removed his jacket and shirt. He changed the angle of the lamp and traced the tip of his finger over the marbled wound on his left arm. The Moor's bullet had sliced in a straight line across the top of his bicep, bursting the flesh into a lump that had healed in a rectangular-shaped welt. The scar neatly crossed the crescent-shaped mark carved by the knifeman in Paris.

'My God, that's the hammer and sickle.' Guy looked back up at Simon and shook his head. 'You never do things by halves.'

'I used to do everything by halves,' he replied and buttoned his shirt. 'Guy, would you do something for me?'

'If it is within my power.'

'Take Alice back with you.'

'Of course,' he replied and his expression changed. 'You know, Alice should never have broken off her engagement to Pipper. When his father goes he'll be the richest man in England.' He stroked his moustache. 'Though he is a bit of an ass. Listen, I saw a bar that's open. Let's have a nightcap?'

'That's a super idea, but there's something I still have to do.'

'Tonight?'

'You know how it is, orders and all that.'

Simon had been nursing a plan for some time and this, he decided, was the appropriate moment to put it into action. He was trying to think of a good reason to leave Guy alone, when Graham Webster arrived from the First Aid post and saved the day. Simon made the introductions and left them chatting beside the dying embers of the fire – Webster, the scholarship boy with a chip on one shoulder, and Guy Bradwell with a chip on the other.

*

He crossed the square to the house occupied by Captain Lewin. The door was unlocked and he slammed it hard enough to announce his arrival. Lewin sat back scratching the stubble on his chin.

'If you've come to lodge a complaint, I'm not in.'

Simon dropped into a chair. 'That sounds like a tongue twister, comrade.'

'Comrade?' Lewin repeated. He slid the top back on his fountain pen.

'How's the arm?'

'Can we get on with it, Sheridan, I've got work to do.'

The captain had written letters of condolence to the families of the fallen, but many wrote back asking for more information. In the quiet night hours, his pen was rarely still.

'Alice isn't herself...'

'Good idea. Send her home with your chum. And do make my apologies. I promised myself I was going to punch the next journalist who turned up. You can't imagine how pleased I was when he said his name was Bradwell.' Lewin pointed at the wooden cabinet in the corner. 'In there you'll find two tumblers and some brandy. Pour a wee dram in each will you?'

Simon did so and pushed the cork back in the bottle. He handed a glass to the captain and sat again. He took a sip from his glass and stretched out his long legs.

'Mmm, not bad,' he said, and looked back at Lewin. 'You're becoming very cynical for an old communist architect.'

'Is it architecture or politics that's on your mind?'

'As far as I know, the Jones brothers are still in Albacete?'

'And?'

'Is there any reason why they can't be repatriated? They're never going to be fit to return to regular duties.'

'You know the problem. The anarchists control the border and they've taken it into their heads to give our chaps a hard time.'

'It's hardly surprising, considering how the communists are behaving.'

'Yes, yes, yes.'

'How can we win the war when the Left is fighting itself?'

'The Left has been fighting itself since the slaves building the pyramids went on strike.'

'Is that true?'

'Probably.'

Simon finished the brandy. 'So, Lloyd and Bowen?'

'The cost? Tickets? Papers?'

'I can cover it.'

Lewin stubbed out his cigarette and coughed.

'You should give it up,' Simon said.

'Are you mad? It's the only thing that keeps me on the rails.' Lewin lit up again as if to highlight the point. 'I'm sure they don't have passports. They still might get turned back.'

'The British Consul in Madrid has remained open. From there, I should be able to make a call to the Foreign Office.' Simon ran his hand over his neck. 'My father would like to see Alice return home.'

Lewin nodded. 'She'll be missed.' He coughed again.

'When do you want to leave?'

'I was going to take Bradwell on a tour of the trenches in the morning, then get the night train to Madrid.'

'Organise a ride to Albacete. I'll arrange to get the Jones boys released. And if Mr Bradwell would like a quote for his newspaper, I'll do my best to say something printable.'

*

It could have waited till morning, but Simon felt as if he had made progress and was impatient to complete the task. He made his way down the street beside the bar to the house Alice shared with Ivy Button. Ivy let him in and he found Alice in bed, her thin frame barely causing a rise in the bedclothes. She closed her book.

'I recognised your footsteps,' she said. 'What have you done with Guy?'

He sat on the edge of the bed. 'You should go home. You're not yourself.'

'Don't be silly...'

'He's been gone a long time.'

'He'll be back.'

Her face clouded. She looked so forlorn, it made him feel wretched.

'I am you and you are me. You said that once. Do you remember?'

'Of course I do.'

'I know what you're feeling. You're in love with him.'

'So are you,' she said, and his eyes welled up in tears.

21

GENERAL SHERIDAN NOTICED a water stain on his knife. He huffed on the blade and polished it with his napkin. He was irritated – with events, of course, but equally with himself for the absurd swell of triumph he'd felt from acquiring the corner table. He glanced out at the cherry trees with their lanterns of pink blossom. The earthy smell of spring drifted in through the open windows alongside the sound of klaxons and the tap of dray horses crossing St James's Square.

He didn't agree with reading at the table in the dining room. That's what the reading room was for. But this was a day for exceptions. He unfolded *The Times* and shook his head as he glanced once more at the lead story:

The Tragedy of Guernica: Town Destroyed in Air Attack
Eyewitness account by George Steer. Bilbao, April 27 1937

Guernica, the most ancient town of the Basques and the centre of their cultural tradition, was completely destroyed yesterday afternoon by insurgent air raiders. The bombardment of this open town far behind the lines occupied precisely three hours and a quarter, during which a powerful fleet of aeroplanes consisting of three German types, Junkers and Heinkel bombers and Heinkel fighters, did not cease unloading on the town bombs weighing from 1,000lb and, it is calculated, more than 3,000 two-pounder aluminium incendiary projectiles. The fighters, meanwhile, plunged low from above the centre of the town to machine gun the civilian population…

Sheridan tucked the paper away as Lord Bradwell made his way through the sea of white linen towards him. Bradwell slid his bulk into the chair and reached for the lunch menu.

'Rum business all round.' He withdrew his spectacles and hooked them over his ears. 'Beef Wellington, roast potatoes and butter beans,' he read aloud. 'I rather fancied some lamb.'

'It's Wednesday.'

Bradwell sat back and drummed his fingers. 'Our correspondent tells me the Condor Legion missed the bridge. Is that right?'

'It is,' Sheridan confirmed. 'More than a thousand dead. Civilians.'

'The town wasn't even bloody defended,' Bradwell observed.

'The Germans are testing their technology.'

'The Cabinet was on the point of recognising Franco as Head of State.'

'We can't have it being said that we're following the foreign policy of Hitler and Mussolini,' Sheridan said, lowering his voice.

'I was beginning to grow fond of the little man. Franco speaks a lot of sense.' He paused. 'For a Spaniard.'

'This business is going to set him back.'

'Hang it all, Dicky, he stands for the right things,' Bradwell said. 'If the same riffraff ever got into power here, I'd expect the army to step in and sort it out.'

Sheridan caught the eye of the wine steward and made no comment. The protocol for such an occurrence was not for public debate. Even with Lord Bradwell.

They ordered the club red. It was served by a bent,

silver-haired sergeant major, a veteran of Sheridan's regiment.

'Afternoon, sir,' he said crisply.

'Good afternoon, Billy.'

Lord Bradwell looked back at Sheridan. 'How's Alice getting on? You must be glad to have her home.'

'Needs some rest, that's all. She's a strong girl.'

'She takes after you.'

'I'm not sure about that. I sent a note to Guy to thank him. I read his piece. He did a good job, nicely balanced.'

Lord Bradwell peered over the top of his spectacles. 'Someone did,' he remarked and let the subject drop.

The old sergeant straightened up after filling the glasses and left the table.

'He's younger than me. He looks ten years older,' Sheridan noted.

'They don't take care of themselves,' Bradwell remarked and raised his glass to his lips. 'About the only good thing that ever came out of France.'

Sheridan ran his finger under his eye. For 20 years the scar had given him no pain but, just lately, the nerves had come back to life. He sipped his wine. His instinct was to swallow it down and refill the glass, but he needed a clear head. He was going straight from lunch to report to the Prime Minister on his early morning meeting with the ambassador at the German Embassy.

Joachim von Ribbentrop was eccentric, a tower of self-confidence and an anglophile. Sheridan had once been his guest at Schloss Fuschl, his summer residence in Salzburg where Hitler was a regular visitor. They had built a solid relationship, not that black coffee and *mohnkuchen* pastries had produced any further insights to explain the Luftwaffe's action in the Basque Country.

The bombing of Guernica had shocked the world. An entire town in ruins. A thousand dead. Hundreds more injured. The justification for the action had been to slow the retreat of the Basque militia by destroying the bridge over the River Mundaca. Three hours of *blitzkrieg* had left it standing. There had never been an aerial bombardment of this intensity before and Sheridan had a premonition that modern weaponry would bring far worse in the future.

*

Alice had missed remarkably few things in Spain. Hot baths were one of them. She filled her palm with Wimbledon Lavender salts and swished them around with more hot water. She laid back and pondered the two letters that had come in the first post, one from Bowen Jones, the other from Hugh Tregarth. By the time the water had cooled, she had decided what she was going to say to Hugh. She was going to say yes. Like her, after Jarama, Hugh had returned to England to recuperate.

She wrapped herself in a towel and pushed her feet into Turkish slippers. She gave her hair a few strokes with the brush. It had been cut short, *à la* Jeanne d'Arc, and she resolved never to bother with curling irons again. She slid into her robe, the red one with fire-breathing dragons, and found the new maid in her room making the bed.

'Thank you, Netty, that's awfully kind.'

'How are you today, Milady?'

'Quite well, I think. And you?'

'You know me, strong as an 'orse. That's what my ol' dad always says.'

'Tell him horses are delicate and intelligent, as well as strong.'

'You know somefink, I might just do that.'

Netty grinned and hurried out. Alice was going to tell Netty she didn't need to call her 'Milady.' But it really didn't matter.

She swung back the doors of the closet. All the clothes Mother had once said were too tight now fit as the dressmaker had intended and she had no plans to seek out the new spring fashions. She chose a creamy white dress patterned with bluebells and cinched in with a shiny blue belt. She stepped into blue shoes and sat at her desk gazing out at the elm tree at the end of the garden.

Her letters were on the blotting pad. Hugh had invited her to describe her experiences as a nurse in Spain when he gave a talk to the latest crop of trainee VADs at Tredegar House. She wrote in her reply that she would come to lend 'moral support,' but doubted that her contribution would be 'overly inspiring.' She addressed the envelope and stuck a penny red Edward VIII stamp in the corner.

The second letter contained two sheets of notepaper and a pencil drawing folded in four. Bowen Jones had sketched a row of shop fronts with smart signs, the three figures in the foreground recognisable in that way cartoonists have of picking out certain qualities and emphasising them. Guy was dressed as a Regency man of fashion. Simon had his head in low hanging cloud. She had the appearance of a mathematical abstraction, all angles with oversized eyes like a painting by Picasso.

In his letter, Bowen began by telling her that they were slowly adjusting to life back in the valleys. Lloyd's mental state had improved and, 'like a child learning to speak,' had begun to annunciate his first words. He told her Simon had pushed £100 into his pocket just as the train was leaving from Madrid and that would last them a year. He had sent the drawing showing Madrid's modern shop fronts to illustrate his plan to become a sign-writer and 'bring something new to the dour ironmongers and greengrocers of the Rhondda Fahr.'

He had signed the letter, then added a postscript. 'Please let me know when you hear news from Robbie Gillan.'

Alice ran two fingertips beneath her misty eyes and read the last sentence again. Bowen had used the word 'when'. He was an optimist, creative. He saw the world as he would like it to be.

In Madrid, they had stayed at the Palace Hotel, the watering hole of spies, black marketeers, war voyeurs and foreign correspondents. The glass domed lounge was always busy, noisy, renowned for its vintage wines, fist fights and the occasional pistol shot that sent *habitués* scurrying for shelter beneath the tables.

The task of acquiring papers for the Jones brothers had turned out to be remarkably straightforward. Tommy Courtenay at the embassy had been a year or two ahead of Simon at Eton. He arranged a photographer, delivered the passports to the hotel in person, then took them out to lunch and a tour of the Prado, Madrid's great art museum.

The city was ringed in barricades and machine gun nests, but around the Puerta del Sol, at the heart of the city, the streets were gripped in a constant state of war fever. People cheered the marching bands by day and, at night, girls in short skirts danced in the new jazz clubs with soldiers on leave. She took Bowen and Lloyd shopping for new clothes. Lloyd chose a large hat that hid his face and Bowen selected a Basque beret, his *aide-mémoire* of serving in Spain.

The ormolu clock on the mantel rang out the hour of seven, the chimes multiplying in a tinnitus of ringing bells through every room in the house with the exception of her father's study, the silence a constant reminder that she had forgotten to relieve Simon of the keys to the grandfather clock. During those days in Madrid it was as if her mind was empty, the contents cleaned out, the past washed away, the future obscure and terrifying.

*

Netty fussed around the table at dinner and twice dropped items of silverware. Alice watched her father shift uncomfortably in his chair. After coffee was served, he sprang energetically to his feet.

'I'm going to have a brandy. Would anyone care to join me?'

'No thank you, Richard,' her mother replied.

He poured a drink in a round, short-stemmed glass and mulled the liquid in slow circles.

Alice stood. 'Excuse me,' she said, and her father peered back at her with a look of disappointment.

'My dear, I never see you smiling anymore. Is there anything I can do?'

She looked coldly back at him. 'Yes, there is something. You can urge the Prime Minister to send aid to the Spanish Government.'

'Alice, I am merely a civil servant.'

'People are suffering because men with the power to do the right thing choose to do the wrong thing.'

'I do not disagree...'

'The boys in Spain are the best of our people. They are all that Guy Bradwell and Pipper Stuart are not and never will be.'

'They are indulged young men whose fathers did not serve in the war,' he said. 'As for me, my dear, my hands are tied...'

She didn't let him continue. 'We know who you are and what you do. You have the power to do good, to do something worthy. You choose not to.'

Her cheeks were flushed. She sat again. Lady Sheridan left her chair and came to her side. The general tightened his grip around the brandy glass. There was bewilderment in his green eyes.

'You are speaking out of turn, my dear,' he said, gently, regaining control. 'I know you are upset.'

'When we were children you made us afraid to air our thoughts, to speak freely. You have imagined this lack of communication is a form of respect. It isn't.' She paused. 'I will have that drink, Daddy,' she added, and he was relieved to turn back to the cabinet.

Alice wondered if she had gone too far and realised that she didn't care. She didn't care about anything very much. She was well, physically, but sensed from the moment she woke each morning to the hour when she switched off the reading lamp at night that a part of her was missing.

Father passed her a drink. 'I have always, to the best of my judgment, tried to do the right thing,' he said. 'I have always tried to be fair.'

'That's the way to treat soldiers. We love you because you are our father. We would have loved you more had you opened yourself to us.'

'You have made yourself unapproachable, Richard,' her mother said. 'Had you have acted differently, Simon would have stayed at Oxford.'

'No, Mummy, that's not true. Simon went to Spain because he believes in the Republic.' She glanced back at her father. 'It may come as a surprise to you, but your son is a jolly good soldier.'

'Just misguided,' Sheridan said bitterly.

'That is an opinion I do not share.'

He finished his drink and placed the glass back on the table. He was a man who did not like scenes and this was a scene. 'If I were to forgive him,' he said, 'if I were to give him leave not to apply for a commission, would he return home?'

Alice shook her head. 'You haven't understood. Simon believes in what he is doing, totally, with his heart.'

'The Republic will lose the war.'

'We know that.' She rose from her chair. 'The sort of thing that has happened in Guernica is not the end. It is just the beginning. Your friend Adolf Hitler is going to drop bombs on the whole world.'

'Alice...'

'You know what La Pasionaria said: Bombs on Madrid today means bombs on Paris and London tomorrow. Just see if she's not right.'

'Even if she is right, there is nothing I can do about it.'

'Yes, I know. You are only a civil servant. It is not your fault. It is not the government's fault. It's not Franco's fault. But someone, somewhere, gives the orders for planes to drop bombs on innocent people.'

'Alice...'

Tears streamed down her cheeks and she brushed angrily at her eyes with the napkin.

'If you and the Prime Minister and the Members of Parliament were to spend an hour in one of our dressing-stations, it wouldn't be complex at all.'

'My dear, I was on the Western Front.'

'Then you should be ashamed not to have learned anything from the experience.'

She turned and left the room. She climbed the stairs and paused outside Nanny's room. It was where she had gone as a child when she was feeling sad or bad-tempered. Nanny Fosse was always kind, always there. It was her refuge, her sanctuary. It had gone. Nanny Fosse had died in February while she was in Spain.

22

HE STOOD BEFORE Lewin's desk with his beret gripped behind his back. His uniform was in rags and he had a full beard with seams of gold in the dark bristles. Lewin waved his fingers below his nose.

'You smell like a pigsty.'

Robbie hunched his shoulders. 'That'll be the goats,' he replied.

'Where have you been hiding? Up in the hills?'

'Aye. Not far from here. About 30 miles.' He lifted his head and made eye contact for the first time. 'Is Simon all right? And Alice?'

Lewin nodded patiently. 'Simon's fully recovered. Thanks to you, I have to say. Alice returned to England.'

Robbie's knees felt weak as he let out the breath he'd been holding.

'Sit,' Lewin said and pointed. 'Over there, so I don't have to smell you.'

He sat and gazed about the room as a visitor might in a museum, the oil paintings on the ochre-coloured walls, the ceramic vases shined by the light falling through the open doors. He had kept his memories of those last days on the Jarama walled up in the back of his mind, but being there now, back where they began, the wall crumbled and the past came tumbling through.

'I imagine you've got a story to tell,' Lewin said.

Robbie began ponderously, like a record winding up. 'It's

the quiet that gets at you. You can put up with the explosions, blokes screaming, the rounds coming in. Then it goes quiet and all you've got is that stuff turning round in your head. That night, the last night, even the wind had stopped. I looked down at the river. It didn't seem right that I was alive when everyone else was dead. I told Dai Jones I was going home.'

The light from the open door to the garden had turned his face into a mask.

'I walked all night. I slept somewhere, then walked again as the sun came up over the hills. I didnae drink. I didnae eat. My legs finally buckled. I must have collapsed. When I woke up and there were all these black eyes staring down at me. I thought I was like all the others, like the dead we left behind.'

'No one was left behind. We buried them. Everyone.'

Robbie looked down and his attention was drawn to a movement by the doors. A bird had followed the line of light into the room. It glanced from side to side, released a high-pitched chirp, then turned back the way it had come. It was a *golandrina,* a swallow. He had watched these small birds congregate at sunset every day in immense flocks that took off from the trees to create constantly changing patterns that spiralled across the sky. The displays were so structured and mysterious you had to believe they contained messages if you only knew how to read them.

'Black eyes staring down at you?' Lewin prompted.

'They were goats, bleating and dribbling over me,' he answered. 'Then this bloke came and shooed them away. He held one of those leather wine bags to my lips. I gulped it down. Every drop. Then my head began to spin.' He scratched at his beard. 'Not for the first time. Pedro liked a drink.'

'The goatherd?'

'Aye. He was a tiny bloke, always grinning. He took me to his hut. I ate some bread and sausage. He kept talking. I suppose he wanted the company. All I could do was shrug and shake my hands aboot. Days went by. Weeks. It was like everything inside of me had died.'

'You were suffering from shock,' Lewin said. 'Time's the cure.'

'I learned how to milk the goats. We put the milk in metal urns I carried to the villages. We exchanged milk for food and wine, some baccy.'

'They knew you were from the International Brigade?'

'Aye, in the end.'

'Lucky no one informed on you. There's a price on our heads.'

'Not up in the mountains. They are all poor as dirt. Good people.'

'Now you speak Spanish, I assume?'

'*Sí, camarada. Franco es un maricón.*' Lewin smiled in spite of himself. Robbie's head dropped. 'I expect I'm going to be court-martialled?' he added.

'Do you deserve it?'

Except for traitors and turncoats, Robbie didn't believe there was ever grounds to punish men who joined the International Brigade. It was contrary to the cause they were fighting for.

'That's not my decision,' he said.

Lewin's face twisted in pain as he reached for a cigarette and slid the packet across the desk with a box of matches. They lit up.

'What made you decide to come back?'

'I'd had enough of goats to last a lifetime. I tried to imagine being home with my family. I couldn't. I couldn't keep them in my head. I could only think aboot one thing…'

He stopped and took a long draw on the cigarette. He couldn't find the words to describe his thoughts. He didn't want to. That night when he set off down the sunken road, he bore the guilt that comes to survivors and the fear of what that would mean in the future.

Lewin flicked his ash. 'There's a truck going to Pozorrubio tomorrow,' he said. 'I want you cleaned up and on that truck.'

'I thought the prison was in Albacete...'

'Pozorrubio's where the brigade trains its officers. I told you before you buggered off. I made you a lieutenant in the field.'

'But I deserted.'

'I put you down as wounded. I knew you'd be back.'

'But I'm not cut out for that sort of thing.'

Lewin drilled the end of his cigarette into the ashtray. 'You can consider yourself lucky you're not going to be shot,' he said. 'The army is a pyramid. You, as a lieutenant, will fill the middle layer. You don't question orders, you obey them. When you carry out those orders, you, in turn, expect to be obeyed. Is that understood?'

Robbie sat back. It was hard to take in: from the firing squad to a pip on his shoulder.

'This is your chance to learn strategy, organisation, leadership. You can't teach intuition.'

'I don't know what to say...'

'You stand up, you salute, and you say "yes, comrade."'

Robbie did just that. He stood and straightened his shoulders. 'Yes, comrade.'

'Some chaps you know are here. Wash off the smell of pig shit. Then go out on the line and see them.'

He came to attention, turned to leave, then turned back again. 'Will I get a new uniform?'

'I don't know about a new one.'

'And one of those peaked caps you officers wear?'

'And there's you telling me you're not cut out for that sort of thing.'

Gillan's bearded face creased in a smile. 'I don't know that

I am. But I don't want me mates to know that.'

Lewin gritted his teeth as he tossed him the half packet of cigarettes. He lifted the telephone receiver. 'Bloody miracle, we've got the phones working. I'll tell the quartermaster to fix you up as well as he can. His name's Norman Beanse. One more thing, don't tell anyone where you've been. Just say you were on sick leave.'

*

Lieutenant Robert Ian Gillan. Who would have believed it? *I am here. Alive.* His senses were bristling, sharp again. He looked down at his broken boots, at the grime under his nails, and what came unwillingly to his mind was Alice that night below the olive trees with the moon watching over them.

A scaffold covered the area above the arched entrance to the church. Men mixed cement while their companions hoisted buckets up on ropes for masons to fit stone blocks back into the damaged façade.

'*Buenos días,*' one of the workers called.

'*Buenos días. ¿Cómo estás?*' How are you? Robbie asked.

'*La vida es lo que es,*' the man replied philosophically. Life is what it is.

Sergeant Beanse watched him approach from the quartermaster's stores set up in an abandoned building beside Bar El Casino. He had an old soldier's sceptical look on a long, drawn face lined like a flattened sheet of screwed up paper.

'You must be the new lieutenant?' he said.

'Aye, that's me.'

'Now I know why more men die in hospital than on the battlefield.' He looked Robbie up and down. 'Let's start with your clothes. I don't want to infest my storeroom. I'll have a bath ready for you in about ten minutes.'

Robbie followed him inside where two metal buckets were heating on an iron range. He stripped and threw everything in the fire. He hesitated when it came to his beret, span it around his finger, then shot it into the flames.

Beanse held up the tangled half-length of tartan scarf. 'What about this?'

'Can it be cleaned?'

'We'll give it a go.' Beanse took an enamel mug from a shelf and gave it to him. 'Get some hot water for a shave. There's a mirror out back.'

He took the hot water and a razor down the hall to a room with windows facing a narrow yard. He was back. English voices. The last three months could have been a dream. He shaved, taking off his moustache, and a man older than his years stared back at him from the mirror. Sergeant Beanse cut his hair and rubbed delousing powder into his scalp.

A tin bath part filled with cold water stood against the wall. They added hot water from the buckets and Beanse left him with a clean towel and a bar of carbolic soap. The heat of the water penetrated his skin as he laid back. The windows misted and the steam rose about him like a ring of ghosts. She was safe. She was home. She was a sweet fleeting memory of something that could never be and you can drive yourself crazy dreaming of the impossible.

Robbie dried himself, tied the towel around his waist and followed Beanse upstairs to a room stacked with boxes labelled with their contents and sizes. They unearthed a good-as-new uniform with a bar on the epaulettes and a peaked cap faintly stained around the inner rim. As he laced up a pair of boots, the phrase 'dead men's shoes' entered his mind and he resolved to close the page on the past. The future wasn't unknown. It was unimaginable.

Wilf Tooley came marching in with a leather belt, cross straps and a holster holding a pistol.

'I thought you was dead,' Tooley said.

'Me, too.'

'Now you're an officer, what about the workers?'

'Fuck 'em,' he replied and Wilf showed a mouthful of broken teeth as he laughed.

'Here, best one I've got,' he said, drawing a Mauser from its sheath. 'Self-loading, ten-round clip. Krauts make bloody good guns.'

'And we'll make bloody good use of them.' Robbie took the wooden hilt. He weighed the pistol in his hands and a memory flashed into his mind. He stared back at the armourer. 'Whatever happened to those horses?' he asked him. 'The white ones?'

'Think the cooks must have got hold of 'em.'

Robbie fastened the straps and clipped the Mauser in place. He heard boots on the stone stairwell and Simon Sheridan ducked as he entered the room.

'So the pauper has finally turned into the prince.'

'You're not still believing in fairy tales are you, lad?'

'You should have seen him when he turned up here. Looked like a bloody vagrant,' Beanse said. He looked Robbie up and down with the respect of his rank. 'I'll put a kit bag together for you with a change of clothes.'

'Thanks, Norman. I'll come by and get it later.'

Beanse threw up a salute Robbie returned and it struck him that it was like being an actor. He was costumed as an officer and would learn to play the role. Simon led the way across the square to a French motorcycle.

'Alice went back,' he said.

'I know. I'm glad.'

'She waited for you...'

'She shouldn't have done.' Robbie changed the subject and looked down at the motorcycle. 'Sure this thing will carry the two of us?'

Simon took a grip on the accelerator. The engine fired on the third kick and he swung his leg over the saddle. Robbie climbed on and the machine puttered off on the rising stretch of highway that led to the sunken road. They stopped beneath the olive trees. The branches swayed in the breeze and he was showered with spots of light like shiny buttons that glided over his uniform. He filled his lungs with the olive-scented air and took a cigarette from the packet Lewin had given him.

'Got a light?'

'Sorry, old man, I'm afraid I don't smoke,' Simon replied.

'You're letting the side down. You're a soldier. It's your duty to smoke.'

'Yes, sir.'

'Comrade,' Robbie retorted, and they burst out laughing.

Simon took a grip on Robbie's arms. 'I'm so glad you're here. It's been dreary without you.'

'I'm off again tomorrow, you know that?'

'Captain Lewin filled me in.' Simon paused. 'She waited for you. I made her go back. She was getting so thin. I thought she was going to die of a broken heart.'

Robbie pulled away. 'People don't die from broken hearts. They die from enemy guns. You did the right thing. She's a good nurse. I hope she carries on serving the cause in England.'

'Robbie, you don't understand...'

'*La vida es lo que es,*' he said, repeating the words of the workman, his expression hardening. 'Now, I hear there're some lads from Glasgae up the hill.'

The tic on Simon's neck drummed as he climbed up from the sunken road. Beyond the trees, they entered the defence channel that climbed the incline to three rows of trenches 200 yards apart, the highest along the crest overlooking the River Jarama. The dugouts were deep with walls protected by sandbags and intermittently shaded by canvas sheets. They stepped out into the sun and paused for a moment. Butterflies hovered over the landscape with its patches of wildflowers. Crippled trees were brazenly coming back to life. The rocks gleamed in shades of grey and blue with seams of red from the iron oxide. He was back on Suicide Hill.

Simon led the way into an underground assembly hall with a wireless set, benches and tables where men read newspapers and wrote letters. It was where he held literacy classes. The troops had made it homely with pictures of flamenco dancers and pretty girls on film flyers they peeled from hoardings when they were on leave in Madrid. They continued up the channel to the next band of trenches. As they turned a corner, Robbie heard voices from the streets of Glasgow.

'Jesus Christ. Just look at you,' Jamie Douglas said.

'Just look at you, sir,' Robbie replied.

'Sod all that, Robbie Gillan. If you think I'm going to start saluting you, you've got a screw loose.'

Robbie shook Jamie's hand. 'You made it, lad, and aboot bliddy time.'

He moved in turn to Hamish McDonald and Nat Cohen, men from home who had stood at his side on the long hunger march to London.

'They made you an officer, then?' Nat said.

'He's always been a lucky bastard,' said Jamie.

'Aye, they made me an officer,' he acknowledged, and his tone grew serious. 'We don't go in for too much saluting, but you still have to obey orders. An army relies on men taking orders. Isn't that right, Simon?'

'Absolutely.'

Robbie had been so wrapped up in his own thoughts, he had forgotten about Simon's injury. He studied him more closely: his hair was longer, the colour of corn, blue eyes as old as the sky. He looked back at his friends from Glasgow. Jamie Douglas with his spiky red hair and blasphemous tongue could have been a schoolboy playing at soldiers.

Hamish McDonald was smaller than he remembered, his features knocked shapeless by boxing and police clubs. Nat Cohen had streaks of grey in his beard.

'Where have you been, mon?' Jamie demanded. 'Someone said you was injured. You don't look injured to me?'

Robbie tapped the side of his head. 'I was injured up here.'

Jamie studied the insignia on his shoulder flaps. 'No one told us you was a big shot?'

'He's not a big shot. He's a lieutenant,' Nat Cohen said. He turned to Robbie. 'I'm right proud of you, laddie.'

'You're right, I'm just a lucky bastard,' Robbie told Jamie. 'Look at Simon, speaks 40 languages and they made him a corporal.'

'Yes, and I've got work to do. It's only officers who can hang about doing nothing.'

As Simon turned to leave, a spray of machine gun bullets rattled across the top of the barricades and showered them in dust. Robbie poked his head out for a quick gander and saw flashes from their own artillery, tit for tat. He remembered the mud, the tanks cresting the hill like prehistoric beasts, the logjam of dead and dying men. Captain Lewin had said the lieutenant is the middle strut of the pyramid, the link in the chain of orders. It wasn't going to get easier. It was going to get harder.

23

THE DAY HUGH Tregarth gave his presentation to the VADs at Tredegar House, an idea dropped into Alice's mind. After terrifying the nurses with blood curdling tales of amputations and wriggling innards, she had lightened the mood with humorous anecdotes that had kept them sane. Hugh's descriptions of front-line medicine coupled with her droll attempts at comedy had gone better than she had expected.

Alice had been cross with Hugh since February when Robbie vanished along the sunken road. He had stopped her from following as if she were a child and he a rational grown-up who knew best, as men always imagine they know best and rarely do. Hugh would not have known that his small act had been so distressing to her and now, three months later, she decided the best course was to silently forgive him.

The young nurses gathered around with questions for her, although their smiles were directed towards the handsome Dr Tregarth. Not that he noticed. They were served tea in stout porcelain cups and left like a pair of music hall performers after a successful show. She took his arm as they made their way down the long staircase.

'I didn't know you had such a ribald sense of humour,' Hugh remarked.

'It's all in the timing. That's what Napoleon said.'

'Did he?'

'I have no idea.'

He burst out laughing and Alice felt lighter having laid her grudge to rest.

They stopped in the entrance hall to see the exhibition of photographs by Dr Hugh Welch Diamond showing asylum inmates taken in the last century.

'You're not related, are you?' Alice asked. 'Hugh and Hugh.'

'We are all related if you go back far enough.'

'Don't tell my father that. He still hasn't forgiven Charles Darwin.'

She moved around the hall studying the photographs. The patients looked lost with dead eyes and puzzled expressions uncannily similar to the look on the faces of the wounded who came down from Suicide Hill. Her heart raced. She trembled. Then, like exiting a tunnel, the sun must have come out from behind clouds. The lobby filled with light and Alice had what she thought of as her eureka moment.

'Did you ever see Bowen Jones's drawings?'

'They were excellent.' He shook his head. 'One of God's cruel ironies that he lost his hand.'

One of many, she was about to say, but didn't. 'Those drawings should be on show, here, and other places.'

'That's not a bad idea.'

Alice grabbed his hand and hurried him back upstairs to Sister McKinley's office. The head nurse rose from her desk as they entered.

'That was very illuminating, both of you,' she said. 'Well done.'

'It wasn't too gruesome?' Hugh asked.

'Nothing is too gruesome for a nurse.' She turned with a tight-lipped smile. 'You managed to be exceedingly entertaining, Alice.'

'It was purely by accident.'

Alice now told her about Bowen Jones's book of drawings and asked if she could use them to mount a similar exhibition to the present show displayed in the lobby. Sister McKinley's took a breath that swelled her bust and Alice was unable to judge whether she was picturing the idea in her mind or seeking reasons to reject it.

'Let's sit,' she said and returned to her chair. 'What's happening in the country these days makes me so angry. I abhor the position our government has taken over Spain.'

'Oh, jolly good,' said Hugh. 'I didn't know…'

'Why would you? People these days are afraid to express their opinions.' Her glance fell on Alice. 'I am proud of you, Alice, very proud.'

'That's awfully kind.'

'Truth is not kindness,' Sister McKinley observed. 'Truth is what it is. I will speak to the Board of Governors about your plan and offer my resignation if they do not agree.'

'We wouldn't let that happen,' Hugh objected.

The sister waved her hand dismissively. 'The current exhibition runs for another couple of weeks. After then, if that's convenient?'

Alice felt a warm thrill of excitement pass through her and that's when Hugh had *his* eureka moment.

'If we were to photograph the drawings and make prints, they could be sold to raise money for the Brigade.'

'That's a smart idea, Dr Tregarth.'

It was all happening so fast, Alice's head was in a spin.

'Don't forget, Bowen lost his hand, and looks after his brother. Perhaps half for the Brigade and half for Bowen Jones.'

'That seems satisfactory to me,' said the sister. 'Give me the dates as soon as you can.'

*

Alice recalled seeing a photograph of Cordelia Stuart dressed as Cleopatra in *London Life*. As the daughters one of England's richest men, Cordelia and Portia were the 'it girls' of the age and as to whom they might marry, it was a national obsession.

There was a copy of the magazine in the library. Below the picture was the credit: Pascual Sabater – High Class Photography. She found the address in the telephone directory and caught a taxi to his studio above the Chain Library bookshop in Shepherd's Market. She took with her the sketch Bowen had sent to her showing the shop signs in Madrid. Monsieur Sabater studied the work while she explained that she wanted him to photograph 20 similar drawings and have them backed and framed.

'And by making one negative from the drawings, you could supply more prints?' she added.

'At very little cost,' he replied shrewdly.

Alice offered her hand, which M Sabater lifted and kissed.

She returned home and sat at her desk with her pen poised over a sheet of writing paper. She dipped her pen in the green ink and described without embellishment what had taken place that day. She invited Bowen to visit her in London with his book of drawings. She would pay for the train tickets, arrange accommodation and take him to see Monsieur Sabater. She concluded:

> *My dear friend, I hope you will not see this as an act of charity, but an opportunity to have your poignant drawings seen by more people and also, to help both yourself and the Brigade, two causes dear to my heart.*
>
> *I have enclosed £5 and will meet you at Paddington Station when you arrive in London, preferably within the next two or three days. Write immediately with your schedule and please say hello to Lloyd for me.*
>
> *In haste, Alice*

24

ROBBIE GILLAN DUG deep for a final burst and ran into the shade of the olive trees. He flopped down, panting for breath and watched his companions on the track behind him. After three months in the mountains, he was in good shape. Not so most of the other 15 new officers on the training course at Pozorrubio de Santiago.

It had just gone four. The sun was a furnace, 30 degrees most days, and rarely a cloud in the sky. When it did rain, it gushed down in torrents that carved channels in the red earth and ran over the walls of their quarters in the Ermita de Nuestra Señora de la Soledad, a stone fortress with views from their monk's cells of the distant slopes of the Sierra de Caldereros.

The Poles, Bartek and Aleksy, followed Robbie, running like two parts of the same machine. The others, bunched in a group, were less familiar with the grind and banality of athletics. They were party men in the two different meanings of the word: union organizers and apparatchiks or, by contrast, the bohemian set more accustomed to sipping absinthe in cafés with fast friends and pretty women. It was said that Franchetti was a count with a palazzo on the Grand Canal in Venice. Alphonse Laurencic was a surrealist painter. Anthony Cribb had won the Pulitzer Prize for his novel The Occasional Fall.

Cribb ran in last, shirt black with sweat. He tripped over a tree root and fell in a heap. Before he'd had time to recover,

Urban appeared, tightly buttoned in rimless round glasses. He pointed first at Robbie.

'You,' he said, and Robbie threw up his hands in frustration. 'Bloody hell, Jacek, I was first back.'

'You do not call me Jacek. I am Captain Urban. I tell you this last time.' He turned, raising his hand to point at Cribb. 'And you,' he ordered. 'We commence in 60 minutes.'

Robbie heaved himself up and set off again towards the stone cross planted on the hill behind the village, a geological eccentricity on the flat landscape. It took 30 minutes to reach the shrine, a little less to get back to the olive trees fringing the hermitage. Cribb went first. Always. Every day, two or three officers were disciplined on the hill and every day, without exception, Urban's finger found the American.

Cribb maintained a steady pace, up the slope to the cross and down with the gradient sloping with them. They carried 20 pounds of ammunition, six grenades and Soviet-made Remingtons. The sun baked their skulls inside their helmets and sweat soaked their clothes, the webbing on their bags, the socks chaffing in their boots.

There was no stopping. If you stopped, Urban sent you straight back up again. Cribb collapsed one time after four tours and spent two days in the infirmary. Robbie had been his only visitor. Politics was new to him. He didn't grasp its riddles and intricacies.

They stumbled into the trees as the minute hand reached the hour and followed their comrades back into the hermitage. The chapel was cool inside thick stone walls and had been set up as a lecture hall with maps pinned to the plasterwork and a table with lead soldiers arranged in battle formations.

The new officers studied cartography, geography, Spanish, radio use; how to attack and when to withdraw. They practised shooting skills with a variety of weapons. Weekly classes in psychology were provided by Captain Anatoly

Sokolov, the Russian Robbie had once seen on a motorcycle in Morata with Simon.

He swept in like a film director in plus-fours tucked into knee-boots and a red cravat beneath the collar of a white shirt. The trenches were manned by workers. But, like Lorenzo Franchetti, Sokolov was from some princely family and the General Staff must have believed these confident men made the best officers. Robbie Gillan was the exception, a token. He was aware of that.

One thing he would not have thought about was what Sokolov called the Golden Rule: an officer's first obligation is his own safety. Needless risks while leading men in battle can jeopardise the success of a mission. To protect 'the rank and file' and achieve results, you will be called upon to order others into danger. This, he said, stroking back his shiny dark hair, is neither ruthless nor cold-hearted. It is fundamental.

Robbie could see the logic but knew in the midst of battle it wasn't easy to put rules into practise. Of the 16 new officers, he was one of only a few who had seen action. He was the youngest and felt like the oldest when he listened to the others talk of the battles to come.

*

They returned to their cells. Robbie stripped off his clothes and stretched out on the straw mattress covering a narrow strip of stone bed. Since his arrival in Pozorrubio, he had been thinking about writing a letter, but his hand froze every time he picked up a pen and stared down at the blank sheet of paper.

He dragged himself up and went down to the washroom where a trickle of water ran from the mouths of stone dolphins and the soap had the smell of walnuts. He washed his uniform in a wooden tub and pressed out the creases with the flat of his hand. It would dry overnight. He dressed in fresh clothes and climbed the stairs to a gallery above an inner courtyard.

There was laughter inside Franchetti's cell, where they played cards and drank the Cardenal Mendoza brandy they had found in the cellars.

'*Amigo mio*. Come. I deal you in,' Franchetti called. 'I need your pasta.'

'It's not so easy to part a Scot from his silver. You're too smart for me, Frankie.'

'My friend. I am losing. I lose everything. I am only lucky in love.'

'And he loves himself most of all.'

The others laughed. It was Marzio Sala who had spoken, another Italian. He was either a photographer or a racing car driver. Robbie was never sure which. Wolfgang Webber, the German, appeared to have been drawn to the cause when the Nazis requisitioned his father's house in Berlin. Jacob Maes, a Belgian, reminded him of Simon. Aside from having the same pale hair and blue eyes, he had defied his father and fled bondage to the family printing business in Bruges.

Robbie continued along the corridor with its paintings of biblical scenes and found Cribb lying on the thin mattress with his hands locked behind his head.

'You can fill my glass and help yourself,' he said without opening his eyes.

'How did you know it was me?' said Robbie.

'I can smell the soap.'

'I spent three months in the mountains without washing once.'

'So you told me. Where's that drink?'

On the table at his side stood two bottles, two glasses and a photograph in an oval frame. Robbie added a splash of port to each of the glasses and filled them with *gaseosa*, warm fizzy water.

'Why does Urban punish you on the hill every day?' he asked.
Cribb reached for the drink. 'Ask him.'

'I'm asking you.'

'I'm American.'

'So's Malone.'

'Tread easy, boy. He's Canadian.'

'Same thing.'

'Not to a Canadian it ain't.'

Robbie gazed out through the window bars. The cells were
small, smaller than the police station lock-up in Glasgow
where he had once spent the night. They baked like an oven
all day and only began to lose the heat as the sun turned red
and sank into the horizon.

'Do they still have wagon trains in Canada?' he asked
Cribb.

'Damned if I know.'

'I saw this picture in a magazine. There were these
immigrants setting out on wagons piled up with their furniture
and cooking pots, their kids. I thought I'd go there one day.
Start a new life.'

Cribb lit a cigarette and Robbie caught the packet when
he threw it across the cell.

'Then do it. You only get one life. Dreams are visions of
where you want to go. Who you want to be.' He flicked ash
in a porcelain dish. 'Life isn't what it is. It's what it can be.'

'It's not like that for most people.'

'Are you most people?'

'Robbie lit up. 'There's a girl,' he began and Cribb broke in.

'There always is.'

'I like her. I like her a lot. And she likes me. But we're like
chalk and cheese. She's real high class. Me...'

'Yeah? And?'

'You know. You take the high road, I'll take the low road.'

'Sounds like a whole bunch of British crap.' He swung his

legs from the cot and passed Robbie the oval frame. 'She had dreams. She wanted to go back to the States, forget about the war. And, you know something, she was right. I was wrong.'

Robbie looked up from the picture. 'She's bliddy gorgeous, mon. Why didn't you go?'

'Life has turning points. You have to make sure you take the right road.'

Robbie looked back at the photograph. 'I'm sure I've seen her somewhere before.'

'You're a riot, you know that? Don't you have picture houses in Scotland?'

'That we do. What we don't have is the money to go see the pictures.' Robbie handed the frame back.

'Eva Delaware,' Cribb said. 'Her last film was The Occasional Fall.'

'Now I get it. That's your book. You're famous. That's what Malone said.'

'Yep, famous for being an asshole.'

'Then it makes no sense that you're here.'

'I've always been an observer. That's what writers are. For once in my life, I thought I'd take up arms for the future.' He smiled for the first time. 'I didn't know the future would wear the face of Jacek Urban.'

'If it were me, I would have lost it...'

'Forget Mechanical Man. He's just a cog in the machine. Just don't start thinking for yourself. It's not healthy for a party man.'

Robbie looked up at the window. The sky pastels had turned black. The early stars were coming out. 'It was a nice dream while it lasted,' he said. 'Without something to believe in, nothing makes sense.'

'Nothing does. We live, we die and everything carries on without a ripple. We do what we think is right, then we die just the same. Only when we are dead do we become equal.'

'At least we won't have too long to wait.'

Cribb laughed. He had been hitting the port and gaseosa. He was more relaxed. He glanced again at the photograph of Eva Delaware.

'She's in Madrid, waiting for me. Waiting for me to get done with this bullshit. Waiting for Ernst Lazar to find her. Find me.'

'I don't understand.'

'She starred in the movie. Lazar married her at 18 and made her a star. He bought the rights, made the film. Film producers are like Franco. They never give up.'

'He wants her back?'

'You got it.' Cribb swung his legs from the bed. 'I'm going to wash up and get some shut eye.' Robbie stood. 'One last thing,' Cribb said. 'Forget all that class shit. Go and get your girl.'

*

Terracotta lamps flickered in niches along the corridor. Robbie paused in the doorway to Franchetti's cell; there must have been 500 pesetas in the pot, 50 days wages for a man on the front line. He continued down the steps and entered the warm night. Sheep with eyes lit by the moon grazed behind stone walls that edged the track leading from the hermitage into the village.

The Moors had been driven out of Pozorrubio de Santiago 500 years before, but the Arab influence endured in the architecture, the irrigation systems, the haughty gaze of the women. Spain was a land of extremes, exultant and melancholic, colder than Glasgow, hotter than hell. The great plain of La Mancha on spring days was painted in primary colours, the red earth, fields of yellow crops, the blue sky.

Robbie felt a sense of belonging on those cobbled streets

that ran down to the plaza mayor, an open air theatre where the absurdity of life played out to the music of raised voices and the African wind swishing through the palm trees. People sat at café tables with jugs of wine and when you looked into their hard, earnest faces, you had to believe the Republic would triumph.

He saw Bartek and Aleksy at a table with Urban and Anatoly Sokolov. The Russian raised a clenched fist. Robbie returned the salute without joining them. He sat on a bench and watched a young woman in a red and white dress dance to the music of two guitars. An older woman created the sound of castanets beating the fingers of one hand upon the palm of the other. The music changed, slowed. The girl sat.

A man sang in the deep voice of *cante hondo*, the roots of flamenco, of all those things that made Spain a land of misery and miracles. The older woman danced, her movements shaping a story – the virgins of Pozorrubio who had committed suicide during the reign of the Moors, or the Nationalist generals who had led their troops from their garrisons to attack their own people. She clicked her heels, her gestures a blend of despair, joy, passion and tears ran down Robbie's cheeks.

25

ALICE RIFLED THROUGH the post, bills, a catalogue, invitations addressed to Lady Sheridan and there, finally, was a letter addressed to her. Her pulse raced as she hurried upstairs. She slit open the envelope and the lines slipped from her brow as it became clear that her prayer had been answered. Bowen Jones thanked her for her 'kind offer' and stated that he would be on the express from Newport arriving at Paddington Station at 11:20 that morning.

Hugh Tregarth was still in bed when she called and his tone brightened when she told him that Bowen was on his way to London. They arranged to meet at the station.

After her bath, she went down to breakfast. Mother poured tea while Alice helped herself to an egg, two rashers of bacon and Mrs Broom's mashed potatoes fried with tomatoes. She buttered two triangles of toast and dipped into the jam they had preserved at their summer house in the Lake District.

'Someone's got their appetite back,' said Lady Sheridan.

'I'm going to have to ask the dressmaker to let out all my waistbands.'

'Hardly.'

Alice looked back at her mother. She was slender and rather beautiful with threads of grey in her blonde hair.

'Why are you always worried about my weight?'

'Habit,' her mother replied. 'It's what mothers do.'

Alice smiled and took her hand. 'I really love you, Mummy,' she said and they squeezed fingers.

She now told her mother about Bowen Jones, the loss of his brothers, the loss of his hand and her plan to exhibit his drawings at Tredegar House.

'You are doing a lot for this man. That's jolly kind.'

'I'm doing it as much for me,' Alice replied. She thought for a moment. 'I can't change the world, that's Daddy's job. We can only do what we can do.'

'Girls your age are usually concerned with other things, their dresses, their beaus.' She paused thoughtfully. 'I'm glad you're not like that.'

'The world is changing. Nothing will ever be the same.' Alice lowered her voice. 'I will send you a secret invitation to the exhibition.'

'Secret?'

'We don't want Daddy to know you're a Fifth Columnist.'

Alice hurried upstairs. She dressed in wide trousers, a matching jacket with broad lapels, a blouse buttoned to the throat and flat shoes ideal for moving fast in tight situations. The ensemble was business-like, her short dark hair giving her the look Coco Chanel called la mode garçonne. Before leaving the house, she called Percy Drew at his office and asked him to book a table for four people at the Café Royal for lunch at 1:30.

'There is someone I want you to meet,' she added.

'Not Guy Bradwell?'

She laughed. 'Not today.'

She took the bus to Hyde Park Corner and followed the path through the park to Paddington. She watched a group of young mounted officers from the Household Cavalry cantering around the perimeter and it suddenly struck her that she should organise a day riding with Cordelia and Portia, names to add to her imaginary guest list.

Hugh waved as she crossed the concourse. He pointed up at the station clock as the Great Western Railway locomotive steamed into the station. Alice felt a rush of excitement as the carriages shunted to a halt. The doors swung back. She looked from face to face and finally saw Bowen Jones among the crowd. He was tanned from his long walks in the May sunshine and wore his Madrid beret with a white scarf tossed over his shoulder.

They all smiled and were unsure what to say. They had been together in the hills above the banks of the Jarama and they were together here, beneath the glass roof of Paddington Station. It was strange and miraculous, Alice thought. She placed her arms around the backs of the two men.

'Viva la República,' she whispered.

'Viva la República.'

They stood back and Alice looked up at the big clock. 'Now come along. We have a lot to do today.'

Hugh insisted on carrying Bowen's case. They exited the station into Praed Street and took a cab to Pascual Sabater's studio in Market Mews. Alice was pleased he had asked the frame-maker, Mr Waverley, to join them. He was an older man in brown overalls with a bony face and fingers covered in small scars.

They shook hands and went through Bowen's sketches. He stopped at a drawing in Paris that captured the ghostly likeness of a beautiful girl clinging to the arm of a grinning Lloyd Jones.

'I could tell you the story of that day, but it might not be suitable,' Bowen said, glancing at Alice.

'Wasn't that the day Lloyd became Jones the Lover Boy?'

'It was, thanks to Robbie.'

The sketchpad was a flick book of the volunteers' journey by train across France. Falling snow as they climbed the Pyrenees. From village to village to Barcelona, Madrid, the trenches above the sunken road. They went back and forth. Bowen had captured the majesty of dogfights on cloudy skies, the terrifying vision of tanks advancing in formation, a brigader curling backwards through the air, thrown from his feet by an exploding grenade.

Alice studied the drawing of Robbie with a rare smile as he counted out peseta notes on a café table. Simon and the five Jones brothers looked on.

'That one,' she said. 'Where were you?'

'Albacete,' Bowen replied and his expression changed as he thought back. 'It was the first day. We'd just watched a man being shot up against the wall. We hadn't eaten for days. Robbie and Simon went to the bank and it seemed like magic when they came back with enough Spanish money to treat us all.' He looked back at Alice. 'They took care of us, the two of them. One way or another, they always had our backs.'

Alice felt her eyes prickle.

Sabater admired the way the crosshatching created pools of light, how in a few strokes each drawing had a vitality, a life. 'Superb. I like.' He glanced at Bowen. 'It is a travelogue, a story without words.'

Mr Waverley spoke for the first time. 'They tell us more about what's going on over there than we read in the papers,' he said. 'I've never seen pictures like these before.'

They continued until 20 drawings were assembled. They had to be cut from the pad in order to be photographed, something Hugh did with a scalpel. Alice paid half the fee. Bowen put the sketchpad back in the case and they left Sabater and Mr Waverley to begin their work.

*

Alice had found a guesthouse in The Strand ten minutes from the National Gallery in Trafalgar Square. Having witnessed Bowen's excitement visiting the Prado in Madrid, she knew that the National would be the first place he went when he had the time. They took a cab to register. Bowen left his case and tucked the sketchpad under his arm. The cab had waited and drove on to the Café Royal.

Percy Drew rose from the table to greet them. They sat and he asked Bowen questions in that naïve way of clever journalists. Bowen opened the sketchpad and went slowly through the drawings until a waiter came to take their order.

'Do you have a Spanish wine?' Hugh asked, and the waiter took in the mismatched group as he glanced around the table.

'I have an excellent Peralada Crianza, sir. From the Republican side.'

'That would be the ideal choice. Thank you.'

The waiter returned in a few moments and poured the wine after Hugh had tasted a sample. They clinked glasses.

'Spain.'

'The Republic.'

'Missing friends.'

A pretty waitress with flushed cheeks and blonde pigtails took their order. When she left the table, Alice outlined their plans for the exhibition to Percy. He was immediately enthusiastic and she put on a show of surprise when he offered to cover the event for the News Chronicle.

Alice had eaten so much at breakfast, she barely touched her sea bass but was pleased to see the men tucking into their lunches. Bowen had judiciously ordered hotpot and tackled it stylishly, changing between a spoon and a fork. He had grown in confidence since he lost his hand, perhaps because of it. He looked up at the ornate green and gold ceiling, the sweeping staircase, the wall of mirrors.

'It is beautiful here,' he said. 'Would it be ill-mannered to make a sketch?'

'Not at all,' answered Alice. 'Artists can do whatever they please.'

'I've never thought of myself as such,' he said. 'When we

grew up, such thoughts never came into your mind. You taste the coal dust in your mouth the day you are born. At 14 you go down the pit. You can't imagine an alternative.'

Bowen used his stump to hold down his drawing pad. As the pencil in his left hand flicked over the white page, Alice remembered seeing prosthetic hands and arms provided to Great War soldiers on the wards during her nursing course. She filed the thought away in the back of her mind. Then another thought came to her, something Pascual Sabater had said.

It is a travelogue, a story without words.

26

June 30th 1937

Dear Alice,
I hope it is not disrespectful of me to be writing a personal
letter to you. I have had little practise in such things.
It remains unclear why, but after being absent for three
months, when I returned to Morata, I wasn't punished,
unless being sent for officer training was a form of punish-
ment. I rejoin the Battalion as a lieutenant tomorrow. When
I saw Simon, I was relieved that he was well and healthy
again. It was a short but happy reunion.
Simon told me that before leaving for London you stayed
at the Palace Hotel. As you will see from the writing paper,
I am staying there now and it seems as I walk through the
long halls that your reflection remains in the many mirrors.
I keep turning, thinking you are there, and feel disappoint-
ed that you are not.

He paused. He had been thinking about this letter for
weeks, but it was still difficult to find the right words. He
dipped his pen back in the ink pot.

I do apologise for any unkindness I may have shown in the
past. I was always afraid to show my feelings. I am unwor-
thy to be writing to you and cannot describe...

Again he paused.

...the fire that burns in my heart. Please forgive me.
I have enclosed a photograph taken in the hotel lounge with
Anthony Cribb, an American author I trained with, and Eva
Delaware, whom you may recognise. There is more that I
would like to say, but the words remain out of reach.
  Your very good friend,
  Robert Gillan

He read through the letter and took an envelope from the
rack of stationery. The hotel was how he thought heaven
might be. It had everything. Even little pots of paste. Captain
Lewin had called Simon for the address. He copied it out on
the envelope and stuck down the flap. He was exhausted. It
was easier fighting Moors than writing letters.

On the desk was a copy of *The Occasional Fall*. The
dedication read: 'For Lt. R. I. Gillan. International Brigade.
Madrid 1937. Anthony Cribb.'

Robbie turned the pages and glanced again at the opening
sentence.

'My father was a lonely man.'

It could have applied to Cribb. To himself. To us all. He
switched off the lamp and opened the blackout curtains. A
tram shot down Plaza de las Cortes spitting out blue sparks.
Searchlights crossed the sky. The Luftwaffe dropped bombs
around the clock. Before the dust settled, the union men
running the tramway cleared the debris from the tracks.
When the banners went up in smoke, they painted new ones.

No Pasarán.

You had to believe it.

The lift took him down from the room he shared with
Malone on the sixth floor to the lobby. It was crowded and

noisy with men in medal ribbons and women in long dresses. Cigarette smoke swirled below the painted ceiling. Everyone talked. No one listened. He waited his turn at the concierge's desk, bought an airmail stamp and dropped the letter in the mailbox. It was done.

He turned away and it wasn't Alice's reflection in the gilt mirrors but some variation of himself in uniform, freshly shaved, the scar on his cheekbone adding a trace of menace to his lean features. He brushed back his dark hair, washed and trimmed by the hotel barber.

The music grew louder as he made his way along the corridor to the bar. As the name promised, the hotel was a palace with huge chandeliers, murals glossed by the patina of time, girls clinging to soldiers savouring the last glimmering days before battle. He was rich. Captain Lewin had approved his pay during his absence, 90 days equalled 900 pesetas, nearly £30.

Malone, Cribb and Eva Delaware were at a corner table. She stood, a finger of flame in a red dress, hair the soft gold of a pocket watch, lips drawn back in a smile. Eva knew without vanity she was a beautiful woman and played her life as if she were being filmed.

'Now, *lootenant*, are you gonna dance with me?' She pointed first at Cribb. 'He's got no sense of rhythm.' Then Malone. 'And he's Canadian.'

'Priest in my town said dancing's for the devil.'

'What town's that, Jack?'

'Calgary, Alberta. Cow Town.'

'So, you're a cowboy and the priest's a celibate. What does he know?' She had taken a grip on her hips. 'I'll tell you something, God respects me when I pray and he watches when I dance.'

Cribb put a match to a Lucky Strike. 'They're all going to be watching you, Gillan,' he said. 'And they're all going to hate your guts.'

Eva shook her head. 'It won't be hate, darling. It'll be jealousy.'

'Same thing, if you think about it.'

She tapped a finger against her cheek. 'You know something, you're right. You're always right. That's why I hate you.'

They exchanged faint smiles, a look that defies description. Eva had run away from the film producer. What was his name? Lazar? That was it. Ernst Lazar. Of course she had. Isn't that what you do when you're in love?

The band had started into 'The Music Goes Round and Round', the Tommy Dorsey song. Robbie slid his arm around Eva's waist and every eye followed as they glided beneath the glitter ball. His feet moved like skates on ice and his feelings were a swirling contradiction of joy and sadness.

'Did you write your letter?' Eva asked.

'Aye, I did.'

'You put the photo in it?'

'Just as you told me.'

'Now, be honest. Did you tell her you love her?'

'Not in so many words.'

'She'll get it. Women read between the lines.' She paused. 'You know, for a Scotsman, you're not such a bad dancer.'

'You're not so bad yourself.'

Eva laughed. The song ended. They sat, hot, content. Cribb filled glasses with sparkling cava.

The band leader clicked his fingers and the musicians ripped into 'It Don't Mean a Thing If It Ain't Got That Swing'. The floor filled with couples who knew how to jive, meeting and parting in crashing waves, the girls ducking beneath the arms of the men, twirling in giddying circles.

Robbie glanced about the bar. Most of the officers he'd trained with were there. Franchetti, Sala, Laurencic, Webber, Jacob Maes. They had pushed two tables together to accommodate the various girls they'd charmed into joining them. Robbie saluted and they raised fists and glasses.

'*Viva la República*,' Laurencic bellowed in his big voice and the singer on stage modified the words to the song:

'It don't mean a thing if you don't *Viva la República*.'

He leaned into the microphone and sang the words a second time. The crowd joined in, chanting the battle cry. The musicians played louder. The dancers danced like whirling *golondrinas*. Franchetti and the card players crossed the floor.

'We run together. Now we dance together,' Franchetti said.

He grabbed Cribb's arm and pulled him into an embrace. They strode to the centre of the floor and stamped their feet in the way of primitive warriors before battle. André Marty had arrived on their last day at Pozorrubio. He had shaken the hands of every officer except Anthony Cribb. Marty had tried to break him and Cribb just stood there, unbroken, steady as an iron statue.

When the sun rose, the new officers would pack their kitbags and join their battalions. They were ready. The days of our lives are quickly forgotten. War days are vivid, protracted, indelible. We are as moths who singe our wings and still fly back into the flame.

27

WHEN BOWEN JONES arrived back in London, he was whisked straight from the station to a surgery in Devonshire Street. Alice had set Hugh on the task of finding a prosthetics expert and his research had led to an appointment with Dr Aslan Aksoy, a Turk fond of tweed suits and wingtip brogues.

While Dr Aksoy studied Bowen's stump, Alice was surprised to be served coffee in a glass with a plate of baclava by a woman in a black headscarf. The doctor then produced a wooden box. From it, he removed a split-hook artificial hand and a harness.

Bowen glanced at Alice.

'For you,' she said, and all his newfound self-confidence evaporated.

'You can't be serious?'

'I most certainly am.'

Bowen shrugged his jacket from his shoulders and Dr Aksoy dressed him in the harness. He explained as he did so how to connect the cables with his left hand. Alice moved closer to watch and it was like a magic feat as Bowen fractionally, almost imperceptibly, moved his right arm to open and close the split-hook.

'It's like being reborn,' he said.

Alice stood and took a pen from her bag.

'That might be a bit awkward to begin with,' Dr Aksoy said.

'But crucial,' Alice replied. She glanced back at Bowen.

'When we leave here, you have to sign a contract.'

'I do?'

'For a book.'

Bowen flexed his shoulders. The hook opened and closed. He took the pen, tightened his grip and made a scribbling motion in the air.

'You have made me complete,' he said.

'Now we must hurry. I have a feeling Mr Gollancz is not a patient man.'

*

The show opened two days later with almost 100 people assembled at Tredegar House. They said there had never been a night like it in London. The daughters of an earl rubbed shoulders with an ex-miner from Wales and, before the lights were dimmed at the end of the evening, the entire collection of framed drawings had been sold.

Alice dressed for the occasion in a pink chiffon dress with red arabesques, red shoes and a red feather fascinator held in place by clips. Her eyes were shiny staring back at her from the mirror and she had an odd sense that she was dressing for someone else.

Mother wore a tailored suit and matching cloche with a rolled brim. The outfit was red, a colour she rarely chose, the same shade as Sister McKinley's evening frock. A year ago, six months ago, these two women of a similar age would have had nothing in common. That night when they met they chatted like old friends.

Hugh Tregarth gave a short speech praising the work of the Red Cross and introduced Bowen Jones, more than ever the artist in his Basque beret and work boots. When the whispers fell silent, he spoke about the ideals of the men who had gone to Spain and reminded those present that part of the proceeds from the sale would go to help the International Brigade. He raised his split-hook hand.

'Long Live the Republic,' he said and, not all, but most of those present returned the salute.

Cordilia and Portia Stuart found it all 'charming.' Each bought two pictures. They posed for the cameras and the articles that appeared in the morning papers encouraged a stream of visitors to Tredegar House and, in turn, a constant supply of work for Pascual Sabater and Mr Waverley.

Alice glanced around the large hall. People stood in front of each image examining the drawings with that expression one has studying a map before starting a journey. The prints in thin black frames were compelling, at times grotesque, the drawn faces of soldiers, the glint of bayonets, the shadows of warplanes at once a reflection and a warning.

Clenching a pen in his split-hook, Bowen had signed a contract with Victor Gollancz's Left Book Club for an edition of lithographs to be published in time for Christmas. Percy Drew had agreed to write an introduction. Sales would benefit Bowen and the Brigade. But Alice's chief objective, however hopeless, however desperate, was that her father and the world were made aware of what was really happening in Spain.

*

Alice went down to the morning room where Mother was attacking the mail with her ivory letter opener. 'I have more bills than invitations, what does that say?' she remarked.

'That you are less popular now you have become a communist.'

Lady Sheridan laughed. She was happy. She was seldom happy, Alice realised. She rarely did what she wanted to do and, worse, Alice suspected she wasn't exactly sure what she wanted to do. Alice helped herself to an egg and a slice of toast.

'Oh, dear, I do apologise. These appear to be for you.'

Alice put the silverware down and took two letters from her mother. They had Spanish stamps. She could smell the sunken road in the mud smears when she lifted one of the envelopes to her nose. Most of the ink had washed off. What remained was 'dan' from Sheridan, 'square' from Carlyle Square and the word 'London.'

'I must say the Post Office does a jolly good job finding us,' Mother said and poured two cups of tea.

Alice slid the note from the envelope. All it said was 'Robbie's back. Love Simon.'

It had taken three months to reach her.

The second envelope was written in a handwriting she did not recognise. She removed the folded sheet of paper and a snapshot fell out on the table. She looked at the photograph and immediately began to tremble. Her heart pounded. She gasped for breath.

'Alice, my God. What's happened?'

'Wait, Mummy, wait.'

She read the letter. She read it again. Tears ran down her cheeks. She looked back at the photograph.

'Mummy, I've been such a fool,' she said.

Her mother stood. They both stood. The sun lit the room like a fire. Lady Sheridan reached for the photograph.

'Who are they?'

Alice pointed at Robbie. 'That's someone I'm rather fond of...'

'I am fond of Mrs Broom, but she doesn't make me burst into tears.'

'You will love him, Mummy. Not at first. At first you'll hate him.' Alice laughed. She felt as if she had drunk half a bottle of gin. 'His name is Robbie. Robert Gillan. He saved Simon's life.'

She gave her the letter to read.

'I am happy if there is someone who makes you happy.' She looked back at Alice. 'You are a strange girl. You never said anything. I knew there was someone...'

'I didn't say anything because... because I didn't know what to say.'

'You'll be leaving again?'

'I have to.'

Lady Sheridan looked again at the photograph. 'He's handsome,' she said, and looked back at Alice. 'Who is he with?'

Alice pointed. 'That's Anthony Cribb. He's an American, a writer, quite famous. The woman is Eva Delaware. I've seen her in the movies.'

'And they're in Spain?'

Alice nodded. 'All the best people are in Spain.' She glanced out at the garden as if to imprint it on her memory, then turned back smiling. 'Thank you, Mummy.'

She crossed the hall, ran up the stairs and stopped at Nanny Fosse's room. She pressed her lips to the door. 'He's safe,' she whispered, and continued along the passage to her room.

28

AFTER 12 MONTHS of withdrawal and retreat, the Republic was going on the offensive for the first time.

The bombing of Guernica had given the Nationalists the impetus to press on and seize the main port of Bilbao on 19 June. The counterattack had two objectives: to delay reinforcements moving north to the Basque Country and to make it harder for Franco to resupply troops dug in around Madrid.

The target was Brunete, a town of 10,000 people ringed by a cluster of fortified villages 20 miles from the capital. The Nationalist position was surrounded on three sides. With a swift pincer movement, the offensive would bring the town back into the arms of the Republic.

The International Brigade was joining a militia force driving south from the slopes of the Guadarramas. They would meet the seasoned regulars led by loyalist General José Miaja as they advanced north from Villaverde. New tanks and armaments had arrived from Russia, defying the Italian blockade, to supply the 20,000 troops deployed in a campaign designed to reverse the tide of the civil war and change the face, even the future, of Europe.

The assault would begin on 6 July.

*

Robbie Gillan nipped out his cigarette and watched Captain Sugden drift back and forth behind a table strewn with maps.

A former railway engineer from Birmingham, Lewis Sugden was a collar-and-tie union official with cropped hair, grey eyes and a passion for the rambling repetition of party slogans. He paused in his marathon behind the map table.

'There were mistakes at Jarama that cost the lives of comrade volunteers,' he said. 'In Brunete, we will stick to the letter of the battle plan.'

Robbie's neck stiffened. He stood.

'When your eyes are blinded by sulphur fumes and there's men screaming, you cannae follow a plan to the letter,' he said. 'Sometimes you have to take the initiative. When the shells come down on you like the rain in Glasgae, you do what feels right.'

Sugden leaned forward. 'Comrade, I am grateful to you,' he said. 'I think I can speak for every man here: we are fortunate to have your knowledge and experience. But let me remind you: we are not a rabble army. We will not be in a defensive position. We are going on the attack.'

Robbie remained on his feet. 'Major Lewin said you need imagination to be a good officer. Imagination means keeping your mind open, being ready for the unexpected…'

'Thank you for sharing that with us, comrade. But we do not need lessons from Major Lewin. He was not considered up to the task set him in Pozorrubio and has been relieved of his commission. As I speak, he is on his way back to England.'

This was news to Robbie. Devastating news. In Albacete they seemed to be weeding out the talent, the freethinkers. What chance was there for Cribb? Or Franchetti? He understood why the men in the ranks had dubbed their CO Father Sugden and his adjutant, Taffy Norris, the Curate. He was another officer who, having seen no action, had no idea that when the first bullets fly, all military plans crumble into chaos.

He lit the saved half of his cigarette, tuned out of the

monologue and put the last pieces of the puzzle together in his mind. He had read, during leave in Madrid, Anthony Cribb's savage analysis of André Marty in *News-Week*. That was the reason for the punishments on the hill. Marty wanted to take revenge. Jacek Urban had failed to break Cribb. Marty had promoted Lewin to major and sent him to finish the job without being aware that the English officer considered physical abuse unproductive. He had been cashiered and Captain Sugden, the inexperienced new CO, would be following Marty's battle strategy 'to the letter' when the British Battalion marched on Brunete.

When the pep talk broke up, Robbie wandered back along the ridge that edged the forest of plane trees that extended for miles along the foothills of the Sierra de Guadarrama. Beneath the tree canopy, 600 men were stretched out on beds of dry leaves, rifles at their sides, their thoughts turned to families at home, to the girls they had left behind.

He lit another cigarette and looked at the time in the match flare. When Reg Foster had fallen on Suicide Hill, his watch had survived and served the cause on Robbie's wrist. The binoculars attached to a pouch on his belt came from Walt Lewin, sent down the hill at Jarama by Dai Jones. In 30 minutes it would be midnight. In six hours the sun would rise and the killing would begin.

He had intended to spend the evening with his friends from Glasgow, but the meeting had gone on an hour longer than was necessary. When he found them, Hamish McDonald and Jamie Douglas were sleeping, side by side, as they would be when they marched into battle. Nat Cohen was still awake.

'It's bad luck to say good luck,' Robbie said. He glanced at Hamish and Jamie. 'Look after these two loafers for me.'

'I'll do my best. You take care, you'll have a lot on your plate tomorrow.'

'Beef and tatties, if we're lucky.'

'We're eating better here than we were at home.'

Robbie continued towards the edge of the camp where Simon was taking care of his kit. As he did so, he became aware of two points of light moving through the trees. He unsnapped the clasp on his holster.

*

The journey from Madrid had taken almost an hour. They were stopped twice at roadblocks by Spanish militia where a folded peseta note passed from hand to hand and they continued on their way. They entered a tunnel of trees and halted again where a military vehicle blocked the road.

A burly soldier poked his rifle through the driver's window. Another soldier with corporal stripes opened the passenger door and Alice threw up her hands as he pointed his weapon at her. The first soldier spoke to the driver.

'Hello, sunshine, and where do you think you're off to?' he said in an accent she was unable to place.

'I'm trying to locate the British Battalion. I assume I have,' Alice answered.

'And who might you be?' the corporal asked.

'My name is Alice Sheridan. I am a nurse. I was at Jarama. Captain Lewin was our senior officer.' She paused. 'I found the driver in Madrid and paid him to bring me here.'

The corporal withdrew his rifle and spoke to his companion. 'Wait here, Phil. I'll take the lady into camp.'

He climbed into the back of the vehicle beside her and gave the driver a tap on the shoulder.

'Off you go then, mate. Easy on the pedal.'

The driver pulled away. He drove another mile along the road to El Escorial before being directed on to a track through the woods.

*

Robbie remembered an afternoon lecture by Anatoly Sokolov and took cover: the first duty of an officer is his own safety. He watched the lights jumping as a vehicle bounced over the track. It came to a halt at the edge of a gulley. A soldier, rifle in hand, climbed out and examined the way ahead.

'What's going on, comrade?' Robbie shouted.

The soldier raised his weapon.

'Who goes there?' he shouted back.

Robbie recognised the voice of Mike Pope, a corporal from New Zealand.

'It's Lieutenant Gillan.'

*

She heard him. She heard him and she couldn't believe it was him. It had been a long journey from London. Not that she was tired. All the tension had lifted from her body. She felt a lightness of being as she stepped from the vehicle.

'Robbie,' she called. 'Robbie. Is that you?'

He heard her voice, it was unmistakeable, then he heard the corporal.

'I've got a girl here, says she's a nurse.'

She was approaching, a slender shadow silhouetted by the car lights. He stepped out from his hiding place and, that moment, the corporal caught up.

'Sorry, sir, I...'

'That's all right, Mike. She's one of us.' He looked at Alice, immobile for a moment, then back at the soldier. 'Who's driving the car?'

'Some Spaniard.'

'I found him in Madrid,' Alice explained. 'He's just a taxi driver.'

Robbie looked back at Pope. 'Give him some grub, Mike. Hold him till morning. I'll take care of the lady.'

'Right you are, sir.'

He fetched Alice's dressing case, then returned to the vehicle. The lights were switched off and they watched in the moonlight as Pope led the driver through the undergrowth into camp. Alice took his hands. They were alone, their faces in shadow. She cupped his cheeks.

'You came,' he said.

'I should have come sooner.'

He took her in his arms and her thin body moulded itself to his as if some part had been torn away and belonged exactly where it was. Their lips met and the kiss took them back through time to Jarama.

'I should never have left,' he said.

'Neither should I.'

'I wrote you a letter.'

'It's in my bag. With the photograph. They are the most precious things I have.'

Her eyes were shiny with tears.

'The battalion's going into action tomorrow,' he said.

'Then we haven't much time.'

They pressed through the woods and found an ancient tree that had fallen and formed a shelter beneath the overhanging branches. They kissed. More tears flowed over Alice's cheeks.

'You're crying.'

'I cry when I'm happy and hide it when I'm sad.'

They knew nothing about each other and everything about each other. Their lips met again. Their fingers moved inexpertly through the buttons and clasps keeping their bodies apart. Alice laid back on the Spanish earth and a flood of tingling sensations ran up her spine and over her skin. He entered her and her whole body burst into life.

When they eased apart, breathless, she leaned up on one elbow and stared down into his eyes.

'We always make love beneath the trees.'

'Then we always will.'

'Even when we're old with arthritis?'

'Even when we're as ancient as the trees.' He shook his head. 'You came back.'

'You must have known I would.'

'I doubted myself. I never doubted you.'

'All the time I was in London I made myself busy, but I wasn't living, I was waiting.'

They talked, hurriedly, words overlapping. Simon. Robbie's training. The Palace Hotel. Anthony Cribb and Eva Delaware. Bowen Jones's exhibition, his new hand, his optimism. As they talked, they touched each other, cheeks and lips, shoulders and hair. The milky glow of the moon shed light over the trees. They made love again, without haste, and she slept in his arms.

He held her tightly, wrapped in his jacket, and listened to the slow beat of her breath.

She had said 'I wasn't living, I was waiting.' He had felt the same without being able to put words to the feeling. The waiting was over and it went through Robbie's mind that they could leave now, run away, make their way to the border. Portugal wasn't far.

29

ALICE HEARD THE dull click of the cicadas in the tree branches and awoke to Robbie's brown eyes looking down at her.

'I will come back for you,' he said. 'No matter what happens, I will come back.'

He heard the rattle of a spoon on a billycan. They dressed. They held each other. They stared into each other's eyes and all that they felt was clear in all that was left unsaid. Robbie carried Alice's case as they made their way into camp. The volunteers were rising like spirits in the dawn light. She saw the fiery tips of countless cigarettes. Men clenched their fists as they passed.

Alice was happy in that way children are happy when they are living in the moment. Her fingertips tingled. She wanted to kiss him, touch him, hold him in her arms. 'One of us,' he had said.

'Did you sleep?' she asked.

'Aye. Like a log.'

'Hardly surprising, seeing as we're in a forest.'

Dave Cooper, the tin miner from Cornwall, one of the old hands from Suicide Hill, raised his rifle in salute.

'*No Pasarán*,' he said.

'*Pasaremos*,' they replied in unison.

Robbie stopped before a short chap with red hair who stared back, first at Robbie, then at her, then at their entwined fingers.

'Fock me...'

'Happy birthday, mon.'

'Mother o' God! How do you do it?'

'It's one of my many talents,' Robbie answered. 'Jamie, this is Alice. Simon's sister. Alice, today's my old mate's birthday.'

'Many happy returns,' she said in her tinkling voice.

Robbie produced a packet of Lucky Strikes he'd been saving. 'Here, lad, don't say I never give you nuthin'. And you'd better give me a couple back, 'cos I'm clean oot.'

Jamie looked again at Alice. Her eyes sparkled and her skin glowed in the morning light.

The men of the catering corps clattered their way through the confusion with coffee and the day's rations: ham and cheese wrapped in greaseproof paper with hardtack and a canteen of water.

Hamish McDonald and Nat Cohen pitched up and they all shook hands again. Jamie opened the packet of Lucky Strikes and gave half of them back to Robbie.

'You look after each other, now. Keep your heads doon. Don't do anything stupid.'

Jamie lit a cigarette and turned to Alice. 'Watch this one, he's a right wee bastard.'

'I intend to,' she said.

They continued, sidestepping men as they drank their coffee and laced their boots. She saw Simon in the distance, a lone figure seated on a kitbag squinting over the pages of a book. The sun had begun to rise. He stood and the light gave him a glow like a saint in a painting.

'I dreamed about you last night,' he said. They hugged. He stood back. He stared into her eyes, at her mussed hair. 'You look marvellous.'

'I know I do,' she replied, and they all burst out laughing.

Robbie turned to Alice. 'I'd best deliver you to the medics.' Then he spoke to Simon. 'I've got to get a blessing from Father Sugden.'

'Father Sugden?' she asked.

'The new co. A communist,' Simon answered.

'Goodness,' she said. 'Sounds like my cup of tea.'

They hurried through the trees and stopped when the ambulances came into view.

'Will you be driving?' he asked her.

'We usually take turns.'

'Pull off the road if you see enemy planes. Find cover. They'll take out the ambulances if they get half the chance.'

She looked up at him. 'I want to kiss you,' she whispered.

'Kisses are rationed. Orders from Stalin.'

They were alone for a moment. They could have been on a walking holiday.

'We could run away,' she said.

'The same thought went through my mind last night.'

'We'd never forgive ourselves.' There was a glistening of tears in her eyes. 'Don't do anything rash, Robbie. It's positively awful when you find something then lose it again.'

Alice turned without another word and he watched as she approached the ambulance crews waiting beside their vehicles. Robbie made his to the front of the convoy where Captain Sugden was surrounded by his officers.

'Comrade Gillan, good of you to join us,' he said. Robbie nodded and Sugden's eyes swept around the group. 'May I remind you that today we take a step along the road to the freedom of Spain and the Spanish people.' He paused to take a breath. 'We shall achieve that by courage, by devotion to duty and by discipline.'

The officers saluted, shook hands, punched the air. They were clean shaven and eager with bright eyes and Robbie knew they had no idea what was coming.

He found Simon and climbed up into the passenger seat of an old Renault. Taffy Norris had a whistle between his lips. He gave it a good hard blow and the line of trucks carrying

600 volunteers in four companies roared to life. They wound their way out of the clearing where they had set up camp and followed the foothills of the Sierra de Guadarrama.

The mist had burned off. The battalion's red and gold flag flapped in the breeze beside the Republican tricolour. Robbie could make out the far-off sound of machine guns. Across the valley, he could see the watchtower in Torrelodones, a pillar of stone pointing at a clear sky that would scorch like fire in the coming hours. It was the last village behind Republican lines. As they rounded the hill, they would enter enemy territory.

The four companies separated on to different routes. Robbie's riflemen scaled a ragged peak, then descended through barren sweeps of rock. The going was tough but the men in the ranks were accustomed to tough times, the grind of hard labour, hunger marches, police batons. Robbie was learning a roster of new names and noble intentions. Bill, Sid, Charlie, Chalky, Smudge, Mike Pope and Ronnie Hollander. They trudged down into the valley shedding their blankets, capes, jackets, gas masks, metal helmets.

'You must save your water,' Robbie shouted at his men, but he might just as well have saved his breath. They were unable to resist taking constant sips from their canteens and by eight o'clock, most had exhausted their supply.

At noon, the temperature reached 40 degrees and the battle still lay ahead like a mirage on the sunlit plains. An enemy plane burst into flames and sailed across the sky hauling a streamer of yellow fumes. The men cheered and, for two steps, forgot they were thirsty.

A motorcycle messenger got through with fresh maps and new orders. A Spanish unit had met savage opposition in Villanueva de la Cañada and had failed to secure the village in the daybreak assault. The British were directed to make a detour and join the offensive in a coordinated attack with the Abraham Lincolns.

Robbie looked down over the stairway of undulating hills. From where they had stopped, he had a panoramic view of the entire valley, 40 miles long and widening from its far point in Madrid into a triangle 15 miles across. Brunete and the villages were clearly outlined in the vivid light.

At two in the afternoon, the hottest part of the day, he led the company in open formation down from the hills into a terrain cut by ravines and dotted with gorse bushes. Villanueva de la Cañada, clear from the distance, vanished in the heat haze.

There was little cover except among the willows along the banks of an ankle-deep river where dead militiamen lay face down, shot in the back. His men topped up their canteens and drank from the bloody flow of their brothers in arms. Sergeant Hollander carried his soaked shirt. He was a muscular ship's stoker from Liverpool with tattoos up his arms and a sailing ship on his chest.

'Give the order, Ronnie,' Robbie told him.

'Aye, aye, skipper.'

He buttoned his shirt as he trotted back to the men bent over the trickle of water like a line of beasts at a salt lick.

'Drink up, gentlemen. Let's be having you.'

As Robbie turned away, he saw a *boina* – a black beret – lodged in the vines. It must have belonged to one of the Milicias Obreras, the workers' units, one of the men dead in the ravine. He beat out the dust, straightened the line across his brow and felt transformed, immune from enemy bombs and bullets.

He glanced back at the men gathered around him and put his finger to his lips. They were about to engage the full force of the enemy and it is best done in the quiet of your own thoughts. They spread out as they made their way through orchards rich in quince and pomegranates. Ahead in the distance, the red and black flag of the Falange quivered in the dry air above the church, a buttressed edifice like a castle, its square tower standing out against the blue sky.

When they reached the Brunete road, Lt Ashcombe's company was waiting with a group of two dozen Spanish militiamen, survivors from the first assault on the village. Ashcombe approached, face burnt red from the sun.

'Bloody hot. I thought it was always cool in the mountains,' he remarked.

Toby Ashcombe had gone through officer training at Dartmouth, the navy college, and taken his skills to Spain. He shaded his brow and looked towards Captain Sugden's column of vehicles descending the curves from a point about ten miles away. He glanced at his watch.

'Someone's going to be livid we got here first.'

'Not at all,' Robbie replied. 'He's as flexible as a tank barrel.'

They lit cigarettes and Robbie's attention was drawn to the knot of people approaching along the road from the village, women, children, old men with walking canes. They were quiet. Strange for Spain. Weddings, funerals, fiestas, Spaniards were always laughing and crying and playing music.

'Where's your commanding officer?' a voice called out in Spanish.

The militiamen went forward to meet the party. Toby Ashcombe hurried to join them. A single shot rang out and he was thrown backwards, half his head blown out of the back of his skull.

Robbie noticed the green uniforms of the Falange among the dusty greys and blues of the villagers. Their job was to take out the Republican officers, the strategy designed to leave the men in the ranks numbed and in disarray. He remembered this from his training, not that it prepared you for the sight of women and children being butchered.

The enemy hit squad opened up with semi-automatics that

produced a rapid response from their combined companies. The crossfire cut people to shreds. Mothers fell with their children, the old men with empty eyes, two girls in stiff white muslin. A third girl, drenched in blood, remained motionless like a statue. An old woman holding a thermos flask was thrown forward and only at the last moment did she relinquish her grip on the precious thing she carried.

In 30 seconds it was over. Ashcombe was dead. A dozen villagers were dead. Six Milicias Obreras were dead. Four Falangists had completed their mission and paid the price. The sudden hush was ominous and it was a relief when one of the Spanish soldiers shot the dead fascists in the face at close range, blinding them to the afterlife.

Two villagers had survived. An old man with a tobacco-stained moustache stood bent over a walking stick. The girl soaked in blood stared down at her mother. She was shaking, washed-out, undernourished, a child of six or seven. Gillan called for quiet and pointed down the Brunete road. He selected two men from Ashcombe's company.

'You two,' he said. 'Look after the old chap and the little girl until Captain Sugden arrives. Tell them what's happened here.'

One of the soldiers took the little girl into his arms. The other looked back with a surly expression.

'But, Lieutenant...'

'Don't discuss it, comrade. Do it. Tomorrow we'll march on Brunete.'

The order Robbie had received from the courier was to rendezvous with the rest of the battalion on the Brunete road. As the four companies advanced on Villanueva de la Cañada, they would meet the American Lincolns marching down from the village of Valdermorillo, to the north-east of Brunete.

That was the plan, the order. But battles aren't won on orders. They would strike now while their tempers were running high, while the shadows stole from the church. Now, before Captain Sugden arrived with his textbook and party card. He had two companies. With the Spaniards, there were more than 200 men.

He raised his fist. The volunteers raised their voices. They punched the air in the loyalist salute and were lifted by a surge of confidence. At daybreak, when they had set out, they had believed they were writing a fresh page of history. That feeling was as strong as ever.

30

FROM THE ROAD leading into the village, Gillan could see a barn with a pair of black crows watching from the roof. It was the ideal refuge for troops ordered to launch a counter-attack from the rear.

He left Hollander in charge of their position and made a diversion with a small unit: Sheridan, Pope, two Spaniards he'd seen in action and four others. They circled the barn from two sides and inched their way towards the half-open doors at the entrance. He pointed at the big Kiwi, playing God again.

Pope nodded and followed his gun barrel into the building. The seconds stretched. There were no shots. Not a sound until Robbie heard a few bars hummed from 'The Internationale', the all clear. He ducked into the shadows inside the barn and stumbled into a row of five dead men, field workers who held their pants up with rope and went without food to feed their families. Their private parts had been severed and shoved in their mouths, the Falange learning from the Moors. Behind the stacked bales of straw, they discovered four women with their numbed children. A girl, no more than 14, her clothes ripped off, sat staring at the golden flecks of dust highlighted by the lowering sun.

Simon found an abandoned jacket to cover her and stood back beside Robbie. He had taken off his beret and gripped it so hard his knuckles had turned white. In this mood, he was capable of anything.

'Robbie. Robbie,' Simon repeated. 'Close your eyes. Take a breath.'

Robbie's head fell forward, then lifted again as he levelled his shoulders. He was shaking and spoke through gritted teeth.

'What's wrong with these fockin people?'

He pulled on his beret and turned to the people cowering in the shadows. They had no water to give them, no food. He spoke to one of the Spaniards.

'Tell them they are safe now. Someone will come to help them,' he said. He spoke in Spanish for the man to repeat. It was better coming from him than a foreigner.

One of the women stood. She brushed straw from her black dress. She was bone thin, face like a mask. Her voice didn't quaver.

'They call us traitors. They rape my daughter. They kill our men like they are pigs.' She stared at Robbie. 'You go. Take revenge for us.'

He nodded his head and swore an oath.

'Lo haré. Le doy mi palabra.'

The crows lifted from the roof as Simon led the way out of the barn. When they reached the pines above the road, Robbie sent another reluctant volunteer back to meet Sugden to ask for help for the women and children.

'We have seen men who bled to death after being mutilated and young girls who were raped. I gave the survivors my word we would take revenge.'

'Venganza. Venganza,' roared the Spaniards.

They checked their rifles and spread out in units of ten to enter Villanueva de la Cañada, one more bleak village with a grand name and broken houses crumbling into the landscape. They seized the outlying buildings with such speed and ferocity the enemy was taken by surprise. The Falange pulled back in disarray. Some of the troopers threw down their arms in surrender, but the Milicias Obreras fighting in the vanguard were in no mood for taking prisoners.

They moved through the backstreets that led to the Plaza de España, the vast stone stronghold of the church dominating the square like a battleship at sea. The only other large building was the town hall with its ornate balconies and arches. The clock in the tower read 8:30 and the black eagle against the red and yellow stripes on the Nationalist flag stretched its wings on the *leveche*, the warm summer wind that comes at night. The sun going down over the western hills painted the sky orange.

The sound of the fountains at the centre of the square provided an absurd counterpoint to the buzz of rounds fired from enemy positions. Robbie led his men from cover to cover along the side of the square facing the church. They seized each building and groups of three brigaders remained behind to set up firing positions. As they approached the bar on the corner, a dozen Falange soldiers burst out and raced for cover behind the fountains.

Inside the bar, drinks lined the shelves. Half-filled glasses stood on the counter. Pope grabbed a bottle.

'Water only,' Gillan ordered. 'We'll get drunk after we take the church.'

'I'll keep you to that, comrade,' Pope said and replaced the bottle on the shelf.

Sergeant Hollander continued to take and hold the remaining buildings. Robbie examined the square through binoculars. The Falange soldiers behind the fountains were protected from the guns in the church but were unable to retreat further due to the field of fire set up in the town hall by what he now realised was the American Lincolns, on time as promised.

Robbie turned the binoculars on the church. He could make out the dead eyes of high-calibre weapons peeking through the windows in the building's façade. The artillery was coming, the British convoy had to be close now, but this was the right time to attack.

With a small force, he could scale the back wall and enter the church from the roof. He was running the plan through his mind when a truck rumbled out from the near side of the town hall and stopped in a position protected from the guns inside the church. He trained the binoculars on the troops sheltering behind the vehicle and felt a rush of adrenaline as he picked out the features of Anthony Cribb.

'You and you,' Robbie cried, pointing at two of his men. 'Run along the back of the buildings, one each way. Tell the lads, when they see me charge, they're to follow.' He looked at the men gathered in the bar, Simon, Pope, the Spaniards. He held each one's gaze for a second.

'Fix bayonets,' he ordered.

The truck began to move again, gathering speed. The driver swerved around the fountain and raced full throttle towards the church. Bullets pinged off the metal bodywork. Incoming rounds turned the square into a dust storm of shrapnel and burning flesh.

Robbie emerged from the bar at a sprint and the combined British and American forces charged, guns firing in a frenzy, the smoke from grenades swirling about them. The truck smashed its way through the oak doors with a hollow crunch like the sound of a ship's hull hitting an iceberg. Machine gun fire crackled from the tower.

He reached the centre of the square at the same time as Cribb. They saw each other through the mass of bodies as if that was what they had expected to see. The enemy troopers stranded behind the fountain had no option but to counterattack in a bayonet charge. The action was over in seconds, so rapid, Robbie thought, you can't be sure what's happening at the time and can't remember the details when it's over. It just happens. Like everything that happens. You see friends mangled in pools of blood and gore, and you could spend the rest of his life wondering if it could have been different. If it could have been you.

A Falange veteran, an older man, bore down on him. He could see resolve in his eyes, coal black and glittery in the dwindling light. He screamed '*Viva Franco.*' Robbie swerved like a bullfighter and slashed at the trooper's throat. The sheer force behind the blade tossed him backwards into the fountains. Robbie may have glanced back at him. Perhaps he just imagined he did. It was unclear, and he was now an open target. The next wolf in the fascist pack was about to run him through.

Anthony Cribb got between them. He came up on Robbie's left side and threw himself forward like an athlete going for the winning tape. He was fast, fit from the hill. He crossed the line and took the German bayonet in his guts. His attacker, in turn, was brought down by Simon Sheridan. He was the last of the Falangists to fall.

It was over.

But it's never over.

It was over for a fleeting moment.

The Internationals had followed the truck as it burst into the church and re-enacted the murals of crusades painted on the walls fighting hand-to-hand with the men inside. The fountain was a red flower that bloomed in the last rays of the dying sun.

Robbie held Cribb in his arms. Cribb smiled.

'You get that girl,' he mumbled.

'Aye, I will. You take it easy. You rest.'

'It's a damn good sunset,' Cribb said and slowly, like a curtain being drawn, he closed his eyes.

The guns fell silent. It was eerie. Unnatural. A shadow crossed the square like a tide. The night turned the shade of purple on the Republican flag and the cicadas clicked and chirped in the plane trees. Men pushed out through the splintered doors of the church, faces marbled in sweat and rifle oil, Americans and British shaking hands, lighting fags. Hollander took charge of the prisoners. The bloodlust had passed.

Jamie Douglas and Hamish McDonald emerged with Nat Cohen suspended between their shoulders, his legs punctured with holes. Mike Pope had a gash down his cheek. He saw Robbie as he crossed the square.

'I'm going to get that drink now,' he said.

Simon slipped down beside Robbie and rested his back against the wet ring of the fountain. Cribb was still in Robbie's arms.

'You know who this is? It's Anthony Cribb,' he said.

'I'm so sorry.'

'He saved my life.' Robbie turned and looked squarely at Simon. 'Then you saved my life.'

The thought was a revelation. It made no sense. Nothing makes sense. You live. You die. Or you don't die. You survive this moment and there is only this moment. This graveyard of men in varicoloured uniforms. This pointless, pitiless war because men with 10,000 acres had no heart to share some land with those who have none.

Robbie came unsteadily to his feet. There was work to be done. The dead had to be separated and identified. He wanted all the food they could find to be put in one place. He promised to shoot anyone caught looting. They had watched him in action. No one doubted his word.

Local people appeared like mice from cellars and lofts. They carried sheets for bandages and water in thermos flasks. A group of convent girls in blue-checked dresses marched up in two files. They were solemn with lowered eyes and burnished black hair, young women with no knowledge of the male anatomy who gently, patiently, stripped and bathed and cared for the cursing, crying, damaged men.

Birds sang as if they had been waiting for the silence. Mosquitoes turned crazy by spilled blood attacked in humming swarms. As the last glimmer of sunlight slid behind the hills, the staff car carrying Captain Sugden rolled into town and Robbie caught a glimpse of the three green ambulances bringing up the rear of the column.

31

WHILE THE COOKS and medical crew went about their tasks, the men who had taken Villanueva were ordered into the church. They sat in the half-darkness grumbling. Robbie was directed to the front row of pews. Simon dropped down at his side.

Captain Sugden hammered his pistol like a gavel on the side of the pulpit and the troops came to a hush.

'Comrade Gillan,' he began. 'No one gave you the order to attack. The order was clear. The battalion was to regroup and storm the village in one body. You put the entire operation in jeopardy.'

He was immediately challenged. 'We took the bloody place, didn't we?' someone called from the back.

'Comrade, that is not the point.' Sugden was controlled. He sucked in breath and took on the look of a wrathful Jesus, like the carved figure on the crucifix behind him. 'There is a chain of command. If that breaks down, we have chaos, failure, defeat.'

'In this case, victory. Change never comes from above,' came the same steady voice.

'It is direction from above that ignites the resolve for the masses to effect change,' Sugden countered.

He licked his lips as if he had an unpleasant taste in his mouth and rattled out chunks of the party canon like a poet in a pub bar. Robbie had heard it all before. He was tired, hungry. He wanted to find Alice. Taffy Norris was earnestly nodding his head like it was on a spring, as was Ian Macaulay, the new Commissar.

Sugden went on about discipline and loyalty, the workers' fight against the vanity of nations. He climbed into the pulpit and took a grip with both hands on the brass rail above the woodwork. Someone lit the altar candles and the image was complete: Father Sugden wasn't holding an inquiry, he was preaching a sermon.

Robbie tuned out. The assault on the church had been precise, efficient and had been achieved with minimum casualties. It was Cribb who deserved the credit. Cribb had made him conscious of who he was, who he could be, not what others or he himself assumed he should be. He had learned from Cribb, from Franchetti, from Alphonse Laurencic, that life could be something else.

Knowing Anthony Cribb, reading his book, he had known what had to be done when the truck accelerated towards the church. It was instinct. Something you can't explain or teach to men with bibles and books of rules. They had triumphed where the shock troops had failed. Villanueva de la Cañada was back in the Republican fold. Across the length of Spain, even such minor victories were uncommon.

The light faded. The bells chimed the clockless hours, then stopped suddenly, a relief for Sugden more than anyone else. He was building up to a dramatic conclusion.

'Your conduct goes against every precept that governs the International Brigade. To disobey a direct order from a senior officer is mutiny, an offence that cannot go unpunished. Simply because the Abraham Lincoln Battalion put in a timely appearance...'

'It wasn't like that,' came a fresh voice.

Sugden raised his fist. 'Just because the goal was subsequently achieved does not excuse Lieutenant Gillan's disregard for my orders.' He paused and stared down at the front row of pews. 'You may imagine that you have acted bravely, Comrade Gillan, but that is not the case. You put the lives of your men at risk by your flagrant disobedience...'

There were more interruptions. Sugden waited for silence. 'We are a revolutionary army, not a mob,' he said. 'I want you to listen to me…'

There was an explosion that echoed over the walls and a clatter of breaking glass as a bullet shattered one of the remaining windows. Sugden peered into the gloom. Before he spoke, the same slow soft voice from the back stopped him.

'No, comrade, I'd like you to listen to me.'

The man who had let off the shot shouldered his way towards the pulpit from the crowd around the demolished doors. It was Dave Cooper, the tin miner, a survivor from Jarama. He nodded at Robbie, then looked back at the captain.

'You weren't there,' he said. 'You don't know what happened. You can't know. We attacked when we did because it was the right thing to do. It was a decision taken in the field. It turned out to be the right decision.'

Sugden seized the opportunity. 'Had Comrade Gillan waited, the anti-tank battery would have rendered the assault on the church unnecessary. Many of our comrades would have been saved.'

'Just as likely more would have been lost,' Cooper countered. 'We would have been a bigger target. Robbie didn't make us do anything against our will. When we saw the old women and little kids being shot by fascists, we wanted to attack.'

'That is not the way to conduct a battle. The Comrade Lieutenant disobeyed a direct order.'

'We…' Cooper slapped his chest, 'the working man, the men here in the church, we need leaders who know how to take the initiative. What you're doing is creating a hierarchy. Those who give the orders and those who have to obey them. Is that the way we're going to build our workers' paradise?'

Jamie Douglas came to his feet. 'We came here to fight

the fascists, not listen to one,' he screamed out.

'The lad's the best officer we've got,' cried Hollander.

Sugden's voice was drowned out as he tried to speak. Taffy Norris had an anxious look about his long thin face and unsnapped the hook on his holster. Before he drew his weapon, Simon moved to his side and locked his hand over his wrist.

'I don't think that would be wise, comrade,' he advised.

Sugden raised his arms in the air. 'Thank you, comrades. Thank you,' he shouted and the congregation grew quiet again. 'The party will not permit insubordination. The party...' he repeated, and the word, and the way Sugden said the word, struck a violent chord that moved Robbie to leave the pew.

They grew quiet as Robbie removed his party card, tore it in half and half again, then dropped the pieces on the pulpit.

'There are a lot of blokes here who are not members of the Communist Party. Still they came to Spain,' Robbie said in a voice so soft those at the back had to strain to hear him. 'There are volunteers from the Labour Party, the trade unions. There are Liberals. Even some Tories.' There were a few laughs. 'It's true,' he added. 'We have all kinds of people, painters, writers, and none more important than the pacifists who came to carry the stretchers and do the dirty work.'

'That's not the point...'

Cooper broke in. 'You've had your say. Let the lad finish.'

'I'm no hero, Captain Sugden. It wasn't me who organised the assault on the church. It was Anthony Cribb, the American officer. He deserves the credit. He died leading the charge. He wasn't a communist. He didn't believe in anything except common human decency. Those are his words, by the way, not mine.'

Sugden scratched his nose as his eyes moved over the rows of pews lined up in the church.

'Comrades. Comrades. You have all had your say. I am sure you are all hungry. I certainly am...'

'What about Robbie Gillan?' came the shout.

'I have come to a decision that I am sure you will agree is the right one. I am going to overlook Comrade Gillan's disregard for my orders. But I cannot permit such lapses to happen again.' He took a breath. 'Comrade Macaulay will lead Lieutenant Ashcombe's company, and Lieutenant Norris will take command of Lieutenant Gillan's company. Comrade Gillan will serve under Comrade Norris.'

The brigaders were quiet as they thought about this. They weren't happy with the compromise and Robbie realised that if he didn't do something, there was going to be a riot. He turned to face the pews.

'The captain has made a fine decision. Now let's go and have some supper.'

'About fockin time,' Jamie Douglas shouted and got a few laughs.

Dave Cooper picked up the four pieces of Robbie's party card and stuffed them back in his pocket.

Simon was waiting. They left the church and entered a starry night lit by a pale, lemony moon. Tables had been set up around the fountains with candles in glass jars. The scent of hot food perfumed the air. Friends they had marched with into battle that morning were no longer with them. They weren't forgotten. They were celebrated by celebrating life.

'I'm famished,' Simon said.

Robbie stopped and hugged Simon tight to his chest. 'I owe you my life,' he said.

'Quid pro quo.'

'There you go, blinding me with your knowledge again.'

They laughed. They looked closely at each other and Simon was suddenly aware of Robbie's similarity to his sister, their colouring, the intense look in their eyes, their faces slender, still forming, like portraits before they age and take on depth and significance.

Men were sitting and filling their plates. They drank wine from the bottles. Someone played a penny whistle and the fountains sang their familiar tune.

'I'll see you later, mon,' Robbie said.

'I'm so pleased you found each other. You're so right together.'

'We're about as wrong as any two people can be. North and south, Scot and Sassenach, the working class and the no-need-to-work class...'

'That's why we're here.'

Mike Pope appeared with a bottle for Robbie, and Simon went to join one of the lads from Lancashire doing a clog dance.

*

The town hall had been turned into a field hospital. Every room was occupied by rows of iron cots requisitioned from across the village. The large chamber at the rear of the building designed for committee meetings had been turned into a surgery where the British and American doctors worked without rest on hell's conveyor belt of smashed and battered men.

Alice applied dressings, checked brows for fever. She took the hands of men in the last terrifying moments before they expired. No man wants to die alone. She sat with a young soldier softly weeping. He turned his head away, then back again, the look on his face so heart-rending the tears she had been holding back ran down her cheeks. His dream had been to play football one day for Manchester United. The doctors had amputated one of his legs.

The soldier in the next cot had lost his eyes. Men had lost hands and arms. Their faces had been torn apart by explosions, their bodies gashed by shrapnel and punctured with searing hot lead. Open wounds quickly smelled rotten.

There was the occasional scream followed by a terrible silence. She kissed the football player's brow and made her way to the next room.

She paused at a tall, arched window and watched the celebrations in the square. Men were dancing together like couples at a wedding. She could see the snail trails of searchlight beams crossing the sky. They would describe their first day of the campaign as a success, territory gained, losses minimal, the pincers drawing in on Brunete. She went downstairs and was about to take a breath in the garden when someone called.

'Miss, could I have some water?'

She recognised the man when she took it to him. He drank the water down in one gulp and she refilled the glass.

'Thanks, Miss, I feel so dry.'

'It's the morphine,' she said. 'We met this morning. I was with Robbie Gillan. It's someone's birthday today. What's his name, Jamie?'

'That seems like a hundred years ago,' he said. 'I remember now. Course I do. You're Robbie's girl?'

She nodded. 'You're Nat?'

'Aye, that's me, Nat Cohen. Doesn't sound Scottish, but that's where I'm from. I've known Robbie since he was a wee bairn. Know his kin. Good people.'

'He's all right?'

'Oh, aye, right as ninepence.' He paused. 'Course, you're Simon's sister. Another good lad. You know, we drove the fascists clean out of the village. They led the way, the two of them, like two peas in a pod they are.'

It seemed an unlikely comparison but she could understand it and it made her feel warm inside. She checked his dressings. The war for Nat Cohen was over. If he walked again, he'd be a lucky man. She went out into the garden and sat below the walnut trees waiting for him to come.

32

SHERIDAN ENTERED THE church with a courier, the man's dark eyes staring from a face coated in red dust. He opened an attaché case and handed over a map with fresh orders in French. Sugden glanced at the communiqué and gave it to Norris.

'What's this?'

Norris read slowly. 'We are to join the rest of the xvth Brigade in an assault on the Nationalist stronghold above the Guadarrama River,' he translated and gave the sheet to Simon to make sure he wasn't wrong.

Sugden glared at the dispatch rider. 'That's it, is it?'

The man patiently removed his flying helmet. 'I do not speak very well English?' he replied.

'These are our orders?' Sugden asked, accentuating each word.

'From Comrade Marty.'

The courier pulled the leather headwear back on and Sheridan followed him back along the luminous spear of sunshine that led from the smashed doors to the altar.

Robbie heard a motorcycle kick over and the engine sound faded as it roared out of Villanueva de la Cañada.

'Who is going to hold the village, comrade?' he asked Sugden.

The CO shook his head. 'That is not our concern,' he replied and glanced at his watch. 'Assemble for mobilisation in 15 minutes.'

As Robbie left the church, his eyes were drawn to the

town hall where he had spent the hours before dawn holding Alice as if there was some way they could weave their bodies together like a basket and never be parted. They had made love, stretching the seconds, and a strange thought had entered his mind. He wanted to make her pregnant, create new life, a bond that could never be broken. It was absurd. Irresponsible. Instinct made him believe he would survive. Common sense told him the odds were not in his favour.

Simon was waiting for him on a bench by the fountains. They fell into step as they crossed the square listening to the guns jabber away on the mountain tops.

'High-calibre,' Simon remarked.

'German.'

'How did they manage to get up there so quickly?'

'While we were clog dancing, the fascists were doing overtime. We'll have to take the heights before we get a look at Brunete.'

'Jarama,' Simon said darkly.

They stopped outside the café and looked up at a pair of Russian 1-16s, new fighter planes with mountings for four machine guns. The Spanish called them *ratas* for some reason. Perhaps because they were always scurrying like rats away from Nationalist anti-aircraft batteries.

They entered the cool of the café and Robbie was startled to find Alice waiting for them at a marble-topped table. She was wearing a white blouse, a dab of lipstick, a red neckerchief at her throat and a matching red beret.

Corporal Pope brought them coffee in white porcelain cups with saucers and warm *madalenas*. He had a white towel over his arm.

'You said it was all down to the American officer, Robbie. I think it was all down to you,' Pope said.

'What are you talking about? It was all of us.'

'I'll settle for that.' Pope glanced at the steaming coffee

cups. 'Now, will that be all, sir?'

'I wish,' Robbie said, and they laughed.

They had never sat together like this – real coffee in a café; people living normal lives. It's the small things that matter, the daily routines. We struggle and dream, strive for meaning, for purpose. But ten minutes having a pint with a mate, chatting with Da in a bed of old newspapers, coffee in a Spanish café. These are the things that make us human, the things we remember.

His gaze shifted from Alice to Simon. Summer suited him. To describe another man as handsome was beyond imagination in Glasgow. But it was the right description for Simon with his saint's blue eyes and hair bronzed by the sun. In Alice's eyes he saw the quicksand of her shifting emotions, her fears, her commitment to those things impossible to articulate. Robbie knew her as a sailor knows the sea and didn't know her at all.

He sipped his coffee. He watched Pope fill a hip flask with brandy and wipe down the zinc counter before he left. The Americans had pulled out at sunrise. The moment was fleeting. Five turns of the minute hand on the town hall clock. As he dipped the *madalena* in the coffee, he heard the shriek of Taffy Norris blasting his whistle.

Alice ran her fingertips over the knuckles of his right hand where it rested on the table. It went through Robbie's mind, as it must have struck them all, to wonder if they would ever sit together again, like this, eating pastries and drinking coffee.

They left the café and stood in the shade below the awning. A crowd of local people had assembled. He saw the woman who had urged him to seek vengeance for the Falange massacre. He had done as she asked, not that it would heal her pain. Nothing would bring back the innocence of her daughter, the lives of her men.

They joined the river of khaki heading for the vehicles

parked along the far side of the square. Simon climbed up into the driving seat of the Renault as the men scrambled over the tailgate. Robbie went to the end of the column where Graham Webster waited in the first of the three ambulances. Alice turned and touched her finger to his lips.

She held his eyes for a second and joined Webster. Robbie squared his boina and strode back along the file of trucks, fist held aloft and the men cheered like they were giving away free money outside the dole office. They shouted '*Viva la República*. They Shall Not Pass. We Shall Pass.'

He stepped into the passenger seat of a staff car driven by Norris.

'Are you ready?'

'More ready than willing,' he replied and saw doubt flicker over Norris's features. 'It's a joke, Taffy. Got to keep our sense of humour.'

Robbie looked up at the sky, an unending stretch of blue with hints of cloud. They followed the lead vehicle carrying the CO as it skirted the Plaza de España. They entered the cramped streets where people waved flags, grateful, he was sure, to see the back of men in uniform.

Norris dropped a gear as they entered the archway of trees that climbed the incline out of the village. They had gone three miles along the Brunete road when Robbie heard what sounded like a sonic boom that echoed over the rocky hillside. The vehicle ahead slowed and the convoy concertinaed to a halt. They stared from their vehicles down into the valley as Villanueva de la Cañada was wiped thoroughly and completely from the map.

No one there that day had seen the bombing at Guernica, but they had read the reports in the press and now watched the repeat performance as wave after wave of Condor Legion bombers released their loads. The church received numerous direct hits. The walls collapsed. The tower shimmied for a moment, then toppled like a felled tree. The houses in the old town turned to debris. The dust rose up and blackened the sky.

The column was protected from the view of the pilots by a ridge rising to the left of the road. There was no Republican air cover and there was barely room in the sky for the endless squadrons of Heinkels delivering 1,000-pound Sprengbombe Cylindrisch, thin-cased demolition bombs that rained down like the fire and brimstone on Sodom and Gomorrah. Their departure from the village minutes before the attack was uncanny, divine if you were a believer.

German fighters arrived like birds of prey to strafe fleeing civilians. The taste of ancient dust reached them and they drove on, following the slowly rising hairpins, 13 trucks laden with men and weaponry, two staff cars and three ambulances emblazoned with the Red Cross.

They debussed in a gorge below an overhanging escarpment easy to camouflage from the air. This was base camp, where the cookhouse boys would ration the supplies and the medics would sterilise their scalpels as they waited for the inevitable. Norris blew his whistle and the British volunteers climbed into the hills beneath the eye of a red-hot sun.

The high ground rose in undulating steps, dominating the plain below. Tucked in under the summit, the guns stared out from a wall of rock topped by sandbags. Shells rained down like hail. Captain Sugden, union man, party apparatchik, was the first to fall. He lifted his arm, looked back at his troops and turned to lead the way up to the first ridge. He died instantly. A bullet to the head. There were snipers up there, dug in all the way to the peak.

Who was in charge now? It didn't matter. They were 500 men climbing an unforgiving hillside to a goal few imagined they would ever reach. Robbie was at the sword-point with the same small squad that had followed him the previous day,

Sheridan, Pope, Hollander, the Spaniards in their forage caps. A deluge of shrapnel fell so close their faces were slapped with showers of scalding earth.

They reached a place of relative calm behind a formation of rock shaped like a bird's beak. Nowhere was safe. They were outnumbered. Outgunned. Outmanoeuvred. Robbie gazed down from his position and watched as a company of Spanish militia on their left flank confronted three low-flying Messerschmitts. They were hacked down. Their cries carried on the dry air like people screaming on a ride at the funfair.

A handful of soldiers reached cover in a windmill with broken sails. The fighter planes turned in graceful loops, dropped packets of grenades and the building disintegrated. A boy who looked too young to shave crawled from the wreckage. He threw down his rifle as he ran for the trees. His arms pumped like pistons. His legs pounded the dirt. A hundred yards separated him from safety. One of the planes peeled off from the formation in an unhurried arc. It swooped low. The guns rattled and the runner fell.

Robbie lit a cigarette in cupped hands and watched the plane slide off like a black needle sewing thread into the blue fabric of the sky.

With Sugden dead, Taffy Norris assumed command and it said something for the man that he didn't let it go to his head. He inched himself towards Gillan's niche in the rocks. Below them, the battalion was spread out, not in companies but chaos.

'What do you think we should do, comrade?' he asked, and Robbie took a long time before he replied.

'We'll wait. Let them run out of water and get bored with waiting. The time to advance will present itself when it's ready.'

It was the answer Norris wanted to hear. He took a peek through field glasses at the sun burnished hillside. As he did so, the earth trembled under a fresh onslaught, batteries firing in unison. They covered their heads, glanced up again and it was hard to believe they were still there, still in one piece.

The peak had been christened Mosquito Ridge. Rounds filled the air in swarms like mosquitoes, a version of Suicide Hill with enemy firepower fiercer than anything they had witnessed at Jarama. They fought through the long day, and got a foothold on the first ridge as night came and the guns fell silent like many of the men who had carried them.

Caterers and stretcher-bearers climbed the rock face with billycans of food and water. Pope shared his hip flask of brandy and Robbie was glad he had bitten his tongue before telling him to pour it away in the café that morning.

You sleep rough and you're not certain that you've slept at all. The sweat pours out of you. You don't wash. Ten men charge forward 80 yards to conquer a new salient. One dead and you call it a victory. A Russian bomber lands a direct hit on an enemy gun emplacement. The long barrel bounces down the incline before stopping a yard from your position and you consider the irony of being crushed to death by a firearm instead of a bullet.

They advanced next day and the next. Spanish divisions, workers' militia and the joint battalions of the International Brigade lumbered like a herd of wounded beasts across a 20-mile front into withering salvos of enemy gunfire. Robbie watched comrades die on the hills and on the plain. They fought against ferocious odds beneath a sun that burned their bodies and cooked their brains. It was a bloody test of wills, a showdown between the rising tide of fascism and Spain's immature hopes of liberal democracy.

By the seventh day, their numbers were too few to keep up the assault. Thousands had died from every country in Europe, American Lincolns, the Canadian Mackenzie–Papineau Battalion. Mike Pope had caught it that morning advancing with Quique Velázquez. Ronnie Hollander, the seaman, had run into a grenade and vanished like a puff of smoke. Hamish McDonald had been carried back down the hill missing an arm and a leg. Jamie Douglas had lost his face and an eye. Dave Cooper, the quiet tin miner, would never raise his voice again.

Robbie and Simon were 200 yards from the summit. The rest of the battalion, fewer than 200 men, spread out in disarray below their position. The sun slipped into the far sierras, splashing the sky in pastel hues. The big guns had grown quiet. Robbie lifted his field glasses to look over the ridge. He was hit twice, two rounds that landed in quick succession. The first passed through his neck, the second shattered his right collarbone.

There was so much blood, Simon thought he was already dead. He rushed to his side and was cut down in the same volley of gunfire. He let out a long gasp and struggled for breath as he gripped Robbie's hand.

Robbie turned his head. He saw a look of serenity in Simon's eyes, peace at the heart of battle, and it occurred to him that Simon had found whatever it was he'd been searching for.

'The stretchers will come. You hang on,' Robbie said, but there was no sound. His throat burned. His voice was silent.

Simon's face was streaked in oil, but the whites of his eyes were unusually white and the blue remained bright. He painstakingly unbuttoned his shirt pocket and removed some items he pressed into Robbie's hand. He slipped the keys he wore around his neck over his head. 'For Father's clock,' he said, and then added, 'Time's going backwards.' It didn't make sense and Robbie couldn't reply.

Simon used the last of his energy to pull closer. He placed his arm around Robbie's shoulders, supporting his head. Their bodies connected in a moment when two men are as intimate as they can be. Robbie knew, he had always known, that Simon loved him.

The big guns started again, but the sound seemed far away. Robbie felt as if his head was under water. Pain consumed his torso and spread through his limbs. His throat was on fire. He thought about Alice. He had promised he would go back. He imagined her hopelessly waiting and the pain in his throat didn't feel quite so bad. He closed his eyes and it was as if someone had turned out the light.

33

GENERAL SHERIDAN STOOD stiffly in his smoking jacket, hands gripped behind his back as he stared out the window. His study looked over the treetops in Carlyle Square where the fading light turned the view into shades of grey.

Newspaper cuttings and reports from his operatives in Spain stood in a file on his desk. It was 25 August. The Battle of Brunete had been over for exactly one month. After taking the city in a lightning attack led by Enrique Líster's division on 6 July, it had taken the Nationalists three weeks to drive Republican and International Brigade forces back to where they had started. The Republic's defeat at Brunete was what he had expected, what his agents had predicted. There had been a time when he would have welcomed the outcome. That time had passed.

There was a double tap on the door.

'Dinner, sir,' he heard, and turned about, the finger of his right hand moving to the scar below his eye.

On top of the clipping's file was a sheet of writing paper containing the telephone number of Ribbentrop in Austria.

*

Forty-two British volunteers had still been fit for service after being driven from Mosquito Ridge. Alice had been evacuated with them to Albacete where the flags rarely stirred in the summer heat and she watched new recruits arriving to fill the ranks of the dead. While she tended the wounded, Alice asked after Simon and Robbie. But memories had grown hazy. The men were in shock. No one had seen them.

Weeks passed without news. Alice had become reed-thin and vomited up what little she ate. When she finally asked the new CO for leave, he granted it without question and she travelled to Madrid. Tommy Courtenay, from the Embassy, was waiting when the train steamed into Atocha Station. He had made up the guest room for her in his apartment on the Gran Via and she slept without stirring for 12 hours in a proper bed with laundered sheets.

Next day, and every day, she visited hospitals and infirmaries across the city where the wards were crammed with so many soldiers with severed limbs and vacant stares she was reminded of the paintings of hell by Hieronymus Bosch displayed in the Prado. She felt nauseous. Her breasts were tender. One night, she couldn't stop crying. Tommy Courtenay must have heard her through the dividing wall and was unusually attentive that morning as he made coffee and toast. They sat in the cool of the semi-circular balcony with the sun lighting the shell-pocks drilled into the wall of the building opposite.

'You ought to go home, Alice,' he said, and she looked at him over her cup for several moments before she answered.

'Men always seem to think they know what's best for a woman.'

'I don't mean it unkindly…'

'I know you don't. But it's still maddening.'

She glanced around the room at the marble figures balanced on the black and white tiled floor, the curios and embellishments. Tommy Courtenay was living in a private museum.

'There is every chance Simon is a prisoner of war. Simon and the other chap.'

'He has a name. Robert Ian Gillan.'

'Go home. Get well. I will call you the moment I know something.'

*

She tried the Spanish composers, Albéniz, Joaquín Rodrigo, Manuel de Falla, but her fingers were incapable of transferring the melodies in her mind to the sounds released in the music room where the summer light gleamed on the glass fronts of the flower prints. One day, when a cloud crossed the sun and the room darkened, Alice closed the piano lid and never played again.

Her room with the door closed was her sanctuary, her feet on a stool, a book wedged open, the lines of black words like marching ants going on and on endlessly from nowhere to nowhere. It was pretty with the windows open. The compass of her stare was brought constantly back to the garden where sparrows swooped in and out of the apple trees.

She looked often at the snapshot of Robbie with Anthony Cribb and Eva Delaware. She read his letter so many times the words smudged from tears falling on the writing paper. Her thoughts were chaotic, random, panicky. There was something wrong with her, something beyond her sense of grief.

*

Sheridan held his breath as Netty lurched over him with a serving dish. He had always regretted that they did not have male servants, as one did in the army. The maid finished her task and he let out a sigh as she left the dining room.

'We really ought to get up to Windermere for a week. The summer's almost over,' he said, approaching the subject like an enemy bunker.

Lady Sheridan glanced at her daughter. 'A change of air will do you good.'

'I shall stay here,' said Alice.

'You can't stay here,' her father argued. 'It's summer. We always go to the lakes in the summer.'

'There is no "always," father.'

He let the subject drop and cut into a slice of lamb.

Alice scarcely touched her food and rose from the table. 'Do excuse me,' she said, and disappeared through the door like a stone through water.

Lady Sheridan sat as if paralysed, her hands trembling as she replaced her silverware on the table. She then did something her husband had never seen before. She cried. Tears rolled down her cheeks. He stood.

'My dear,' he said. 'My dear...' He moved cautiously to her side, where he remained for several moments before going to the drinks cabinet. 'Can I get you something?'

She clenched her fists to regain control. 'It won't help. I am sorry,' she apologised. She dried her eyes with her handkerchief. 'I am so unhappy.'

He poured a drink and returned to his seat. His wife's few words hung between them like cobwebs in a disused house.

'Charlotte, I...'

'Don't say anything. My life is over. I only care about Alice.'

'And I no less.'

They became quiet, sharing for a few moments the intimacy of their common regrets.

'You are aware what's wrong with her?' she then asked.

'She is troubled by what she has seen and because we don't know what's happened to Simon...' Lady Sheridan was shaking her head. 'Yes, I know. There's a young chap she has feelings for.'

'Richard, your daughter is in love.'

She pushed back her chair and went to the drinks cabinet. She stared at the rows of decanters and finally poured a drink without knowing what it was. She turned to face her husband.

'She's in love with a Scottish boy,' she said with a catch in her breath.

'I did know, although she didn't exactly spell it out,' he replied.

'You have not been told because you show little interest in anything other than your very important work. His name is Gillan. Robert Ian Gillan. He is a lieutenant. He was last seen with Simon on some place called Mosquito Ridge. It was all in *The Times*.'

'I am aware of that.'

'Of course you are. It is the fact that they are missing that makes it so much worse. You can't grieve. If we only knew.'

'There are hundreds of families in the same position.'

She hammered her fist on the table. 'Good God. We are not hundreds of families, are we Richard?'

He accepted the rebuke and remembered the telephone number on the file on his desk. He knew what had to be done and had been putting it off for any number of reasons, pride, shame, his resolve to never take advantage of his position.

'Alice has your nature. Or your strength, I should say. Simon was mine. I will never get over it.'

'He should never have gone to Spain. The boy has been being fighting his birth right.'

'Is all this anguish for our son, or what he has failed to achieve?'

'Really, Charlotte. I have never heard you speak like this.'

'You were never comfortable with him.'

'That's preposterous.' His finger moved as if drawn by its own will to his cheekbone. 'He should have gone into the regiment. We all have obligations. Young people don't appreciate that.'

'Perhaps they do.' She paused. 'Alice is committed to the Spanish cause. I gave her the money they needed for the ambulance.'

He drew breath and calmed himself. He had known that. Of course he had known. That was the problem with his work, his position. There was very little that he didn't know except the whereabouts of his son.

'We have to do what we believe is right,' he finally said.

'None of that matters now, Richard. We must look after our daughter.'

Sheridan wasn't sure what to say and it was a relief when Netty waddled in with a pot of coffee.

'Thank you. You can leave it on the table,' he said. 'Would you be so kind as to bring me a pencil and some paper.'

They sat without speaking until she returned. Netty's hands shook as she poured the coffee. Sheridan had come to a decision, one of the hardest in his life.

'Gillan?' he asked.

'Robert Ian, a lieutenant. Aged 25. Alice has a photograph.'

'I'll get it copied.'

'Richard, I do understand. More than you know. You are not a man who bends the rules. I admire that. But it is beyond that. If you have the power to find these boys, please, please find them.'

She rose from the table. He did also, and they took a step towards each other. He held her for a moment and kissed her cheeks.

'I will,' he whispered.

He returned to his study. He glanced at the grandfather clock from habit, forgetting that the hands had not moved since Simon left. The sheet of paper on his desk contained the direct line of the German Ambassador, Count von Ribbentrop, at Schloss Fuschl, his summer home in Salzburg. They had known each other for a long time. They would count each other as friends, men of equal rank who appreciated the burdens of national responsibility each carried.

It was too late to call him now. He went to bed early with a book, slept restlessly as if keyed up for a morning attack on an enemy stronghold and ate breakfast alone. He made the call at one minute past nine. Ribbentrop answered after two rings.

'Why, good morning, Sir Richard, what a pleasant surprise. How are the lakes?'

'I'm still stuck in London. How's the family?'

'We are exceedingly well. And Lady Sheridan?'

'She's not at her best, to be honest.'

'I'm sorry to hear that.'

'That's why I am calling. I have a favour to ask. I would like to come and see you in person, if it doesn't interrupt your holiday, of course. I would only take an hour or so of your time.'

'Richard, you are always welcome.'

'Would it be convenient to come tomorrow?'

'Let me know the time of your arrival. I will have a car waiting.'

'Joachim, that's very kind. I will get back to you later today.'

It was done. He called the CO at Biggin Hill to arrange a flight to Salzburg and went for a long walk around the lake in Battersea Park.

34

THE FIRST THING that touched his senses was the smell: chemicals, ether, most probably. There was a dry, sour taste in his mouth. Doors opened and closed. Chains rattled. A lock turned. He heard the muffled sound of voices speaking Spanish.

It must have been late afternoon. Through the bars on the high window he watched the light turn orange and slowly darken. The dressing around his neck was so thick he was barely able to move his head. His eyelids felt heavy and he drifted into sleep.

*

Rifle fire woke him. His heart pounded. The light rose quickly, bouncing from the walls like sun from snow. The echo and retort from the gunshots receded. He heard the faint sound of birdsong. He was alive. He wondered if Simon had made it and remembered dully that he had not.

Tears slipped down his cheeks. He drifted into a surface sleep where he saw a girl in a dream removing a long dress splashed with blood. Her gaunt body was marked by bullet holes. She drew back and kept moving away until she was out of sight.

He woke with a start, trembling and afraid. He tried to call out but had no voice. Then, it didn't matter. A nurse appeared at his bedside in a white habit. She took his pulse and temperature. She wrote the results on a chart attached to a clipboard and hooked the board over the metal bar at the end of the bed. She left the cell and returned shortly with a bowl of soup. She fed him without haste and left with the empty bowl.

The door as it clicked shut made the sound of a hammer striking the bullet casing on a rifle. He was lying on his back. He tried to roll over, but his right arm was pinned down by a splint. His mind as he drifted in and out of sleep floated from the white cell room to patchy scenes on the battlefield, the images etched into his retina. Mosquitoes bit his hands and feet, waking him from bad dreams.

Days passed marked by the hourglass of light changing in the rectangle of barred window. He tried to remember how many days had gone by but lost count. Not that it mattered. They were all the same: the dawn light as sharp as the rifle fire that woke him, the nurse who changed his dressing and tended to his toilet. Every morning she gave him two tablets with the sweet, sulphurous taste of morphine and held a tin mug with water to his lips. She never looked into his eyes. He wondered if she were a nun, vowed to silence, and was grateful for her attention.

When the splint was removed from his arm, Robbie was able to sit up and feed himself. His body healed, but his mind was besieged by violent dreams. He saw Simon and Cribb and Dai Jones running into enemy gunfire. He saw Paddy O'Hay dressed as a doughboy with his lips crammed with cigarettes. He saw a mountain range with wounded soldiers crawling like maggots between the twisted arms and legs of the dead. Alice moved frantically from one to the next, binding their eyes with strips of gauze, masking the horror.

*

Every day the nurse examined the wound on his neck. Another week must have gone by when, one day, after unwinding the dressing, a satisfied look entered her features. With this abrupt change of expression, he realised she was young, not an older woman, as he had supposed. *'Está bien,'* she said, removing another assumption, that she was vowed to silence.

He smiled in appreciation for this droplet of human feeling. He was about to speak, but before he could summon the breath, the door bolt clicked back into place behind her. With the bandages removed from his neck, his entire body felt liberated. Supporting his right arm, he eased himself up and swung his legs from the metal cot. He stood. After a few seconds, he became dizzy and had to lie down again.

The following day, he was able to explore his surroundings. Apart from the cot where he slept, the only piece of furniture was a three-legged table on which stood the enamel water mug the nurse regularly refilled. A simple cross hung from the wall. The oak door with iron hinges contained a porthole of opaque glass at eye level in which he could just make out the ghost of his bearded reflection. Opposite the door, the window was too high to provide a view other than the sky.

That night at sunset, he saw an enemy fighter, a brief glimpse like an omen that filled him with a sense of unease. Forks of lightning split the sky, with an interval of a second or two between the rolls of thunder. Rain fell, swishing against the building. In the morning, there were water stains around the window and a sweet taste in the air.

He only ever saw the same nurse. She was stiff like a carving, face pale as wax in the white garments that covered her head and fell in swags that swept the grey flagstones as she entered and retired from the cell. After her one terse comment, she never spoke again.

When the nurse stopped giving him painkillers, he experienced a period of anxiety, but his head cleared and he was finally able to piece together the passage of their ascent to Mosquito Ridge. He remembered his men dying, one after the other, snuffed out like candles. He remembered being hit and Simon collapsing into his arms. Everything after that moment remained hazy until the following morning when the firing squad woke him and those final moments washed up on the shore of his memory.

Night had fallen. The guns rested. He felt a tap on his leg, a kick without malice from a soldier who must have assumed he was dead. When he opened his eyes, the man jumped back in surprise. His throat and neck were on fire. He had a faint recollection of being lifted on to a stretcher and a feeling of relief that he was alive.

When it first occurred to him that he was in enemy hands, it didn't matter. Now his wounds had healed and he was free from the fog of morphine, the cobwebs cleared from his brain. International Brigade volunteers never fared well with the Nationalists. The men in the ranks had a chance of being exchanged for enemy prisoners. The officers were shot.

He had no idea why he had been diligently nursed and no desire to find out. He was fully conscious again. The skin around his neck remained tender, but his collarbone had mended. As night fell, he broke the legs from the table. He leaned the bed against the wall below the window and mounted the frame in his bare feet. The table legs must have been riddled with woodworm and turned to dust immediately he tried to prise at the bars.

He descended and took the cross from the wall. It was made of walnut, not pine. He tried again, digging into the base of the first bar. Before he had even scratched the surface, the door burst open and two guards charged in screaming in Spanish. He climbed down the bed frame. One of the guards retrieved the cross and hung it reverently back on the wall.

He then turned and mimed firing a rifle shaped by his two arms.

35

HE FELT UNCOMFORTABLE in the evening suit loaned to him by his host although, he had to admit, it was a surprisingly good fit. A platform had been erected beside the lake where a 20-piece orchestra played lively dance tunes. He stood in the shadows with a glass of Riesling watching women in shimmering dresses like birds of paradise in the arms of men with grandiose sashes and the confidence of those to whom life denies nothing.

After Ribbentrop had offered to help trace his son, he had felt obliged to attend the end of summer party. The invitation was genuine, well meant, but he was aware that the inclusion of General Sir Richard Sheridan on the guest list would do no harm to Ribbentrop's reputation. The Germans were no less enamoured of titles than the English and those in the know knew exactly who he was.

The music paused. The dancers clapped. He noticed a young couple hurry into the trees holding hands. The girl had milk white arms and wore a silver dress with bare shoulders. The sparkling wine was too sweet to his taste. He returned the half-filled glass to a tray carried by a waiter. His gaze took in the crowd meandering over the lawns and it occurred to him that his presence that night at the heart of Nazi society provided sufficient insights to justify his journey to Schloss Fuschl. The master race had risen again, more powerful than ever. Two years, he said to himself, two more years and we'll be facing each other again on the battlefield.

The band struck up with a piece of Wagner and the air

seemed to vanish with one mass intake of breath. The roll of kettle drums resounded over the lake and the guests rushed forward to greet Hitler as he made his way down the path from the house with Eva Braun, his mistress. Men clicked their heels. Women trembled with emotion. The mood grew feverish and Sheridan felt a combination of unease and incredulity to observe what amounted to worship for this small, neat, vaguely comical figure in a grey suit with a moustache like Charlie Chaplin.

The Chancellor had travelled to Salzburg from Berghof, in the Bavarian Alps, where he had been making plans for the Nazi Party Congress opening on 6 September in Nuremburg. It had become an annual event, attracting the likes of Lord Bradwell and a growing number of senior Tories who saw in National Socialism a political model that would provide tax cuts and control public unrest during times of unemployment and depression.

That still didn't explain his government's neutrality stance towards Spain. The strategy was appropriate to preserve trade with the Spanish market, the majority of the economy was controlled by the Nationalists. But it had created a vacuum filled by Hitler and Mussolini, the time and space for them to test their weapons and whet the appetite for conquest.

Had his son detected something in the political landscape he had missed? His daughter, too? His finger went unconsciously to the war scar below his eye. God damn it. Love of country was at the core of his being. But nothing, no duty or obligation outweighs the needs and hopes of your children. He glanced across the lawns. Hitler had reached the table beside the marquee where the string of swastika pennants swelled on the surge of expelled air. Ribbentrop caught his eye and made his way towards him.

'Keeping a low profile, Richard?' he asked pleasantly.

'Habit, I suppose.'

Ribbentrop smiled. 'You know, for a moment, it felt like I was seeing myself standing there in the shadows.'

Sheridan brushed down his lapels. 'Perfect fit, old boy.'

'Of course, we share the same tailor.'

Sheridan laughed politely.

'How's your German?' Ribbentrop then asked.

'Passable.'

'Come. Let me introduce you.'

They made their way towards the marquee. Sheridan saw the girl with white arms curtsey before Hitler, her silver dress shiny against the navy-blue backdrop of the sky.

'By the way, I managed to get through to some of our people in Spain,' Ribbentrop said. 'I should have some information in the next 48 hours.'

Sheridan stopped and turned to his host. 'That is amazing...' he threw his hand out over the lake, the Chinese lanterns, the tables where waiters were serving food. 'You've had such a lot on your plate.'

Ribbentrop swatted away the compliment. 'Three phone calls. Twenty minutes.' He shrugged his big shoulders. 'You can't imagine how pleased the officers were to receive my call, what is it you say: out of the blue?'

Sheridan was momentarily nonplussed. 'Joachim, you are extremely generous. It is something I deeply appreciate.'

Ribbentrop clicked his heels. 'Thank you, Richard. I appreciate your saying so.' He smiled. 'Now you are in for a treat.'

It was apparent as they approached that Hitler knew exactly who he was. Rather than offer his hand, he slid it into his jacket and gave a sharp nod of the head. According to the SIS profile on Sheridan's desk, the Chancellor was paranoid, narcissistic, terrified of germs and had suffered shell shock during the Great War. Sheridan was struck by the man's incongruous blend of magnetism and lack of emotion. He was sleek like a shark, with a shark's clever dead eyes that drove into him like a bayonet.

A photographer appeared. Sheridan moved to Hitler's side and they were immortalised in the flash of the magnesium bulb. They exchanged a few polite, empty words and Sheridan would remember this brief meeting with the Führer for the rest of his life.

36

HE WAS MARCHED from the cell down a corridor to a brightly lit office. A clean-shaven man with a bored expression sat at a desk, empty except for a telephone. He stared at Robbie from this position for a long beat, then sat back, folding his arms.

'You may sit.' He motioned him to the chair and waved away the guards. 'I am Captain Josef Baumann,' he said, and Robbie noticed the glimmer of a gold tooth. 'You like to smoke?'

From a drawer at the side of the desk, he removed a packet of cigarettes, a glass ashtray and a box of matches. Robbie lit up, less from desire than instinct. When the smoke hit the back of his throat, it was painful and made him feel nauseous.

'It is a reward for the human spirit. Your body is debilitated. You have no shoes. Yet you try to escape. You are not strong enough. But you try.'

Robbie glanced down at his cotton bed smock. The German wore a dark suit with a black tie pinned by a gold swastika. He removed from the desk a dog-eared form filled in with black ink and placed it before him.

'This is yours?'

Robbie glanced down at Simon's army papers and shook his head. 'No,' he replied.

The German watched him for several moments, went back into the drawer and produced a Communist Party card torn in four. He placed the pieces on the desktop and fitted them together.

'And this?'

'Aye.'

'Of course, the Scottish brogue. You are an officer in the International Brigade. A party member. A good communist?'

'I suppose. What's the difference?'

'What is the difference?' the German repeated. His face twisted as if a raw nerve had sprung from his golden tooth. 'If you are not sure of your beliefs, how can you be certain you are right?'

'I don't know that I am right.'

'If you are not sure what is right and what is wrong, how can you justify your presence in Spain?'

Robbie puffed gingerly on the cigarette. He thought about Simon, about Cribb. When he spoke, he was aware that his reasoning was muddled.

'We wanted to build a better world. You know, where everyone gets a fair crack of the whip, somewhere to live, the chance for a decent life.'

'A fair crack of the whip.' Baumann repeated the words. He then opened a different drawer, took out a notebook with a German eagle stamped on the cover and wrote the phrase down. He looked up. 'This can only be achieved by planning. By strong leadership. The masses do not require power. They require guidance. Communism exploits your vanity by making you believe we can all be equal. This is a lie.'

'People in Spain didn't vote for communism. They voted for democracy.'

Baumann laughed. 'Democracy is not based on rationality but feelings. People in elections are not asked what they think. They are asked what they feel. We have come to understand in Germany that this is not the way to run a government.'

'But it's not our place to tell Spain how to run their government.'

'Then what are you people doing here?' he said irritably, raising his voice for the first time. 'The International Brigade is a Comintern Army. It is a tool of Soviet expansionism. Only Germany can save Europe.'

Robbie wasn't sure what to say. The German hammered on.

'Our very civilisation is under threat from the Jews, the Reds, the black tribes of Africa, the undesirables, the unbelievers. You are on the wrong side of history.'

Robbie ground out his cigarette. His throat was on fire. He watched as the German dipped back into the drawer and withdrew two small brass keys on a leather thong.

'What are they for?'

'They come from a clock that belongs to my mate.'

'Mate?'

'Aye. Do you know what happened to him?'

'Mate,' Baumann said again and wrote the word down. He looked up. 'Do you think I am here to answer your questions?'

'I was just curious. I would like to know why I have been cared for?'

'Do you think we are barbarians?' He sat back and his tone softened. 'When were you enlisted by the SIS?'

'I'm not sure what that is.'

'Come, come, Lieutenant. Do not play games with me. Lying will not save your life.'

'I'm not lying.'

'The Secret Intelligence Service.'

'It rings a bell, but I'm not in the British army. I'm a dockworker from Glasgae. I don't know nuthin'.'

'"Rings a bell." Thank you.' He wrote it down. 'It is a phrase I forgot.' He put his pen to one side. 'Tell me about your mate.'

'There's not much to say. Is he dead?'

'I have told you. I am not here to answer your questions. You are here to answer my questions. Simon Sheridan?'

'He was one of those nice people. Everyone liked him. He read poetry. He introduced me to reading. He was just decent.'

'Where did you first meet?'

'In Paris. We travelled to Spain together. We climbed the Pyrenees and got the train to Albacete. There were ten of us, I think. They're all dead.'

'And you are still alive.'

'For now.'

The German smiled. The cross-examination continued. Robbie answered instantly, with total honesty. Baumann asked the same questions again, in a different way, but was unable to catch him out in any inconsistency. He had nothing to hide. He was just a man on the line, he said. He had no knowledge of battle plans or strategy.

'If you are just "a man on the line", why did they make you an officer?'

'Some kind of luck, I suppose,' Robbie shrugged. 'I survived Jarama. There wasn't anybody else.'

'And you led men to their deaths in Brunete.' He held his fist aloft. 'No Pasarán,' he mocked. 'You shall not pass. We have passed.'

'No, Captain.' Robbie shook his head. 'We shall pass. One day. People will wake up and build a world fit for us all. It is destiny. We shall pass.'

'You are a believer. You will not shed a tear when your time comes. Nor will I. We have that one thing in common.'

We have nothing in common, Robbie thought. He kept the thought to himself.

Captain Baumann took another dip in the drawer and withdrew Simon's volume of poetry. He poked his finger through the bullet hole in a way that appeared sinister and strangely obscene. He opened the book and read the inscription. 'Be safe. Be well. Be happy. But most of all, be yourself.' He looked up. 'A little sentimental, I think. Who is this Alice, his girlfriend?'

Robbie had a feeling the German knew exactly who she

was, that this game of cat and mouse had a subtext he didn't understand.

'His sister,' he replied.

'Sister?'

'Aye.'

'The children of your commander.'

'No, that would be Captain Sugden.'

'When did you first meet General Sheridan?'

'We've gone through all that.'

'You have not answered my question.'

'He's some bigwig in the British establishment. I don't know him. I've never met him. I'm a docker. I load and unload boats. You know I'm telling the truth.'

'What I do know, Lieutenant Gillan, is that you hide your intelligence very well.' He paused and leaned forward. 'Tell me about this Alice Sheridan?'

Robbie wondered for half a second if he could get across the desk and tear the man's throat out with his bare teeth.

'Way out of my class. Don't really know her.'

'You don't know Alice Sheridan?'

The terrible thought struck him that she, too, had been captured. The Nationalists had overrun their position and scooped up the medical staff, the orderlies, the injured. He closed his eyes and took a deep breath.

'She's a nurse. Just a nurse. That's all.'

Baumann sat back and stared at him across the table. He shuffled the book and cigarettes towards him, then gestured with his fingers. 'Keep them,' he said. He rose, opened the door and shouted in Spanish, '¡Vengan!'

The same two guards appeared instantly.

Baumann yawned and covered his mouth. 'Excuse me. Perhaps I will see you in the morning, Lieutenant Gillan.'

The guards led him down a flight of stairs to a room stacked with clothes, shoes, suitcases, hats, walking canes, underwear. Attached to the room was a bathroom with soap, towels, a shaving kit. He scraped the bristles from his face with a blunt razor, useless as a weapon, not that there was any chance of escape.

He took a bath in cold water and remembered that day when he arrived back in Morata after three months in the mountains. He had thought there was something important for him to do, some role, some purpose he had to serve. But that's just vanity.

On the shelf stood a pair of brown brogues, shoes of a style he could never have afforded and he felt as he reached for them as if someone else was guiding his hand. He chose a pair of green corduroy trousers, a plain white shirt, a tweed jacket that looked like it could have belonged to a Scottish hill farmer. He thought about Maw and Pa, Billy, his sisters. It had all been for nothing. He looked at the hats, the berets, but everything reminded him of the past and the past had gone.

The guards marched him along the corridor and he was locked in a cell occupied by four Spaniards. Two wore the uniform of the Milicias Obreras. There was a sturdy, overweight man in a suit with a bold moustache, the former mayor of a small town loyal to the Republic. His wife was a slight, elegant woman in a black dress with white trim who sat passively with her hands in prayer.

Robbie shared his cigarettes. The men were surprised he spoke Spanish and oddly proud that he was a volunteer in the International Brigade. It made them feel braver. They talked for a few minutes, but there was nothing to say and they withdrew to enjoy a last smoke with their own thoughts.

He sat on the bench. He closed his eyes and Alice appeared in a flicker of images, below the trees on the sunken road, looking up into his eyes and saying 'I want to kiss you', in a café in Villanueva de la Cañada. She wore a flash of red lipstick. Her green eyes sparkled with life.

In turn, they stretched their legs and urinated in the wooden bucket. The stench was awful. It was a part of everything: the quiet, the iron bars on the two narrow windows, the abstract sense of waiting. It was hot. Robbie felt the sweat rising from his skin and soaking his clean shirt. They didn't expect soldiers to shoot a wounded man in pyjamas.

He remembered Simon's last words on the ridge: time's going backwards. But it wasn't. It was racing towards the last tomorrow. He clutched the book of poetry as if it were a holy relic. They would come before dawn. He wanted to get it over with. It was better to die in battle with your mates. Better to die on your feet than live on your knees.

The woman prayed. The big man, the ex-mayor, sat beside her staring at the window watching for the light to change. The soldiers sobbed and hugged each other. When the lock snapped back and the cell door opened, they dried their eyes and brushed down their uniforms. The mayor took his wife's hand. She looked around at the four men with her.

'*No Pasarán. Pasaremos,*' she said, her last prayer.

The guards had entered the cell. One of them pointed at the exit and the other led the way along the passage and up a flight of stairs into a courtyard with a silent fountain at one end. The air tasted sweet. They would die with dignity. When the time had come, they had stood up to be counted.

The light came quickly, frosting the walls of what Robbie now realised was a monastery. An arch at the centre of the colonnade across one wall contained a life-sized crucifix and, at each side, marble statues like a small audience staring out from the shadows. Bullet scars peppered the surface of the facing wall.

Robbie heard the bark of orders in Spanish and eight men with rifles angled over their right shoulders marched into the courtyard. They were accompanied by an officer with a sword, two orderlies and a priest.

The prisoners were spread out a yard apart. The orderlies produced blindfolds and lengths of rope. The militiaman on the extreme left of the line – Pepe, Robbie recalled, a small, undernourished man with drawn cheeks – argued and shook his fist. The mayor joined in and they all began shouting until a compromise was reached. They would have their wrists bound in front of them, but their eyes would be left uncovered. You want to look into the eyes of the man before he shoots you dead.

The task was completed and the priest stood before each of them in turn. He made the sign of the cross and murmured the prayer, 'In the name of the Father and of the Son and of the Holy Spirit. Amen.'

'Is this God's work?' the mayor asked without anger and the priest carried on, completing the ritual.

The prisoners turned their heads and nodded to each other. He was in the centre of the line, facing the crucifix. The woman was next to him. She smiled. She was ready. Good luck, they said. 'Buena Suerte. Viva la República.' Robbie felt tears on his cheeks. He wasn't afraid. But he didn't want to die. He was crying for her.

The firing squad commander called his men to attention. He gave the order to present arms. Take aim. Then, without pause, the command:

'Fire.'

The blast was deafening. Robbie slipped to his knees. He didn't feel any pain, just a terrible regret that he would never see Alice again.

37

THE CAR WAS waiting on the landing strip in Biggin Hill. The driver placed his bag in the front and opened the rear door.

'Good trip, sir?'

'Yes, Douglas, I suppose it was.'

Sheridan climbed into the back seat. After four hours being shaken half to death on the flight from Salzburg, he was exhausted. As they pulled out of the base, he closed his eyes. He felt moderately satisfied. If nothing else, he had seen Reich style close up, a disturbing picture at the least, and terrifying to imagine the consequences if that little man in the grey suit ever unleashed his malevolence on Europe.

It was unfortunate that Ribbentrop was leaving that day for the Nazi extravaganza in Nuremburg. More than likely, he would hold back his report until he could provide it in person on his return to the embassy in London. It was the nature of intelligence. It rarely came at the right time. Sheridan went straight to his office and called Tommy Courtenay in Madrid. He had not expected any results and got exactly what he had expected.

He did ponder whether or not to tell Alice about his journey but thought better of it. To give her hope then dash it would make matters even worse. It was like being in the trenches. Waiting.

*

There were nights when she couldn't sleep and there were days when she closed her eyes reading in the afternoon and woke when it was already getting dark. She had enjoyed pulling weeds with Netty in the garden one morning and, then, another day, she could barely drag herself from the bed.

She had exchanged letters with Hugh Tregarth two or three times and finally arranged to meet him at Tredegar House the following day. At least that was something to look forward to. She had not been to the Red Cross centre since the exhibition and was pleased that the project had achieved more than she had ever hoped. Small sums of money were still being raised for Bowen Jones from the sale of prints and the edition of lithographs was under way.

Alice knew by her waistbands whether she had put on or taken off a few pounds. She had not been eating a great deal, but still her skirts seemed tight and she didn't know why. She didn't feel ill, just lightheaded and strange. This is what she wanted to talk about with Hugh.

It took more than an hour and three buses to get to Bow. With the tingling in her bladder, she rather regretted not having taken a taxicab. She went straight to the lavatory in Tredegar House. A trainee brought tea in the big white cups the moment she sat down with Hugh and Sister McKinley in her office.

They went quickly through what she thought of as the *unpleasantries*. No. There was no news. Only bad news ghoulishly reported in the daily press. The Brunete offensive had failed. The Republican army had been unable to prevent Franco's Nationalists from completing the conquest of the north. With jurisdiction over the Basque ports, Spanish raw materials were being shipped to Germany in payment for the effective campaign led by the Condor Legion.

Sister McKinley sneezed and wiped her nose. 'Enough of politics. I must say, in spite of everything, you look rather perky, Alice.'

'I don't feel it. In fact, I feel oddly odd.'

'My dear, you are in the right place. Let's have a look at you.'

'I need to pop to the lavatory again. I won't be a second.'

They waited for her in the consulting room. Hugh went through the usual procedure when Alice returned. He looked under her eyelids, held a flat stick on her tongue while she said 'ah'. She took deep breaths while Hugh, with his stethoscope, listened to the rhythms of her heart and the gurgling of her lungs.

'Can you lie down, please.' Alice removed her shoes. 'Your skirt and blouse, too.'

She stretched out on the couch. He felt her abdomen. 'I'm a bit swollen,' she said.

He turned to Sister McKinley. The sister stood and did the same, kneading her abdomen with her soft fingers.

'Are you using the bathroom more often than usual?' she asked.

'Yes, rather more than I like.'

Alice was surprised again when the sister squeezed her breasts.

'When did you have your last period?'

'I'm not sure.'

'Are your breasts sore?'

'Yes.'

'Do you have any other... symptoms?'

'I'm tired all the time. I keep getting headaches and I feel sick.'

'In the mornings mostly?'

'Yes.'

Sister McKinley glanced at Hugh. 'Turn your head for a moment, doctor. He did so and the sister unclasped her brassiere. 'Her breasts are full with a darkening of the areolae.'

'Ah!' he exclaimed.

Alice dressed and they returned to the office.

'I have one more question,' Sister McKinley said. 'Are you a virgin?'

Alice raised her shoulders. 'No,' she answered.

'When was the last time you had intercourse?'

'In Villanueva de la Cañada.'

'About eight weeks ago,' Hugh calculated.

The sister glanced again at Hugh. 'Are we agreed, Dr Tregarth?'

He nodded his head and turned to Alice. 'You will need more tests, but I am inclined to believe you are with child.'

'Oh, I see. So I'm not suffering from some terrible disease?'

'On the contrary, what you are suffering is completely normal,' Sister McKinley continued. 'That is, normal for a married woman.'

'I think I'm pleased,' Alice said after a silence. 'I wonder what Daddy is going to say.'

'I suggest you don't say anything at present. You need more tests. Then you must think about what you are going to say and what you intend to do.'

'I know what I intend to do,' Alice replied.

38

THERE WAS NO pain except the noise in his head as the explosion from eight rifles bounced over the stone walls. He had held his breath at the command to fire and gasped frantically for air. The retort echoes softened into the dawn and he heard the sound of blood gurgling from bullet wounds.

'Just my little joke, Lieutenant.'

He opened his eyes and stared at the buffed toecaps on a pair of black leather riding boots. He raised his gaze. Baumann was standing over him.

'Come,' he said. 'It's time to get up from your knees.'

Robbie was trembling, alive, unhurt. He glanced at his fellow prisoners with blood pumping from massive chest wounds. The mayor twitched like a beached whale, his great body reluctant to let go without a fight. The firing squad stood down, about turned and marched away.

'You fockin bastard,' Robbie spat.

Men with stretchers arrived to cart away the bodies. The orderlies carried buckets of sand to absorb the blood running amongst the cobbles. Baumann produced a black-handled knife and cut through the bonds around his wrists. Robbie struggled to his feet and followed him back up the stairs to the office.

On the desk was a mixture of both his own and Simon's possessions: two sets of army papers, Simon's passport, the keys to the clock, the volume of Blake's verse, Anthony Cribb's book *The Occasional Fall*, a wallet containing £40 and a torn party card. Baumann handed him a signed document with a wax seal and an ink stamp of an eagle with spread wings. Below the swastika at the top was his name, Lieutenant Robert Ian Gillan.

'Your travel permit.' He looked at Robbie with a grudging respect. 'You play a dangerous game, Lieutenant.' He tapped the telephone. 'I was not aware that you had, what do you say: friends in high places.'

Robbie had no idea what he was talking about. His relief was touched by bitterness, with a feeling of having failed his comrades. They were dead. He had survived.

'A car is waiting to drive you to the station. You will be escorted to the frontier.' He glanced at his watch. 'I need to get a start before it is too hot.'

Baumann was wearing jodhpurs and carried a riding crop. He put the crop down and produced a small case and an overcoat that looked new.

'I remember the English autumn comes early and can be chilly.'

*

Father had been away on one of his trips and she had not spoken to him for a couple of days. That night, at dinner, his jaw seemed to have softened and in his eyes that matched her own was a sadness she had never seen before. He looked weary. It was easy to forget that, while she was anxious, so was he. So was Mummy.

'You were in Germany, Daddy?' she said.

'Well, Austria, actually.' He broke off, then added. 'It was jolly hot, hotter over there than it is here.'

'We always get a breeze in the afternoon,' her mother said. 'I can feel autumn in the air.'

They did not continue the conversation. Alice sensed that there was more that her father had wanted to say but stopped himself from doing so.

Mrs Broom had made kedgeree, not one of her favourites, but she ate rather more than usual. The evening was warm. They went outside and sat together around the table in the gazebo with a jug of lime cordial. Father had his brandy. The birds settled in the trees.

'I met Hitler,' her father said. 'The Chancellor.'

'We know who he is. And we know what he's capable of.'

'I fear you may be right, Alice.'

She was surprised by his response. As their eyes met, she knew he was thinking about Simon. She was about to continue when they were disturbed by Netty. She came hurrying into the garden with a wild look about her face.

'There's someone outside, sir,' she gasped. 'He asked if this was the Sheridan house. I told him to wait.'

General Sheridan glanced at his watch. Perhaps it was someone from the office, he thought.

'I'll deal with it,' he said.

He marched back through the house and opened the door. He stared at the man standing there for several long seconds before he spoke.

'Lieutenant Gillan?'

'Aye.'

There was another brief pause until Sheridan slightly bowed his head and extended his hand. 'You are very welcome, sir, very welcome,' he said. 'She's waiting for you.'

Robbie left his case in the hall and followed Sheridan through to the garden.

The lowering sun hovered above the rooftops lighting Alice's face as she stood. Tears glazed her eyes. Her voice came in a whisper.

'You came back for me. You said you would.'

He stepped forward and she ran into his arms.

Lady Sheridan took her husband's hand. He pulled her closer and she rose up to kiss his cheek.

'Thank you,' she said, and glanced back at Robbie. Sheridan did the same.

'Simon?' he asked.

'He was a good soldier,' Robbie replied. He felt Alice tremble. 'He didn't suffer. It was quick. I wouldn't be here if it wasn't for Simon.'

Robbie kept his arm around Alice's waist as he took from his pocket the keys to the grandfather clock. He handed them to Sheridan.

'Simon asked me to look after them for you.'

Sheridan stared down at the two brass keys and looked back at Robbie Gillan. They had lost their son. They had not lost their daughter.

Time would start again.

Epilogue

THE SURVIVING BRITISH Volunteers returned to England after the International Brigade was disbanded at the end of 1938. Among the cheering crowds who met them at Victoria Station was the Labour Party leader Clement Attlee.

Attlee led Labour to a surprise victory in the 1945 General Election with a pledge of full employment, the creation of a National Health Service and a system of social security, policies promoted by the Spanish Republic in 1931.

Spain was briefly a republic from 1873 to 1874. What became known as the Second Republic was proclaimed on 14 April 1931, when King Alfonso XIII went into exile. Two general elections, in 1933 and 1936, resulted in Popular Front coalitions made up of liberal and socialist deputies with a handful of communists.

The Republic set about modernising Spain with laws securing workers' and women's rights, a minimum wage, a programme of land reform and the creation of a national health system. The reforms were considered too slow by the urban workers and agricultural labourers who had supported the Popular Front, and too extreme by the Nationalist alliance of monarchists, the military, the landowning classes and the Church.

Three years of street protests and polarisation culminated in the military uprising on 17 July 1936. The resulting civil war ended on 1 April 1939 with a million Spaniards dead or in exile. The Nationalists established a dictatorship under

General Francisco Franco that lasted for 36 years until his death on 20 November 1975.

Democracy in Spain was slowly restored. In the General Election on 28 October 1982, Felipe González led the Partido Socialista Obrero Español to victory. The PSOE – Spanish Socialist Workers' Party – was the same party that had led the Popular Front coalition in 1936 and González campaigned on the same policies.

During 14 years in office, the PSOE created a minimum wage, equal pay, pensions, women's rights and unemployment protection, the ideals of social democracy that spread across Europe and were first promoted by the Republican Government almost 50 years before.

A call for volunteers at the outbreak of the civil war drew 50,000 men and women into the International Brigade from across the world. More than 15,000 remained in Spain with the Spanish soil their shrouds. Some 2,500 volunteers came from Britain, the majority urban workers and labourers, but also well-known artists, writers and intellectuals.

Also published by **LUATH PRESS**

Homage to Caledonia
Scotland and the Spanish Civil War
Daniel Gray
ISBN 978-1-913025-36-6 PBK £12.99

The Spanish Civil War was a call to arms for 2,300 British volunteers, of which over 500 were from Scotland. The first book of its kind, *Homage to Caledonia* examines Scotland's role in the conflict, detailing exactly why Scottish involvement was so profound. The book moves chronologically through events and places, firstly surveying the landscape in contemporary Scotland before describing volunteers' journeys to Spain, and then tracing their every involvement from arrival to homecoming (or not). There is also an account of the non-combative role, from fundraising for Spain and medical aid, to political manoeuvrings within the volatile Scottish left.

Using a wealth of previously unpublished letters sent back from the front as well as other archival items, Daniel Gray is able to tell little known stories of courage in conflict, and to call into question accepted versions of events such as the 'murder' of Bob Smillie, or the heroism of 'The Scots Scarlet Pimpernel'.

Homage to Caledonia offers a very human take on events in Spain: for every tale of abject distress in a time of war, there is a tale of a Scottish volunteer urinating in his general's boots, knocking back a dram with Errol Flynn or appalling Spanish comrades with his pipe playing. For the first time, read the fascinating story of Caledonia's role in this seminal conflict.

Daniel Gray's important and powerful book Homage to Caledonia *tells the story of those deeply committed and courageous Scots who volunteered to fight for democracy and socialism against General Franco and his forces.*
TONY BENN

Told through the words and experiences of those who were there, this meticulously researched and beautifully written book is simultaneously heart-breaking and uplifting.
MAGGIE CRAIG

Daniel Gray has done a marvellous job in bringing together the stories of Scots volunteers – in [this] many-voiced, multi-layered book.
SCOTLAND ON SUNDAY

Moving and thought-provoking.
THE HERALD

A new and fascinating contribution.
SCOTTISH REVIEW OF BOOKS

Gray deserves applause for shining a light on a lesser-known aspect of the nation's character of which we should all be proud.
PRESS & JOURNAL

Our Fathers Fought Franco
Scotland and the Spanish Civil War
edited by Willy Maley

Willy Maley, Tam Watters, Lisa Croft, Jennie Renton

ISBN 978-1-80425-040-2 PBK £12.99

There was no good speaking of the menace of fascism, and not going to fight it myself.
JAMES MALEY, GLASGOW

It was an atmosphere I will never forget – there was the sense of freedom in the air, of workers' power.
DONALD RENTON, PORTOBELLO

You fight for your beliefs, not medals.
GEORDIE WATTERS, PRESTONPANS

There have been reports that [when we were released] we shouted 'Long Live Franco'. Not on your life!
ARCHIBALD CAMPBELL MCASKILL WILLIAMS, PORTSMOUTH

A resonant piece of working-class history, this book is a living link to four extraordinary stories.

Why did these young men put their lives on the line and go to Spain to fight with the International Brigades?

How did they all end up in the same prison cell?

And what is their legacy today?

This wonderful and moving book adds something completely original to the Spanish Civil War narrative.
DANIEL GRAY, from the Foreword

An extraordinary example, and an unforgettable, essential book.
ANGUS REID, *The Morning Star*

Such openness connects us readers to the vulnerabilities of a family, life in all its complexity and difficulty. This is a virtue of all four accounts in Our Fathers Fought Franco... *What comes through persistently is a sense of how much we have to learn from the past.*
ALAN RIACH, *The National*

Part first-person history, part war memoir, part working-class polemic, it is a valuable addition to the canon.
RICHARD BATH, *The Scottish Field*

Too often their experiences went unrecorded.
THE PENNILESS PRESS

Each of the authors calls us to read the signs for our own times in the legacy of these men of the IB. This book is a fine tribute to them and their comrades.
LESLEY ORR, *Bella Caledonia*

Details of these and other books published by Luath Press can be found at:
www.luath.co.uk

Luath Press Limited

committed to publishing well written books worth reading

LUATH PRESS takes its name from Robert Burns, whose little collie Luath (*Gael.*, swift or nimble) tripped up Jean Armour at a wedding and gave him the chance to speak to the woman who was to be his wife and the abiding love of his life. Burns called one of the 'Twa Dogs' Luath after Cuchullin's hunting dog in Ossian's *Fingal*. Luath Press was established in 1981 in the heart of Burns country, and is now based a few steps up the road from Burns' first lodgings on Edinburgh's Royal Mile. Luath offers you distinctive writing with a hint of unexpected pleasures.

Most bookshops in the UK, the US, Canada, Australia, New Zealand and parts of Europe, either carry our books in stock or can order them for you. To order direct from us, please send a £sterling cheque, postal order, international money order or your credit card details (number, address of cardholder and expiry date) to us at the address below. Please add post and packing as follows: UK – £1.00 per delivery address; overseas surface mail – £2.50 per delivery address; overseas airmail – £3.50 for the first book to each delivery address, plus £1.00 for each additional book by airmail to the same address. If your order is a gift, we will happily enclose your card or message at no extra charge.

Luath Press Limited
543/2 Castlehill
The Royal Mile
Edinburgh EH1 2ND
Scotland
Telephone: 0131 225 4326 (24 hours)
Email: sales@luath.co.uk
Website: www.luath.co.uk